THE LAST FRIEND

A NOVEL BY

DARRAL WILLIAMS

Words Matter Publishing
P.O. Box 531
Salem, Il 62881
www.wordsmatterpublishing.com

ISBN 13: 978-1-947072-06-0
ISBN 10: 1-947072-06-4
Library of Congress Control Number 2017945629

Except for recognized historical figures, all characters are fictional, and any resemblance to persons living or dead is strictly coincidental.

ACKNOWLEDGEMENTS

To my editor, Kimberly Coghlan, coghlanwriting.com, for cleaning up my manuscript. Kudos to you, Kim. You're the best!

To Perry Green for his technical assistance on how the wiretap of a telephone line would be performed in the early 1960's.

DEDICATION

This book is dedicated to the late Captain Roy E. Segers, without whose encouragement and outright demand that I write, this story would probably still be banging around inside my head. Thank you, old friend.

CHAPTER 1

The deep orange glow of the sun had just slipped below the tree line and was slowly disappearing as Joe Carter sat in his favorite rocker on the front porch of the small clapboard house that he and his wife, Millie, had shared for over two decades. Soon the sounds of the rural Southeastern Arkansas nighttime would be heard all across the bayou on the other side of the narrow country road.

As he gazed at the landscape that had been so much a part of his life for all of his forty-three years, his mind drifted back to his childhood when he and his friends from along the ridge enjoyed hours and hours on the bayou fishing from its banks.

He and his closest friend, David Squire, had been inseparable in their youth during the depression years of the 1930's, often staying in the woods on the other side of the bayou for hours after dark just sitting and listening to the crickets, owls, and an occasional far-off crying panther. Both boys lived and worked on the small farms owned by their parents, and since Joe had no siblings and David had only sisters, they had become like brothers to each other.

Today was a particularly sad day for Joe, as he wrestled with a decision he never imagined he might have to make. Since all of his family and extended family were gone, and there was no one left to turn to, he was faced with having to decide if he should call on his old friend, David to help him out of a grave predicament.

As the darkness of the evening wrapped around him, Joe arose from his chair and stepped off the porch, strolling slowly down the driveway toward the gravel road that separated his house from the bayou. A cool gentle breeze washed over his face bringing the familiar smell of all sorts of early autumn fragrances known only to the southern Mississippi River delta.

A half-moon low in the eastern sky reflected off the bayou and momentarily eased his troubles. As he stood at the edge of the road staring at the reflection in the water, he remembered the time he and David had attempted to convince David's younger sister, Elizabeth, that there were people on the moon. The two boys had gone through a long spiel about how the atmosphere on the moon caused everybody to be bigger than earthlings and that scientists had said that someday the moon people might invade Earth and kill everybody. Joe and David were eleven, and Elizabeth was nine. When she ran home crying hysterically, David's mother threatened to thrash the daylights out of both boys until they finally, reluctantly, apologized to Elizabeth for the yarn.

The reminiscent thought, however fleeting, gave Joe a small lift and brief diversion from his awful situation. It had been four weeks since his doctor had presented the bad news to him and Millie. Joe had inoperable cancer, and the prognosis was grim. To survive more than a few months would be a miracle, and Joe was already feeling the effects of the malignancy. His level of energy was dwindling, and he was getting weaker daily.

To make matters worse, there was the situation with the mortgage. Joe had lived on the 400-acre farm all of his life, and now it seemed that he was going to lose it to a less-than-hospitable lien-holder. For the past five years, cotton prices had suffered because of abundant crops and an increase in imported cotton from South America. It had become more and more difficult for small family-owned farms to survive, but farming was all Joe had ever known, and he just couldn't pick up and leave, especially after three generations of Carters had owned the land. However, the undeniable fact was that the mortgage was now seriously past due, and the mortgage company was breathing down his neck for the money.

A foreclosure would mean all he and Millie had ever dreamed of would be gone with the stroke of a pen. If he died without resolving the crisis, where would she go? What would she do? They had no children, and she had been his bookkeeper and a homemaker all of her adult life. Their future retirement had depended on someday leasing the land to some other local farmer who would pay a substantial rent for the use of the property.

In light of his health and financial situation, Joe was faced with the unthinkable prospect that his soon-to-be widow might end up homeless. The thought of that was almost too much for him to bear. That was the reason—the only reason he was pondering the idea of calling on David.

So, torn between pride and need, Joe, while staring into the bayou below, decided to make the call. With a heavy heart, he turned and walked slowly back up the driveway toward the house. He was grateful for the darkness so Millie couldn't see him wiping away the tears with the sleeve of his shirt.

The faint shadow of his six-foot frame glided slowly ahead of him as he approached the house. As he made his way up the steps, his thoughts were suddenly interrupted. Millie had stepped through the doorway and was about to call him to dinner when she saw the silhouette walking toward the house.

"I was just about to call you," she said. "Supper is ready." Then, in the faint light filtering through the living room window, she saw the grim look on her husband's face. Millie knew the look. She had seen it many times over the years, but she knew the reasons behind the expression were far more ominous than anything they had ever faced together.

As they stood there in the quietness of the moment, the crackling sound of gravel under the wheels of an automobile driving along the ridge broke their thoughts. The car, a Mercedes sedan, turned off the road into the Carter's driveway and stopped a few feet from the front of the house. A fat little man stepped out wearing light colored slacks, a long-sleeved white shirt, and a red bow tie. Joe Carter could see the shine of the patent leather loafers even in the dim light of the early evening.

Clyde Bayless always fancied himself a classy dresser, often traveling over a hundred miles to add to his wardrobe. He liked to brag that you could tell a lot about the importance of the man by the clothes he wears.

To Clyde, the respect he received from others was a vital part of his persona. He had few friends, mostly vain men of less prominence who hung around just so they could be seen mixing with the upper crust. This was their way of showing everyone else that they had standing in the community.

Clyde's awareness that he wasn't very well liked among the common folk was the underlying cause of why he had decided long ago that if he ever got in a position to wield power over his neighbors, he would have no sympathy for their plight. He had carried this bit of cynicism around with him since he was a young boy when his classmates made fun of him because of his short, physical stature.

On this night, he was feeling especially proud of himself, as he was one step closer to accomplishing a small goal that he had been pursuing for the past five years. He was about to inform an old schoolyard antagonist that he was moving to collect an unpaid debt by foreclosing on the collateral.

As Clyde made his way toward the porch, Joe nodded for Millie to go inside. She gladly accepted the gesture as an opportunity to leave the scene. Without a word, she stepped into the living room and closed the door behind her.

"Good evening, Clyde," Joe said.

"Good evening," Clyde said with an almost giddy smile in his voice.

"What brings you out here this time of night?" Joe asked, knowing the answer before he asked.

Stopping at the bottom of the steps, Clyde said, "There's something I need to discuss with you, Joe. That's a nice swing up there on the porch. Do you mind if I sit in it while we talk?" he asked.

"Yes I do mind," Joe said with a matter-of-fact tone. "You

can sit in my swing after it belongs to you, but not before."

"Very well. If that's the way you want it, I'll make this short," Clyde said, attempting to hold back his anger. "I spoke to my attorney today, and I'm here to inform you that we are foreclosing on the Carter farm. You have sixty days to vacate the premises."

"Okay. Is there anything else?" Joe asked slowly.

"No, that about does it," Clyde said with his usual flair of arrogance.

"Then get your short, little dumpy butt off my land," Joe said bluntly.

Clyde hated being reminded that he was short, but he knew that he would end up on the unpleasant side of any physical confrontation with Joe, so he quickly retreated to his Mercedes and drove away.

Millie had been in love with Joe since they were twelve years old. He had come to her rescue on the school bus after an older male student tried to force her to move and take her seat. Joe intervened, and although two years younger than the other boy, he didn't back down. When the bully tried to push him out of the way, Joe planted a fast, hard right straight to the jaw. As the boy fell back, stunned from the shock of the blow, Joe quickly stepped forward and hammered him with three more jabs to the head and face before the bus driver pulled Joe off the other boy. From that very moment, Millie Fraser knew that Joe Carter would always be her guy.

They started dating as soon as they were old enough. By the time they turned twenty-one, the Japanese had bombed Pearl

Harbor and Joe and his best friend, David, had enlisted in the US Army. A week before they were to leave for basic training, Joe and Millie decided to tie the knot. They were married at the Fraser home in a small ceremony just four days before the two young men had to report for duty.

After the war, David decided to leave the farm behind and go to college. He earned a degree in Business Management from The University of Arkansas in 1949.

Within a few weeks of graduation, David had secured a position as an investigator for a large Chicago insurance company partly due to his military background. He worked there for four years until he had saved enough money to open his own private office specializing in investigating insurance clients who were attempting to defraud the companies he represented.

The investigation business had been a good career choice for David. He now had four investigators working for him and had recently expanded his services to include investigations into employee fraud of large corporations.

A few times over the years, David did have to resort to force when suspects got violent, usually when he was closing in on their dirty dealings. At six foot three with huge biceps and the strength of an ox, however, few people were ever foolish enough to attempt to take him down.

Although Joe and David hadn't actually seen much of each other the last fifteen years because of the eight hundred miles that separated them, they had stayed in contact. Joe and Millie always received a Christmas card from David, and the two men talked on the phone two or three times a year. They usually managed to visit once every eighteen months or so, which reassured Joe and Millie that David was still the same country boy who grew up on his family's farm about a mile north along the ridge.

When Joe Carter was discharged from military service after the war, he and Millie settled on the four hundred acre farm that his grandfather had bought for fifty cents an acre in 1884 at a tax sale at the county courthouse. They cared for Joe's parents and Millie's mother until, one by one, they were all gone.

Farm crop prices were never very high in the early days, but any farming family that stayed within a modest budget could make a decent living. The last few years, on the other hand, had been a nightmare for everybody in the business. Many of Joe and Millie's friends had lost everything and had moved out of the county seeking employment elsewhere.

Joe and Millie had their dinner in silence that night, as both were in deep thought. Millie was not worried about her future. She did not yet know how she would make it on her own, but she knew that somehow she'd be okay. Her main concern was the prognosis of her husband's condition.

"Do you think you can find David's telephone number for me?" Joe asked his wife.

Millie looked at her husband of twenty-two years, and with a lump swelling in her throat said, "Yes, I have it in my address book."

"I guess I'll give him a call," Joe said.

The sadness in his eyes told Millie all she needed to know

about why Joe wanted to talk to David. She knew that Joe would never lean on his old friend for help if it weren't for her and that only added to her pain.

"It'll be alright," she said as she leaned forward and gently placed her hand on his arm.

Millie stood up slowly and walked over to the buffet, pulled open the top drawer, and retrieved a small spiral bound notebook. She handed the book to Joe and disappeared through the living room and onto the front porch. Millie knew her husband well, and she knew he needed his privacy.

As she sat in the swing listening to the sounds of the night, she could hear the faint mumbling coming from the dining room. She really didn't want to know what was being said between the two old friends, but she was certain of one thing; Joe was dying in more ways than one right now.

David Squire was sitting in his favorite lounge chair having a glass of tea, attempting to wind down after a busy week while reading the sports page of the newspaper. Anna-Marie, his housekeeper, had arrived later than usual, and as was sometimes the case, had brought along her ten-year-old daughter, Alicia. Anna-Marie had just finished mopping the kitchen floor and was walking through the living room when the phone rang. She answered and spoke to the person on the other end for a moment.

"Mr. Squire, It's a Mr. Joe Carter from Arkansas," Anna-Marie said.

David thanked her, got up, walked across the room, and took the receiver. "Well it's about time you called," he said with a slight mischievousness in his voice. "It's been so long I thought you'd forgotten about me."

"Well, no I haven't forgotten you," Joe said trying to keep the weariness out of his voice. "It's just that a lot has been happening down here, and I haven't had time to sit and talk until now."

David knew Joe as well as he knew himself, and immediately, he sensed that something wasn't right. Feeling in his gut that he was about to hear some bad news, David sank into the sofa next to the telephone table and gently leaned his head back against the cushion. "This is not going to be good is it, Joe?"

"I'm afraid not," Joe said with a slight shakiness in his voice.

"What's wrong, my brother?"

Joe took a deep breath and just blurted it out. "I'm dying of cancer, David. My doctor says I only have a few weeks of good living, and a few months until I'm gone."

Joe sat patiently during the long silence to give David time to absorb the news.

Finally, with emotion welling up inside of him David said, "You've got too much living to do for this to be happening, old friend."

"I know, but except for suicide, the time of our death is not something we have the luxury of choosing," Joe said with a forced level tone to his voice.

"What can I do to help?" David asked.

"I really hate to ask, David, but I need to speak with you

about my situation. Do you think you could come down? I have some things I need to talk to you about."

Feeling the subtle tone of urgency in Joe's voice, David's response was quick. "Of course I can. I'll be there sometime next week, as soon as I can clear up a few things here and make flight arrangements."

"Thank you so much. Millie and I will forever be grateful," Joe said.

"I'll be in touch," David said and hung up the phone.

David hated ending the conversation with his oldest friend so abruptly, but he knew if he didn't he would get emotional, and right now Joe needed him to be strong.

Within minutes, David had flight arrangements for Monday to Little Rock, Arkansas, and a rental car waiting for him to make the 100-mile road trip to Joe and Millie's farm.

When Madge Bellows, David's longtime secretary arrived a few minutes before eight on Monday morning, he informed her that he would be leaving on a ten o'clock flight to Little Rock on personal business. He asked her to postpone all meetings and appointments for the next three days. He gave her Joe's phone number in case she needed him but told her to call him only in case of a business emergency. She said she would take care of everything. Knowing Madge would reschedule his meetings and appointments, David left for the airport.

Millie had finished washing the dinner dishes and was sitting in the swing on the front porch when she saw the headlights of an automobile coming down the ridge road toward the Carter farm. As the car slowed in front of the house, Joe stepped onto the porch, and with a puzzled look, asked, "Who do you think that might be?"

"I don't know, but I guess we're about to find out," Millie said as the car turned off the road and headed toward them. The late model sedan came to a stop in front of the house, and a tall, muscular built man wearing Khakis and a navy blue golf shirt stepped out.

"I've lost my way, and I'm looking for a place to stay the night," David said as he closed the door of the car behind him displaying a warm smile.

"You've come to the right place," Joe said as he stepped off the porch with a broad grin.

The two men embraced for a long moment, not saying a word.

Joe spoke first. "It's been a while old friend. I'm grateful that you came. It's good to see you."

"It's good to see you too," David said. "I came as quickly as I could." David then noticed Millie sitting in the swing at the end of the porch. "Well, hello gorgeous," he said.

"Hello handsome," Millie said with a bit of a blush on her face.

For the next two hours, the three of them enjoyed what they all knew might be one of their last pleasant visits. As they sat on the porch and with the help of a cool, autumn breeze, Joe and Millie brought David up to speed on all that had happened in the community since he was last there.

"I have a freshly baked apple pie," Millie finally said. Would you be interested in a piece with some of my special homemade vanilla ice cream topping?"

"Why of course. That's the real reason I came all the way down here," David said with a big grin. "I tell all my friends up north that they just don't know what apple pie is until they've had yours."

Millie smiled as she disappeared into the kitchen. When she returned with the pie, she excused herself and left the two men alone. After they finished and talked a while longer, David decided the time was right to get to the point.

"Well Joe, why am I here?" David asked with a soft but deliberate assertiveness.

After a noticeable pause, Joe said, "Because I'm losing my land, my home, everything to Bayless Farms. Never mind that I have terminal cancer. Dying is part of life, and I accept that. You and I long ago reconciled our fate on the battlefields of Europe, but I just can't bear the idea of my Millie being homeless."

Noticing David's motionless silhouette, Joe continued, "A few years ago Clyde Bayless' company began loaning money to small farm owners to use as operating capital after bank credit tightened. Farm prices began to go south about five years ago. Millie and I, like many other local, small farming operations, have taken it on the chin year after year until almost all of our savings have been depleted. Now, I can no longer pay Bayless Farms the money I owe them.

"As you know, Bayless Farms is owned solely by the Bayless family. Clyde Bayless was elevated to Chairman of the Board after his father died about ten years ago. Since then, the company has expanded its operation in several directions, financing is one area that seems to have been very lucrative for them. I suppose there's nothing better than having the backing of old money. Inherent wealth, if used at precisely the correct moment by an evil man can put a lot of good people on their knees at his feet."

"What exactly are you saying, Joe?" David asked.

"I believe Clyde Bayless knew all along that the small local operations would not be able to pay back the money we owed. He charged us higher than market interest rates, but the money was available, and some of us were forced to either take the loans or go out of business. Whenever a farmer could no longer repay the loan, Bayless Farms moved in and took over the land," Joe said with a distant gaze in his eyes.

"But that's not the worst of it. When a couple of my neighbors complained that he had mortgaged their land without them knowing it, I checked into my own agreement with him. Without asking me and without my knowledge, he mortgaged our land. By the time I knew about it, the statute of limitations had passed. My attorney told me I had no case. For that reason, I couldn't file protection under federal bankruptcy laws. He had, as collateral, that very seat you're sitting in. I had no recourse whatsoever, and now I'm losing everything. At least I could have sold the land to someone of my choosing if Clyde hadn't blatantly lied to me about the collateral he requested for the loan. I honestly had no idea that he was that dirty, so I didn't read the agreement as closely as I should have."

"Well I see that little Clyde's unashamed disregard for others hasn't changed," David said.

"No, it hasn't. It's actually gotten much worse," Joe said. "But never mind him, David. His kind always eventually get what they have coming to them. What I need to talk to you about is Millie. She won't have any place to go if we lose the farm. We still have some money in savings, but not enough to buy a house. I need to know that Millie will never have to worry about a house payment. If I could just scrape up enough money to buy her a small cottage, at least she would have a home."

Seeing that his old friend was about to lose his composure, David quickly interrupted, "I'll see to it that Millie has a home for as long as she lives on this earth, Joe."

That's when Joe lost it. The bottled up emotions he had held back for so long burst open, and the tears flowed. David sat quietly and just let his old friend get the release he needed.

CHAPTER 2

David visited with Joe and Millie the next day and night. On the morning of the third day, David said his goodbyes to them, promising to be back in a week or two. In the rental car, he drove down the ridge toward the small town of Delta Ridge a few miles away.

Clyde was at his desk going over the previous day's cotton gin receipts when one of his office girls gently knocked on the door before opening it. "There is a mister David Squire here to see you," Sallie McLarin said.

Clyde had not heard that name in years. *What on Earth would David Squire be doing here*? he asked himself. "Show him in," he said.

David entered Clyde's office, walked over to his desk, and held out his hand. Clyde extended the courtesy with caution, shaking David's hand while trying to figure out why David would be here to see him. One thing was certain; it wasn't a social visit. Clyde had never been sociable with any of the boys from west of the railroad tracks when he was growing up, and he hadn't missed David one bit since he moved out of the county shortly after the War.

"Hello Clyde," David said. "How ya been doing?"

"I'm doing fine. You get homesick for some good old southern fried chicken?" Clyde asked with a guarded smile.

"Well, that's part of it. Actually, I came down to visit my old friend, Joe Carter. It seems that he's been diagnosed with cancer, and the prognosis looks very grim."

"Yes, I'm aware of that," Clyde said with a bit of caution. "I found out a couple of weeks ago. A very unfortunate situation."

Clyde was no fool. He had a keen sense of knowing when an unpleasant request was about to come at him, and before David said another word, Clyde had it all figured out. David was here to beg for mercy on behalf of Joe, and he was beginning to relish the thought of turning him down flatly.

"Actually Clyde, that's why I'm here to see you," David said. "I learned after I got here a couple of days ago that you hold the mortgage on the Carter farm."

"That's right, I do," Clyde said with all warmth leaving his voice. "Joe Carter has been delinquent for some time to Bayless Farms. I have, unfortunately, been forced to issue him a notice of eviction. It's very sad, but that's just business. I'm sure you understand," Clyde said with a thin, wicked smile.

"Yes, I do understand, Clyde. I just thought..."

"He'll get no more time, David," Clyde said cutting David off mid-sentence. "I have been as patient as anyone could ask for. He'll just have to pick up and move on."

"Joe doesn't have anywhere to go," David said softly, suddenly remembering one of the many reasons why he always detested Clyde. "I've got a long drive ahead of me, so I have to get going. I just thought I'd stop by and ask."

"Sorry I couldn't help you," Clyde said, forcing himself to hold back his delight.

"Here's my business card. If you decide you may want to negotiate, please give me a call," David said as he handed Clyde his card.

"I will," Clyde said.

David turned, walked out of Clyde's office, and closed the door behind him.

As he made his way past the receptionist, a female voice interrupted his thoughts.

"Mr. Squire?" Sarah Jennings asked as she approached David.

"Yes?" David said as he turned around.

"I'm Mrs. Jennings, Sarah Jennings. I'm a friend of Millie Carter's. She's told me a lot about you. I just wanted to say hello," she said.

As she shook his hand, she slipped a small piece of paper into his palm. He casually took it and discreetly dropped it into his jacket pocket, so as not to alert the other office personnel.

"Jennings... I don't believe I remember any Jennings folks when I lived here back in the forties," he said.

"We're not originally from here. We moved here about twelve years ago from Greenville, Mississippi," she said.

"Well it's nice to meet you," David said with a warm smile. "I have to be going now. I have to catch a flight later this afternoon out of Little Rock."

"It was nice to meet you too," Sarah Jennings said as she stared directly at David. Noticing the intensity of her gaze, David gave her a slight nod, turned, and left.

Once he was a few blocks away, he pulled into the parking

lot of a grocery store and retrieved the piece of paper from his jacket pocket. On it was written, *"565-0311—Call me at 2:30 p.m. today…please."*

As he sat there looking at the note, the previous fifteen minutes came thundering back into his mind. The brief meeting with Clyde whereby he reacted exactly as David had figured he would and Sarah Jennings slipping him the note added a puzzling new dimension to the situation. What did she want to talk about? She had mentioned that Millie was a good friend, which was enough to cause David to think she may have something to tell him that might help the Carters with their plight. After all, she worked for Bayless Farms. Maybe she had information that could shed new light on the Carter mortgage that David could use to help them.

After a few moments of pondering on the events that had just unfolded, he decided to miss his flight. Joe was his oldest friend, and his better judgment was screaming at him to stay and hear what Sarah Jennings had to say before leaving Arkansas. He turned the car around and headed back toward a small café on the other end of town.

The owners of *Sally's Café* were relatively new to the community and did not know David. He was glad that no other patrons were there because he knew that he could very well encounter any number of old acquaintances. Right now, he was on a mission and in no mood to talk about old times with anyone. He took a seat at a corner table farthest away from the window. After reading all the news in the latest edition of the weekly county newspaper and drinking a couple of cups of coffee, David looked at his watch and saw that it was 2:25. He stood up, paid his bill, and stepped outside where a phone booth stood a few feet down the sidewalk. He reached into his pocket, pulled out the piece of paper, and dialed the number.

Sarah Jennings was sitting at her kitchen table looking over photos of a document when the phone rang. She had left work early stating that she had some personal business to attend to.

"Hello," she said.

"Mrs. Jennings?"

"Yes."

"This is David Squire. I got the note you passed to me in your office this afternoon. I figured it must be important, so I decided to stay awhile and call you before leaving town," David said.

"Yes, it is important. Actually, I would rather not talk on the phone. Do you think we could meet at my house?" she asked.

"That would be fine. Where do you live?"

Sarah lived in the old Howard home that was once owned by the family of a schoolmate of David's. Ten minutes later, he turned into her driveway.

The old house looked very much the same as it had twenty-five years ago when he and Joe used to hang out with Bill Howard, the oldest of the Howard boys. To the left of the front porch stood the giant, live oak tree, which had been a favorite place for the boys to sit and talk about girls. Its majestic branches bowed toward the ground as if to be speaking to a long lost friend as David stepped out of the car.

"It's been there a long time," Sarah said with a smile.

Observing him from inside the doorway, she noticed his prolonged gaze, but there was no way she could have known the memories that flooded his mind as he stared at that old tree.

"Yeah, I know. I used to hang out in the shade of her when I was a teenager," David said, realizing that she was watching him. "The oldest Howard boy was a good friend of mine," he said.

"Come on up and take a seat," Sarah said, nodding toward a row of Adirondack chairs placed around a round cypress table a few feet from the balustrade. "I'll fix you a glass of lemonade."

"That sounds great," David said as he took a seat in one of the wooden chairs.

"I'll only be a moment," Sarah said as she disappeared.

Inviting him to sit on the front porch instead of the living room was a keen reminder to David that he was now in the South where a female simply would not invite a male stranger into her home. A Southern lady demanded and always received respect from a gentleman. It was just the way things were.

"I hope it's not too tart for you," Sarah said as she came through the screen door with the serving tray.

"I'm sure it'll be fine," David said with a smile as he rose from his seat.

Sarah placed the tray on the table next to David and handed him a glass filled with ice. As she poured the lemonade from a clay pitcher, he was pleased to observe that she had made it from freshly squeezed lemons. He was hoping for that since he had consumed countless glassfuls of Mrs. Howard's fresh squeezed lemonade on this very porch many times during his youth.

He pondered on whether he should reveal that small piece of his boyhood to Sarah but decided not to as he sensed that something heavy on her mind.

"Well, Mrs. Jennings, I'm sure you have things to do, so I suppose you would like to get right to the point of this meeting," David said.

"Yes I would," she said. "But before I say anything else, I must have your solemn promise that you will never reveal your source of the information I'm about to share with you."

A long beat passed as David absorbed the weight of what she had just requested of him. Finally, he spoke. "Your secret is good with me," he said. "I give you my word of honor that I will tell no one."

"I believe you," she said with a glimmer of relief in her eyes. "Millie has told me a lot about your lifelong friendship with her and Joe. The two of them consider you like family."

His warm, thin smile was all Sarah needed to assure her that his feeling towards the Carters was mutual. She then reached into her apron pocket, retrieved a small envelope, and placed it on the table next to the serving tray.

"What's this?" David asked.

"Photos of the hard evidence you'll need to negotiate a deal for our friends," she said.

David opened the envelope and began to look at its contents. The black and white photos appeared to be of a small record book containing initials, amounts of money and dates next to each initial on the list. As he slowly scanned through the photos, he found no initials he could place with a name.

"How on earth did you acquire this?" he asked.

"Actually, quite by accident," Sarah said. "A while back, our offices flooded on the weekend due to a mistake made by a plumber who installed a new water heater late on a Friday afternoon.

"When we arrived on Monday morning, water was flowing under the front door and into the parking lot. As soon as we unlocked the door, a local farmer who was there waiting to meet with Mr. Bayless found the source of the flooding and turned off the water valve.

"It took two days to clean up the mess, including removing carpet and moving all the furniture out of the offices. Sometime in the afternoon of the first day, I was removing files in Mr. Bayless' office when an envelope fell to the floor from under the middle drawer of his desk. It had been taped underneath the drawer, and apparently, the moisture from the flooding had loosened the tape.

"I opened the envelope and found a pocket ledger with four initials recorded in it and amounts of money next to each of them," Sarah Jennings said.

"I'm counting seven here," David said as he scanned through the list again.

"That's correct," Sarah said. "He's added three initials to the list since I first discovered the ledger. About twice a month I have retrieved the book and looked through it to see if there are any new entries added to the list."

"If this is what I think it is, a payoff scheme to possibly shady people, you could be taking a huge risk here," David said.

"I don't really care, Mr. Squire," she said as she stared at her half-empty glass of lemonade. "You see, Clyde Bayless did a terrible wrong to me, and when I stumbled onto this information, I knew I had what was necessary to make him pay for his deed. All I needed was to find the right person in whose hands I could place the information. Are you that person, Mr. Squire?" Sarah asked.

After a long moment of silence David slowly looked up from the list of names, and with a cold stare, he said, "I'm him. Yes. I'm him, Mrs. Jennings."

A wave of relief and exuberance rushed over Sarah as the chance for the vengeance she had craved for so long began to settle in on her.

David decided not to ask what Clyde had done to Sarah. At this point, he didn't care to even speculate. He figured he would know about it soon enough.

"I want to warn you of one thing, Mrs. Jennings. Clyde has always been a very cunning person. If I were you, I would not underestimate him. Just remember, a cornered rat can be a dangerous little animal under the right circumstances. Do not take any unnecessary chances with snooping around in his business," David said.

Looking down at the photos again, one thing had suddenly become very clear to David—the leverage he needed to negotiate the Carter mortgage had just fallen into his lap. That is if he could match the initials on the list with names of real people. He was also sure that he would not give up until he had given little Clyde Bayless the investigative anal reaming of four lifetimes. If Clyde was dirty, David Squire was going to know it. And if it meant taking down the fat little clown in the process, he would do so with no reservation.

CHAPTER 3

"Good morning," Chance Martin said as he approached the showcase where Sarah and her friend, Janie Shaw, were admiring a large assortment of necklaces. "May I interest you in a necklace today?"

"No, I'm actually here to pick up a pocket watch that I left for repairs about a month ago," Sarah replied.

Pattison Jewelers was a long established Little Rock jeweler and had been Sarah's favorite jeweler since they repaired a locket for her twelve years ago, which had been in her family for over a century. After Chance Martin had retrieved the watch, Sarah thanked him and paid him for the repairs.

Back on the sidewalk, Janie suggested they stop by The Guarantee Shoe Store a short distance down the sidewalk and look at a pair of Wing Tips for her husband. The two women were about to enter the store when Clyde Bayless came walking out accompanied by another man. Sarah and Clyde saw each other at about the same time, and both were equally surprised.

"Well hi, Mr. Bayless. I see you also buy at the best shoe store in Little Rock," Sarah said.

"Yes, nobody can ever say I don't have good taste in clothes or footwear," he said with a nervous chuckle.

Sarah knew Clyde well, and immediately, she noticed that he seemed to be uneasy at the coincidental meeting. The man with him, however, was clearly looking the two women over with the look that a man gets when he's interested in more than just a friendly "hello." Seeing that Clyde was not going to introduce Sarah and Janie, James Benton stepped forward, tipped his hat, and introduced himself.

"You didn't tell me you knew all the pretty girls, Clyde," he said as he first shook Janie's hand then Sarah's. "My name is James Benton."

Clyde told Benton that the two women were from his hometown, Delta Ridge and that Sarah worked for him. He attempted to nudge Benton toward the next street where their cars were parked, but Benton was clearly not ready to move on just yet.

"It surely is a nice day for a couple of lovely ladies to be out shopping," he said. "Are you girls up here for the big game tonight?" he asked. "I hear the Arkansas Razorbacks are playing the Missouri Tigers at War Memorial Stadium."

"No, I'm afraid I'm not a fan of football. We're just doing a little shopping," Sarah answered, noticing that Clyde was attempting to hide his nervousness. "You speak with an accent, Mister Benton. Where are you from?"

"I'm originally from a small town in Montana, but I now live in Alexandria, Virginia. I'm in the real estate business there," he said.

Clyde was clearly uneasy about where this conversation was going, and Sarah had already figured out why. Sarah knew she was onto something and was determined to find out as much as she could about this James Benton fella.

"Well, it was good to meet you Mister Benton," she said.

"It was good to meet you too," he said.

Clyde motioned for Benton to follow him down the sidewalk toward their cars. Benton made another small gesture toward Sarah and Janie, turned, and walked away toward the street corner a half block away. Sarah and Janie stepped inside the foyer of the shoe store and waited as a crowd of shoppers cleared the doorway.

With a smirk on her face, Janie turned to Sarah and said, "You must have seen something you liked in that Mr. Benton. You couldn't seem to keep your eyes off him."

Sarah laughed aloud. She knew she could not possibly reveal to her friend why she gave James Benton such a thorough look from head to toe, so she just smiled at Janie and said, "You mean you didn't think he was handsome?"

The two women giggled like teenagers. Janie had no way of knowing that the giddiness in Sarah's voice was not because she thought James Benton was handsome. The initials "JB" were the most prominent initials in Clyde Bayless' little record book. She now had a real person to put with at least one pair of the initials she had discovered two years ago.

After the crowd of shoppers had cleared the doorway, Janie stepped inside the store. Sarah stayed outside watching the two men who were talking a half block away. She waited to see which way they went.

At the corner, Clyde let Benton know that he was not pleased with his exchange with the two women. "What were you thinking, back there, James?" Clyde asked, obviously irritated.

"Clyde, you are just entirely too nervous about little things that don't amount to anything," Benton said with a weariness in his voice.

"I've told you in the past that I do not want a single person who knows me to see us together. Now one of my very own office workers has met you, and she knows you're in the Real Estate business in Alexandria Virginia," Clyde barked. "To a trained ear, that could be enough to link you, me, and the Senator together. So I just wish you would keep your mouth shut around someone who is acquainted with me," Clyde said as he turned and began walking toward his car.

"Don't be so paranoid, Clyde," Benton shouted with a grin as Clyde walked away at a rapid pace.

Clyde walked two blocks, crossed the street, and made his way to his Mercedes. On his way down the sidewalk, he couldn't stop thinking about Benton's recklessness outside the shoe store with the two women. Clyde may not have been a Harvard graduate, but he was no fool when it came to deception.

Benton can think what he wants, he thought to himself, *but that kind of behavior has got to stop, or I'm going to have a word with the Senator.*

Clyde had been close to the Whelan family since Clyde and Senator Benjamin Duff Whelan's son were classmates at The University of South Carolina in the early 1940's. When Whelan's son was killed in an automobile accident in 1943, the Whelan family looked at Clyde as one of their own. Whelan was a shrewd businessman, and Clyde had learned many valuable lessons from him. The two of them had been involved in many business deals in the years after Clyde graduated from college and moved back to Arkansas to join his family's business.

When Whelan was elected to the United States Senate in 1952, he saw to it that Clyde got as many political favors from Washington as the senator could safely provide, often allowing Clyde to front for him on sweet, discreet investment deals that required inside knowledge that only those in power would be privy to.

During the election cycle of 1960, the buzz around Washington was that it didn't matter if Richard Nixon, or John F. Kennedy won the election; the defense department was going to get the lion's share of funding to keep the Soviet threat at bay. Both candidates were known to be hawks when it came to military strength.

Since Senator Whelan was in line for the chairmanship of the Committee on Armed Services, it would give him a golden opportunity to expand his small time dealings to a larger, much more lucrative deal. After he was elected to the Chairmanship in 1961, he began to make contacts with a small number of defense contractors who were known to "play the game." After he had things worked out with a couple of contractors, he brought Clyde into the deal to handle all the money.

Clyde was determined to make this deal as smooth for the Senator as all the others before, and he was not going to let one flawed cog in the wheel damage the whole well-oiled machine. Benton was going to have to learn to follow Clyde's rules or else.

James Benton turned and walked the opposite direction

from Clyde. Sarah had been observing this, and as soon as Benton disappeared behind the corner building, she quickly crossed to the opposite side of the street and walked rapidly to the corner. Once there, she peeked around the cornerstone of the building and saw James Benton gazing in the window of the second store down the sidewalk. She watched for a minute or two until he turned, walked away from the window, and crossed the street. Dissolving herself into the crowd on the sidewalk, she discreetly moved as close as possible to where James Benton had made his crossing. From where she stood on the opposite side of the street partially blocked by a parked car, she could see the tag on Benton's sedan. As she was retrieving a pen from her purse and something to write on, Clyde, who had been parked two blocks away on the same side of the street as Benton, pulled up beside Benton and said something to him through the passenger window of his Mercedes.

Clyde had stopped to tell Benton that he was serious about his recklessness and would no longer tolerate it. As he began to pull away from Benton's car, he glanced around to see if the street was clear of traffic. Then it caught his eye. Something familiar. *Someone* familiar.

That was Sarah Jennings standing on the other side of the street, he said to himself. *I thought she was in the shoe store down the other street. What is she doing up here? Why would she be following James Benton? Was that really her? I'm, not sure, but it surely looked like her,* he thought to himself as he drove away.

Sarah had seen Clyde glance around just in time to turn

her head to the opposite direction from him. She hoped he had not recognized her. She was well aware of his peculiar actions around the office. Clyde was a very suspicious man. He thought because he couldn't be trusted that no one else could be either, so the office atmosphere was always clouded with a little bit of uneasiness. Sarah knew if Clyde thought he had seen her, he would wonder why she was there, across the street from James Benton's parked car, and would let her know subtly on Monday that he had seen her. He would then ask her a few thinly disguised, prodding questions as to why she was there.

After Clyde was at a safe distance up the street, Sarah quickly wrote down the tag number of James Benton's late model Chevy and hurried back to the shoe store where Janie Shaw was waiting just inside the door for her. Sarah explained that she had to catch Clyde and talk to him for a moment about company business. Janie turned to Sarah with an amused look and accused her of chasing that Mr. Benton.

As the two girls stepped through the door and onto the sidewalk, Clyde, who had driven around the block, passed by and saw the two women coming out of the shoe store laughing. They did not notice him as Janie was playfully harassing Sarah for information about Mr. Benton. Seeing this, Clyde was satisfied the woman he had seen near Benton's car was someone else.

Clyde had a way of living under the shadow of Murphy's Law. He was convinced that if something could go wrong, it would. He made it a point to cover all the bases. He had made a lot of money in his life following that one simple rule.

As James Benton drove away from the curb, he thought, *what was so wrong with telling those ladies who I am? They're so far removed from my dealings with Clyde, they'll never suspect anything. Clyde is simply afraid of his own shadow.*

James Benton met Clyde Bayless after he became the liaison between Senator Whelan's aide, Frank Rubenstein, and Clyde. Rubenstein had contacted Benton two years earlier and had offered him the job for a nice little piece of the action. The senator had given Rubenstein a sealed envelope to give to his courier and had ordered him not to open it. Rubenstein gave the envelope to Benton during their first meeting to discuss how the deal would be executed. Inside the plain business envelope was typewritten instructions on how to get to the location for the pickup, and who the contact was. The instructions were very specific in saying it would be better for everyone involved for Benton to never reveal to Rubenstein who the contact was or what state he was located in. Likewise, Benton did not know the name of the Senator involved in the deal, although he suspicioned it was Whelan because Frank Rubenstein did, indeed, work for Whelan. He had never asked because that wouldn't have been prudent, and besides, Rubenstein wouldn't have told him anyway. Therefore, he only knew Frank Rubenstein on the Washington end and Clyde Bayless down in Arkansas. It was better for all parties involved for this to be the execution of the deal.

To this day, Frank Rubenstein did not know who James Benton's contact was or where he was. He only knew that it always took about five days after he called Benton and told him the pickup was ready before Benton returned with the money.

Frank Rubenstein chose Benton to be the courier for two reasons. Benton was a naturally shady character, and that was exactly what Frank Rubenstein needed for this job. If there was a way to make a quick buck, Benton might go after it, but if it involved the excitement of playing around the edges, then count him in. He loved the thrill of the chase. It didn't matter if he was the hunter or the hunted. Just give him the mission. The more dangerous it was, the greater the thrill.

Frank Rubenstein and Benton had served in Naval Intelligence during the War, which was the other reason Frank chose Benton as his go-between. Benton had proven to Frank many times during the war years that he was always a team player and would not let Frank down. Frank knew that Benton would deliver the goods and would never take more than his share. Frank had always viewed Benton as just a simple crook, but one with at least a measure of honor toward the other crooks on the team. He would not lie to or steal from them.

So Frank had approached Benton with the task of driving to the location from time to time and collecting money from the contact there. Senator Whelan was adamant about the liaison driving to the destination rather than using commercial airlines. Driving would create no travel record. He always said if there's no paper trail, there's no record of wrongdoing.

Whelan knew that if his deal was to go undetected, he had to collect the "contributions," as he called them, far from Washington. No meetings in restaurants or bars around town to conduct business. That was entirely too risky.

He also knew he had to have people working for him he could trust. He was comfortable with Clyde, but not Frank Rubenstein. His angle on Rubenstein was actually very basic. It was just simple, old fashion blackmail. He had hard evidence of a scandal on Frank that had been swept under the rug and was holding it over his head. He knew of Frank Rubenstein's deep desire to serve in the United States Senate. Whelan knew that as long as he had the goods on Frank Rubenstein, he would have no trouble asking special favors of him. But he also knew that if given a half a chance, Frank Rubenstein would burn him to the ground. That's why the information he had on Frank was so important. It would crush Frank Rubenstein's dream of someday serving Pennsylvania, his home state, in the Senate.

****

"Mr. Squire," Sarah Jennings said.

"Speaking," David said as he placed his coffee cup on the small table next to the sofa.

"This is Sarah Jennings. I have some good news," Sarah said, enthusiastically. "I have information for you."

"You mean information concerning our case?" David asked.

"Yes, I have a name to put with the most prominent initials in Clyde Bayless' record book," she said bursting with excitement.

Sarah proceeded to tell David exactly what had occurred outside the shoe store in Little Rock earlier that day. She told him how James Benton had introduced himself and how Clyde had immediately shown uneasiness that James Benton had given out information about himself to Sarah and her friend, Janie. She went on to tell David how she had followed the two men and had gotten the tag number from James Benton's car. She gave David a thorough description of James Benton.

"How do you know Clyde was uneasy about this Benton guy talking to you?" David asked.

"Mr. Squire, I have spent eleven years of my life working in close physical proximity to Clyde Bayless. I know everything he's going to say before he says it," Sarah said matter-of-factly.

Hearing that put a broad smile on David's face. That was just one more confirmation to him that Clyde had not changed a single bit since childhood other than his receding hairline and a few wrinkles in that fat little face of his.

With a chuckle, David said, "I believe you, Mrs. Jennings. Clyde always has been quite transparent in attempting to hide his intentions. Otherwise, investigations of this sort are always unpredictable, and innocent people can sometimes end up in harm's way very quickly, so be careful. You've stumbled onto a real piece of luck here, Sarah. This is very good news. I'll get to work on it immediately. I'll be in touch," David said and hung up the phone.

Sarah leaned back on the sofa and stared at a framed snapshot across the room on the fireplace mantle of her husband and their daughter in happier times. They had been on a trip to the mountains a short time before his accidental death in a tragic two-car accident.

Sarah sat quietly and pondered on what she would say to Clyde if she ever got the chance to invoke the revenge on him that she so desperately wanted for what he had done to her. Unmitigated revenge was the only reason she had continued to work for him. She had vowed silently to find a way to get him no matter what, and she felt she had a far better chance of accomplishing that if she remained near him on a daily basis.

Changing her focus back to her conversation with David Squire, she thought, *At last, David has a solid lead he can work with. I just hope he's as good as Millie and Joe have always said he is.*

Somewhere deep inside her, Sarah knew that David would squeeze every drop of usefulness out of the information she had stumbled onto. She knew that he would not let his oldest friend down. She had seen the icy cold stare in his eyes on her front porch only four short days ago. It was an unmistakable look of resolve that she knew in her heart would be absolute.

CHAPTER 4

Walt Austin had just finished a meeting, something he didn't typically do on a Sunday morning but had agreed to do so because of the urgent need of the client. As he made his way to the door and was about to turn off the lights, the phone rang. He almost ignored it but thought it might be his wife, so he decided to answer.

"Austin Investigations," he said.

"You sound like you'd rather be somewhere else on this Sunday morning. Since you own the place, why aren't you?" David Squire jokingly asked his old friend.

After a short silence, Walt asked, "Major Squire, is that you?"

"Well, I see you haven't lost your hearing. You recognized my voice after two years of not bothering to call me," David said.

"Well, I think Joanne might beg to differ with you on the hearing loss, especially when she requests the honey do's," Walt said, laughing.

David and Joe had both served in the OSS with Walt Austin during World War II. The three men had remained friends in the years after the war and had stayed in contact with each other from time to time. Walt Austin had gone into the investigation business and had done quite well. The Washington D. C. area had provided a rich environment for private investigators, and Walt had certainly realized his share of the business, boasting clients from politicians to divorce attorneys.

"Walt, I want to apologize for calling on a Sunday morning like this, but there's a bit of urgency to a case I'm working on," David said.

"No problem, Major Squire. What can I do for you?"

"I need you to put a tail on someone for me. He lives in Alexandria, Virginia, and I suspect that he'll be arriving at his home sometime today with a sack full of dirty money. I hate to ask this, Walt, but I need to have a sticker put on this guy as soon as he arrives," David said. "I need to know where he makes the money drop and the identification of the person who receives it. I think we need to tail that guy also."

"Sounds simple enough. Do you have an address?"

David gave Walt James Benton's name and his automobile tag number. He also gave Walt the physical description of James Benton that Sarah had given him. Walt didn't ask David what the case was about.

"This involves our old friend, Joe Carter," David said.

"Captain Carter? Is he in some kind of trouble?" Walt asked.

David told Walt all about Clyde Bayless and the financial trouble Joe was in as well as the bleak prognosis concerning his health. The two old friends talked for a few minutes about their mutual friend and his plight.

Walt assured David that he would find the address from the automobile tag number David had provided and would have a stakeout at James Benton's home within an hour or two. David thanked him and asked Walt to call him at his office as soon as he knew anything he thought might be helpful.

"You still in Chicago?"

"Yes, same number. Thanks, Walt. By the way, Joe doesn't know that I'm involved in any investigation like this, but if he did, I know he would be grateful for your help," David said.

"I wouldn't have it any other way, David. You may not know this, but Joe saved my bacon on two separate occasions in Paris during the German occupation. If it hadn't been for him, you and I wouldn't be having this conversation. I owe him my life, Major," Walt said to his former commander. "I'll be in touch."

After he had hung up the phone, David thought about what Walt had said concerning Joe saving his life behind enemy lines. Although the three of them had been close friends during the war jumping into occupied France together on numerous missions, Joe had never mentioned that to David. He wasn't surprised. Joe was never one to brag on himself, not even in a joking manner at a pub over a beer. Finding out from Walt what Joe had done for him in combat just gave David more determination to resolve Joe's problem. Heroes like Joe should never be forced to give up anything, *anything* to a scumbag like Clyde Bayless.

****

Elizabeth Gardener had just finished the final arrangements for Senator Whelan's trade mission to several South American countries when the Senator stepped into her office.

"Everything's set to go, Senator," she said as he approached her desk. "The President called to give you a thumbs up on the mission."

Senator Benjamin Duff Whelan had been in the United States Senate for eleven years, had worked his way up through the ranks to the chairmanship of the powerful Committee on Armed Services, and was the Vice Chairman of the Committee on Commerce. For the next eight days, he would be touring several countries in South America to promote trade and shore up relations with various countries in the Western Hemisphere. The Soviet threat had shown its ugly head less than a year ago during the Cuban missile crisis, and the President had asked Senator Whelan to lead a mission through several South American countries just to let the neighbors to the south know that the United States was firmly behind their free market capitalist governments.

No one could ever say that Whelan was a humble man. His ego was as big as his 6' 4," 250-pound body. He enjoyed being important and relished the knowledge that President Kennedy had called to wish him well on his mission. All of his life, he wanted to be somebody who others looked up to. That was the reason, the *only* reason he had run for the vacant Senate seat when his South Carolina predecessor had died unexpectedly in office. He just wanted to be important. Never mind the country. It would practically run itself.

Over the years, Whelan had become comfortable in his role as one of Washington's power brokers, and he was known to flaunt his stature on the national stage whenever it suited him politically. Right now was one of those times, and he was going to milk it for all it was worth.

Back at his desk, Whelan was going over legislation that was coming before the Armed Services Committee in a few weeks when there was a knock at the door. Frank Rubenstein appeared and requested a short meeting with the Senator.

"Senator Whelan, I have that report from Mr. Benton you asked for," Frank Rubenstein said, using the usual code.

"Oh good. I've been expecting that. I talked to his supervisor, and he told me it was on the way," Whelan replied.

Frank handed Senator Whelan a large, brown envelope containing the cash that Benton had given him when they met at Martha Washington Library in Alexandria Virginia the night before. The Senator took the envelope and thanked Frank for getting it to him before he left town. Whelan dismissed his aide, placed the envelope in his safe, and went back to studying the upcoming legislative proposals. There was no need to count it. He knew it would be the right amount.

All the men in my pipeline from the contractors to Frank Rubenstein are honest in all their crookedness, he thought with a chuckle, realizing the oxymoron for what it was.

As Frank went back to his desk and began preparing to write some legal documents, the haunting thought of what he had allowed to happen to his honor was once again eating at him. He had been told many times since arriving in Washington seven years ago that all who participate in the political game do so after checking their conscience at the door with their coat. He thought about the idealistic Frank Rubenstein who had served honorably during the War and had gone on to earn a law degree from Harvard University. He pondered on how he had been a Naval Intelligence officer participating in the collection of intelligence that was directly responsible for the defeat of the Japanese at Midway Island. He had served with men of impeccable character and courage under fire.

Now look at me, he thought. *I've taken an astoundingly hard fall from the pinnacle. From serving with men of exceptional honor to being subservient to a scoundrel of the first order. A man with no integrity who would throw his own mother off the ballroom balcony for a few pieces of silver.*

Frank was becoming more depressed with each passing day. Every time he made a delivery of cash to Whelan, the loathing for his boss cranked up another notch. He had been eyeing a Senate seat from his home state of Pennsylvania that would soon become vacant, as Senator Joseph Clark had expressed privately to friends that he might retire after his present term.

Why did I let this happen to me? Did I sell my soul just like all the rest? I've become what I've always despised the most, just a common criminal, Frank thought as he sat there staring at the keys of his typewriter.

"Wanna have lunch?" a familiar voice asked from over his shoulder.

Frank was so deep in his thoughts that he hadn't noticed Elizabeth Gardener standing next to his desk.

"Yes, I guess so," Frank said as he snapped out of his deep thought.

Elizabeth and Frank had been good friends since she joined

the staff as Senator Whelan's executive secretary five years ago. They usually had lunch about once a week and enjoyed each other's company. She was attracted to Frank's gentlemanly manners and the self-confident way he carried himself. Lately, however, she could see that something was bothering her friend. She sensed that it was far more than anything mundane. She had come to know Frank well, and this was, no doubt, far more than the usual stresses of life.

At lunch, they sat quietly except for small talk as Elizabeth pondered whether she should ask Frank what was going on. When the waiter brought the check, Elizabeth reached for it, but Frank, in his usual manner, would have none of it. The bantering back and forth that ensued finally ended in Elizabeth just allowing Frank to pick up the tab.

After the waiter had left, she looked Frank straight into the eye, and with as much restraint and softness, as she could muster, she asked, "What's bothering you, Frank? You haven't been yourself for weeks now. You hardly ever laugh anymore. I mean, really laugh."

Frank returned the gaze of his close friend, and with weariness in his voice, said, "The boss is up to no good, Lizzy. And I do not mean the usual political posturing kind of underhanded dealings. He's into some very bad stuff."

Elizabeth looked at Frank for a long moment before saying anything. She sensed that she should choose her words carefully. "How do you know this, Frank?" she asked.

With sorrow in his voice, Frank sighed deeply, and just said it, "Because I'm involved also."

Elizabeth could not believe what she had just heard. She was stunned and simply could not think of a single thing to say in response. *My close friend has gone over. He's joined the underbelly of Washington Sleaze,* she thought.

Finally, it hit her like a powerful cold wind against her face. The revelation of what was happening to her friend immediately became clear.

"Somebody has something on you, don't they Frank? Maybe a mistake you made sometime in your life, and now they have the goods on you. I know you, Frank Rubenstein. You are not like the others."

"I always thought that too, but this town has a way of corrupting the very soul of everyone who participates in the process, Lizzy," Frank said quietly.

"What are you saying, Frank?" Elizabeth asked.

Without revealing any details of his youthful mistake years before, Frank spent the next few minutes explaining the blackmail that Whelan was perpetrating upon him and the reasons why he bowed to the pressure from the senator. He did not want his family back in Pennsylvania to be hurt, and he badly wanted that Senate seat in his home state. It was as simple as that. Just another dirty trade-off in a town where everything was for sale including humanity.

Frank profusely apologized to his friend who sat stoically listening and hanging onto every word he said to her. He went over each little detail of the scheme that Senator Whelan was running. He told Elizabeth he did not know who James Benton's contact was, and he did not know what state the contact was located in. All he knew was that Benton would call him to arrange a meeting to deliver the package a few days after Frank sent him out for the collection.

After he was finished, Elizabeth leaned back in her chair, took a deep breath, and told Frank that she understood at least part of why he had succumbed to the bribe. She would have done the same thing to protect her family from the actions of her private life.

"But Frank, you are mistaken to think that if you ever become a senator that Whelan isn't going to hold votes in the Senate over your head as long as either of you is serving as an elected official."

Frank sighed and rubbed his forehead.

"There's one thing I need for you to clarify for me, Frank. As I said, I understand why you did what you did, but what I'm having a hard time understanding is why you're telling me this. Now I know firsthand about criminal dealings between you, Senator Whelan, and others. I could bury you with what you've just revealed to me," Elizabeth said.

"But you won't."

"How do you know that?"

"Because you love me, Lizzy, and you wouldn't do that to me."

Elizabeth was stunned. She had always been incredibly fond of Frank but had not allowed herself to admit it to him. She sat there for a moment until she regained her composure. Finally, lowering her head slightly and staring at the food scraps on the table, she quietly said, "You're right, Frank. I do love you. I guess I always have."

Frank resumed, "I wanted to tell you face to face, Lizzy, instead of having you read about it in the papers after Whelan's handpicked investigators twist things around to make it look like I acted alone. This thing is about to get messy quickly, and it's not going to end well for all involved, including myself. It's just a matter of connecting my end of the pipeline to the source end of it. I have to find a way to get the name of the man who collects the money from those who are paying the bribes. Benton won't tell me. He's always been a team player and won't break the rules of the game. The boss expressly said in the introductory letter to him that he was to keep it confidential, and that's what he's going to do. So, I have to find out the connection on that end some other way.

"Finally, I told you because I wanted you to hear the facts, Lizzy. It's important to me that you know what actually happened, and I knew if I didn't tell you, then you would never know the real truth. If you know the accurate story, then it won't matter to you what Whelan attempts to do to squirm out of the mess that will immediately follow the first news release. You will know in your heart that, in the end, your friend did the honorable thing," Frank said.

"I just don't know what to say to comfort you," Elizabeth said, almost weeping. "All I ask is to please leave me out of it. I have no one who can help me. My parents are in their final years and have no money or connections. I'm on my own, Frank, and would have nowhere to turn if I became tangled up in this."

"I will not involve you. I just need you to believe in me

right now. I need the moral support. No one has to know that you and I are close. I've never told anyone about our friendship. Have you?" Frank asked.

"No, I've told no one," she said.

"I'm glad to hear that. It should be easy to keep you above the fray when the bad stuff starts coming down. I swear to you, Lizzy, I'll bring down Whelan if it's the last thing I ever do," Frank said.

"It just might be, Frank. The last thing you ever do that is," Elizabeth said quietly.

"So be it," the former decorated Naval officer replied.

****

Elizabeth was reviewing a letter she had just finished typing when Senator Whelan came through the doorway of his office and over to her desk.

"I just got a call from Senate Majority Leader, Mike Mansfield. I'm going down to his office to meet with him and Senator Everett Dirksen for a few minutes. I shouldn't be gone more than a half hour," Whelan said.

"Okay, I'll hold down the fort while you're out," Elizabeth said with a smile.

Whelan always liked Elizabeth Gardener. She had good looks, was well mannered, and was efficient. Particularly interesting was how quickly she had caught on to how things got done in Washington. She was able to wade through the entanglement of misstatements by those opposing his positions on various legislation, and she always made his letters sound a lot more professional than what he actually delivered during dictation. He figured she had a bright future on his staff, and if he ever decided to run for President, he would probably take her with him to the Oval office.

Twenty minutes later, as Elizabeth was putting the finishing touches to a second letter she needed to finish for her boss's signature, Frank appeared and asked to see the Senator.

"He's down the hall at Senator Mansfield's office in a short meeting. He should be back in about five or ten minutes," she said, glancing at the clock on her desk.

"Well, would it be okay if I just place this legal opinion on his desk? I have a dental appointment in a little while and don't really have time to wait for the Senator," Frank said.

"Sure, go ahead," Elizabeth replied. "By the way, are you doing okay? I mean, you were in a bad way at lunch, Frank, and I've been kind of worried about you."

"I'm fine. Thank you for asking, and thank you for being my friend, Lizzy," Frank said.

"You're quite welcome, 'Senator Rubenstein'," she said playfully.

The upbeat gesture from his friend gave Frank a nice lift. As their eyes met, he clearly saw 'the look.'

If I ever get out of this mess, I'm going to pursue this girl, he thought.

As Frank entered the senator's office, something unusual caught his eye. The door to the walk-in closet containing the senator's tape recorder was slightly open.

Senator Whelan secretly recorded all of his telephone conversations so he would have an account of what was said during any given conversation. If he needed to verify the content he had with a colleague, then he would have a record of it. He had installed the reel-to-reel tape recorder a few years ago. It was set to start recording phone calls as soon as he flipped a switch under his desk. Likewise, he could flip another switch and record anyone in his office that was sitting across the desk from him.

Senator Whelan had been inside the closet changing a reel of tape on the recorder when Senator Mansfield called, and he had forgotten to lock the door. Frank saw this as a golden opportunity to lift possible evidence from the senator's closet that just might be incriminating to him.

Very quickly, Frank moved over to the closet door and stepped inside. The shelves on both sides of the small room were stacked with dozens of large reels of audio tapes, each placed in its own box. They were neatly arranged upright like books on a shelf and were dated from March 1959 through August 1963. Frank knew that a large part of the business Senator Whelan had conducted pertaining to the money scheme had transpired in 1963, so he proceeded to take five reels dating from April through August. After exiting the closet, he made sure the door was slightly open just as he had found it.

On top of a filing cabinet next to the door leading back into Lizzy's office was a stack of unused large paper bags. He retrieved one and quickly placed the reels of tape inside it. As he walked by Senator Whelan's desk, he picked up the folder containing the legal brief that he had brought to the senator. He did not want Whelan to know he had been inside his office. In another life, Frank had been a spy, and he knew how to cover his tracks on a mission.

Frank stopped by Elizabeth's desk on his way out and placed the legal brief on her desk. "Tell the senator I brought this by," he said.

"I thought you were going to leave it on his desk," she stated with a puzzled look.

"I decided I don't want the senator to know I was in his office."

"Should I not ask what's going on here? And should I not ask what's in that paper bag?"

"You're right. You should not ask, and I'd appreciate it if you did not tell the senator I was in his office," Frank said as he gave his friend a long, stern gaze.

"I won't," Elizabeth said as she returned the look.

As he was closing the door leading to the main hallway behind him, Frank heard the senator's voice as he was coming through Elizabeth's door leading from his to her office. He had entered his office using a direct access door to the hall and had immediately locked the closet door as soon as he realized he had left it open.

"Has anybody been here to see me?" he asked.

"Yes sir, Frank Rubenstein came by for a moment to drop off this legal opinion brief for you," she replied as she handed him the folder containing the brief.

"Did he go into my office?" he asked.

"No sir, he just dropped it on my desk and left. Said he had a dental appointment," she said as she kept herself busy to mask the blatant lie she had just told her boss.

"Oh, okay. I hate going to the dentist. Don't like taking shots in the mouth," Senator Whelan said shaking his head.

"Me either, but if you're going to keep that Bucky Beaver smile, Senator you have to go," she said smiling.

Senator Whelan stepped inside his office and closed the door behind him.

Elizabeth did not know what Frank had retrieved from the senator's office, but she knew it must be very important. Then she realized that she did not need to know what was in that paper bag. She instinctively felt that it could be dangerous information to possess. Suddenly, she was glad she didn't know.

CHAPTER 5

On his way to his private office, David stopped by Madge Bellows's desk to get any messages received while he was at lunch.

"Mister Walt Austin called while you were out. He said he had something for you," she said as she handed him the note.

"Thank you," David said as he turned and went into his office.

Once behind his desk, David dialed Walt's Washington DC number. Walt's secretary stated that Walt was expecting his call and passed David through to him.

"Walt Austin here," he answered.

"Walt, this is David. My secretary said you have something for me," David said.

"I surely do, and it's pretty good stuff, Major," Walt Austin replied.

Walt explained to David that he had placed a stakeout at James Benton's Alexandria, Virginia home and that Benton arrived midafternoon on Sunday. After about three hours, Benton came out of his house and drove to the Martha Washington Library. There he met a man in the parking lot and handed him a large brown envelope that appeared to be full of paper, maybe cash.

Walt's detective tailed the second man after he and Benton

went their separate ways. Using his automobile tag number, Walt ran a check on the second man and determined that he was one 'Frank Rubenstein.' Walt told David that he was tailing Rubenstein now and had learned that he worked in the Capitol Hill office of Senator Whelan of South Carolina. He also said that he would be tailing Rubenstein for the next couple of days to learn his after-work leisure habits. Walt thought tailing Rubenstein during his nighttime activities would be helpful if David wanted to approach Rubenstein during his investigation. David asked Walt to provide him with a complete bio on Frank Rubenstein and Senator Whelan. Walt agreed and assured David that he would have what he needed within twenty-four hours.

Walt Austin was a very thorough investigator, and David was thankful to have him on the case. He thanked Walt and told him that he would be in touch within a day or two.

After hanging up, David began to piece together what he suspicioned was some sort of bribe scheme between Clyde Bayless and Senator Whelan. He was sure he was onto something big and only needed to gain the confidence of one person somewhere in the food chain of this organization in order to obtain the leverage he needed over Clyde. He was beginning to conclude that person to be either Frank Rubenstein or James Benton.

But how am I going to get either of them to talk? he thought.

David decided to worry about how to make that happen when the time comes. The truth was he couldn't care less if Clyde had involved himself with dirty Washington politics or was on a secret mission for the CIA. He really didn't care. His only interest was how to shove the little pig into a corner and choke the deed to Joe and Millie's property from his grubby little fingers. If it meant the senator's empire along with Clyde's came tumbling down in the process, then David Squire was okay with that.

****

After his afternoon dental appointment, Frank stopped by Erol's TV repair shop to secure two reel-to-reel tape recorders. He was disappointed to learn that Erol had only one available but had another one due back in the store on Saturday. Frank decided to rent the one recorder and use it to find and mark the portions of the tape that were pertinent to his objective. He would then be able to duplicate what he needed after he received the second recorder. He knew this was going to put him on a short timeline before Senator Whelan returned on Tuesday from his South American trip, but he had no choice. Erol's TV repair shop was the only electronics store in the area that rented large reel-to-reel tape recorders.

Frank loaded the machine into his Ford sedan and drove back to his apartment. After he plugged in the tape recorder and listened to a short portion of the tape dated April 1963, he was satisfied that he had everything set up properly.

It was five thirty, and his friends from various Capitol Hill offices would be at Martin's Tavern for an afternoon drink by now, so Frank needed to get on down to the pub. He needed to find a way to get back into Whelan's locked closet, and the right guy who could connect him with someone to pick the lock would probably be at Martin's Tavern by now.

Frank knew he must have the tapes in their original places on the shelves sometime before the Senator returned. If past habits were any indication, Whelan would probably not pay any attention to the closet, but he had recently mentioned that he was going to have to find a larger space for the items stored inside as soon as he got back from his trip. That would mean an accurate inventory of the closet contents would take place before he moved it to the new storage location.

Frank knew Elizabeth could end up in a bad fix because she was the guardian of Senator Whelan's office while he was gone, and she had seen Frank remove a paper bag containing something from the office. Frank wasn't sure Elizabeth could stand up to the Senator's interrogation if he were to bear down on her. That's why he had not told her what was in the paper bag. If she didn't know, she couldn't tell the senator.

Martin's Tavern was busy with the usual crowd of congressional staffers, lobbyists, and a couple of Congressmen. As Frank approached the table where several of his friends were unwinding, he was pleased to see that Paul Herron at the table. If anybody could help Frank unlock the closet, Paul Herron would know him and would have his name in the ever-present address book he carried in his jacket pocket.

Making it a point to sit next to Paul, Frank ordered a draft beer and relaxed while the comedian of the group, Ellard Whitmore told the latest funny story of the day's activities around the hill.

When the laughter died down from Ellard's anecdotal

monolog, Frank took the opportunity to get Paul Herron off to the side to talk to him about a possible locksmith that Paul might know that could pick the lock on a door. Without telling Paul the details, Frank suggested that great discretion had to be observed on this thing, and he needed someone who would forget about it ten minutes after doing the deed. Paul pulled out his address book, and Frank copied the name, and phone number of a locksmith that Paul suggested would be the perfect man for the job.

Frank had a couple of beers, thanked his friend, said goodbye to the group, then got up, and made his way to the door. Sitting three tables away, a man dressed in a sports coat and tie sipped a cup of coffee and went unnoticed by Frank as he walked past the table.

Gene Somers was Walt Austin's most reliable detective, especially when it came to tailing someone. He would stick to a subject like glue and would not turn him loose until the boss gave him the order. He had been parked a few spaces away from Frank Rubenstein's car all morning until Frank left the office and had followed him to the dentist's office. He then watched as Frank loaded a large tape recorder into his car at a TV shop and had taken it to his apartment and unloaded it. Now he was about to follow Frank wherever else he was going.

****

By the end of the second day after Frank rented the tape recorder, he had marked several places that could possibly implicate Whelan and others in criminal bribery charges. He was not comfortable that he had enough evidence for a conviction, however, and felt he needed more. This was not a case of two goons bragging about how they had robbed a liquor store. This was a powerful United States Senator involved in bribery with those paying the bribes being enormous beneficiaries of the senator's subsequent favors. The evidence against them had to be very clear and irrefutable.

There was one thing that Frank Rubenstein was determined to uncover. The recorded conversations so far had not revealed the Senator's contact on the other end of the deal. It was imperative for Frank to know the name of that contact if he was to go to the FBI with charges as serious as these against a high-ranking member of the Senate.

Frank had listened long hours and knew that he had several more hours of listening. He had two more tapes to monitor, so he decided to skip his afternoon beer at Martin's Tavern.

****

It was midafternoon on Friday, and the mood around the office was more relaxed than usual since Senator Whelan was not scheduled to be back until Tuesday. Elizabeth Gardener had three more letters to type to various constituents who were concerned about an assortment of legislation that might affect South Carolinians. After that, she would be able to relax and just take messages from colleagues who needed Senator Whelan's assistance for whatever reason. As she was about to start on the first of the three letters her door opened, and Frank came in carrying his briefcase.

"You look like you're on your way to the golf course," Elizabeth said.

"Actually no, but I've finished the last of my work, so I think I'm going to slip out the door while no one is looking. You won't squeal, will you?" Frank asked playfully.

"I promise I won't tell a single person until the senator returns on Tuesday. Then I'll tell him everything the entire staff was up to while he was gone. After all, this is Washington, where all advancement is based on brownie points. I need a few more added to my collection if I'm going to get that raise I'm expecting in December," Elizabeth said with a smile.

"Oh, I see. Well, in that case, I think I'm coming down with a cold," Frank laughed.

"Okay, I'll put you down for sick leave," she said returning the cheer.

Frank looked at his watch as he left the office. He felt like he would have enough time to finish listening to the last tape tonight, and tomorrow morning he would get the other tape recorder and begin the duplications.

On his way home, Frank decided to stop by Erol's TV shop just in case the other rented tape recorder had been returned early. To his dismay, the owner, Erol Onaran, informed him that the man who rented it had called to inform him that he would not be returning the machine until Monday morning. Frank now knew he was on an even stricter timeline to make the duplications. He decided to attempt to secure a recording machine from surrounding cities, even if it was a two-hour drive. It didn't matter at this point. He had to make the duplications before the senator returned on Tuesday or he had no corroborating evidence to support any accusations he was to make against Senator Whelan.

After a half dozen phone calls, Frank finally found a tape recording machine in Richmond, over a hundred miles away. He decided to pick it up the next morning and dub the tapes through the weekend. He figured he could have them back in their proper places by Monday morning, a full day before Senator Whelan would be returning. It would be a tight squeeze, but Frank had been in tight situations before, so he was comfortable that he could make it happen.

****

As soon as he entered Elizabeth's office early Monday morning, Frank knew the situation had significantly changed. Standing next to her desk laughing about something that had happened on his trip to South America, Whelan saw Frank, smiled, and continued with his story. Frank had the tapes tucked away in his briefcase and was about to persuade Elizabeth to allow him to enter the senator's office during the noon hour when most of the staff would be out. He had made arrangements with the locksmith to meet him there at just past noon. Whelan's appearance had suddenly changed everything. Frank had duplicated the important segments of the tapes, and in the process, he had discovered a mountain of evidence that would drive all the nails into the political coffin of Senator Whelan. Now he was in big trouble and so was Elizabeth if Whelan discovered the tapes had gone missing before Frank could return them to their proper places.

Practically speaking, Frank had played it too close. It was just a matter of time before Whelan decided to make good on the comment about moving the contents of his closet to a larger storage location. He had returned a full day ahead of schedule, and now Frank was worried that if the senator discovered his blunder, this was going to be a very bad situation. Senator Whelan knew that hard evidence existed on the tapes that could send him to prison, and he would do whatever was necessary to get the tapes back into his possession.

Whelan had never been known to order bodily harm to anyone, but he was an incredibly mean-spirited politician who took no prisoners when he felt it was time to drop the hammer on the opposition. It had once been rumored that he was responsible for a rendezvous between a popular congressman who was in line for Speaker of the House of Representatives and a woman that the congressman did not know was a prostitute. She had been throwing herself at him for weeks until he finally decided to meet her for intimacy. A photographer was in an adjoining room of her apartment behind a one-way mirror taking photos of the whole thing. Whelan did not attempt to blackmail the congressman. He just simply leaked the photos to the Press, and they proceeded to destroy the man. Whelan showed no mercy when it came to political enemies. If he needed to destroy someone to advance his agenda, he would do so in the blink of an eye.

The stealing of the tapes, on the other hand, was far more dangerous than simply opposing Whelan on a piece of legislation. Frank knew this, and he was worried for the safety of Elizabeth, and to a lesser degree, his own safety. He simply had to figure out a way to return the tapes before the senator began the process of moving the contents of the closet. Whelan was a stickler for details so he would arrange for a close accounting to make sure each tape was placed in chronological order in the proper packing boxes for easy access. There was no doubt in Frank's mind that he would discover the discrepancy.

CHAPTER 6

David was finishing a phone call with a client when the intercom on his desk buzzed. Madge informed him that Walt Austin was holding for him on line three.

"Good morning, Walt. Tell me you have something for me," David said.

"Yes, I do, Major. I have a complete dossier on Senator Whelan and one on Frank Rubenstein, including the whereabouts of their next of kin. In Frank's case, I was able to get his military record and his brother's military record as well," Walt said enthusiastically. "I also have a dossier on James Benton including his military record, and a couple of family members. I think now might be a good time for you to catch a plane to DC. I believe we have enough information on most of the principal players to plot our next move, Major."

"I'll be there later today or tomorrow morning. Do you have a loose plan of action for going forward?" David asked.

Walt Austin always had a plan to go forward. That had been one of his strongest assets as an OSS agent during the War. He always knew the next step to take at any given time. He had brought that quality into the investigation business, and it had served him well. Walt Austin was always a few steps ahead of his targets.

There was the other element that was heavy on Walt's

mind. This was not just another routine investigation. This was for his old wartime friend, Joe Carter, to whom he owed his life, and Walt was not going to let David down on this thing.

"I do have a plan, Major. Just get here as quickly as you can. I believe I have what you need to begin making progress. I'll be lending you all the support I possibly can. You have my assurance on that, sir," Walt said.

"I have no doubt you will," David replied. "Thank you in advance, and thanks on behalf of Joe too."

"The pleasure is mine, sir," Walt said as he hung up the phone.

Like many men who had become friends after the War with higher-ranking officers they had served with, Walt had never become used to addressing David by his first name. David had always considered it the highest form of compliment for his old friend to address him by his Army rank.

****

Frank Rubenstein took a seat on his sofa, opened a beer he had just retrieved from the refrigerator, and took a long pull. His mind drifted as he stared at a framed photo on the fireplace mantel of himself and President John F. Kennedy that was taken in the oval office on a cool November afternoon less than a month after the end of the Cuban missile crisis last year. Senator Whelan had invited Frank to meet the President because of Frank's possible future run for the Senate.

As Frank sat there gazing at the photo, he remembered how personable President Kennedy was during the twenty-minute meeting. The President had been a naval officer during the War, with a well-documented record of heroism in the PT boat command. When Senator Whelan mentioned Frank's service in Naval Intelligence, President Kennedy immediately turned to Frank and began communicating with him as though the two of them were former comrades in arms chatting on a park bench. For the next several minutes, President Kennedy had asked Frank all about the intel that he had been involved in during the weeks leading up to the Battle of Midway. The President had listened with keen interest, Frank remembered, as he explained in detail just exactly how the Navy had verified that they had broken the Japanese code. The President had stood quietly, listening intently to every word that Frank said about the mission. Not a single person in the Oval office dared interrupt his monolog to the President.

After Frank was finished, President John F. Kennedy quietly said, "And I was awarded a couple of medals for getting my boat split into two halves by an enemy destroyer. Something that I should have seen coming. It doesn't take much for a skipper to lose his ride like that. You, on the other hand, were the real heroes. Your unit saved thousands of lives on both sides with that one piece of intelligence. My hat goes off to you, Frank."

For a year now, Frank had savored those words from the most powerful man on Earth. He would never forget the humble look in the President's eyes as he praised the actions of Frank's unit.

But now, Frank was at the lowest point of his life. He had hard criminal evidence on a scoundrel who was not qualified to shine the shoes of a great man like John Fitzgerald Kennedy. The decision Frank had to make now, *right now* was whether he, a former officer and a gentleman, who had served his country with honor, was willing to give up his future and probably even go to prison, to expose the criminal enterprise in which a powerful United States senator was the central player. This was Frank Rubenstein's day of reckoning, the moment to do the right thing or take the low road and continue to wallow inside the awful void of conscience in which he had found himself.

After draining most of a six-pack, Frank slowly stood up, walked over to the mantel, and gently took the framed photo into his hands. While staring into the eyes of a smiling President John F. Kennedy, the former decorated naval officer made the decision that he had to go through with this. He had been having an agonizing debate inside his very soul for months now about the scam perpetrated onto the American people of which he was an integral part. Now was the time for him to come clean with the law and most importantly himself. He didn't much care what happened to him. He accepted that he deserved whatever the government decided to do with him. And so did Senator Whelan, whom he quietly made a solemn vow to bring down also.

****

Harold Gersen had just finished filling a Christmas display on an end cap of a shelf in his hardware store when he heard a familiar voice a few feet away. Frank Rubenstein had stopped by to ask a favor of his longtime friend. Frank knew the favor could cause a disaster for Harold and his family. The truth was that he had no one else to turn to with the evidence he had on the Senator. Harold Gersen was an old friend from college whom no one in Frank's political or social world knew about. For that reason, he figured Harold would be the perfect person to temporarily hold onto the audiotapes until the immediate situation passed. Frank felt uneasy about the fact that he had not been able to return the tapes to Senator Whelan's closet before the Senator returned from his South American trip. He knew that any day now Senator Whelan could begin the inventory of his closet, and if that happened, the explosion that followed would not be pretty. No one on his staff would be safe.

"Good morning, old friend. Looks like you're getting into the spirit a bit early this year," Frank said.

"Well, we have to get an edge on the competition, you know. The hardware business is much more competitive than it once was," Harold said with a smile. "So, what brings you down from the Ivory tower?"

"Oh I just thought I'd stop by to say hello to the little people," Frank said, chuckling. "How's my roommate doing?"

"He's doing fine," Harold said. "He never complains, is never late for work, and always gets along with the customers well. Everyone likes him."

"That's good. I'll tell Helen when I see her. I'm sure she'll be pleased to hear that he's doing well," Frank said.

A couple of years earlier Jay Booker, the son of a female friend and high school classmate of Frank's, had moved in with him at the request of Jay's mother. Frank had originally decided to allow Jay to stay with him for a few weeks until he could get his feet on the ground, but the weeks ended up being months, and now, two years later he was still there. He caused Frank no problems and was a very neat, well-groomed young man who pretty much kept to himself. He had expressed to Frank that he would like to save money for a down payment on a house, so Frank decided to let him stay as long as he needed to save the money for the house. Jay was a simple young man who was a little slow to learn, but he was very dependable and a good worker. Right after he moved in, Frank introduced him to Harold. Harold hired him and was very pleased with his job performance.

"Harold, I actually have something important I'd like to talk to you about if you don't mind," Frank said.

"Of course. Private?" Harold asked.

"Yes, could we have a minute?" Frank asked.

"Sure, follow me."

Harold led Frank into his private break room upstairs over the warehouse in the rear of the store.

"Coffee?" Harold asked as he reached for the pot on the counter next to a small sink.

"No, thank you. I don't have much time," Frank said as he took a seat across the table from Harold. "This is not actually a social visit, Harold. I won't waste your time, so I'll just get right to the point," Frank said. "It seems that I'm in quite a fix over at the so-called Ivory Tower. I'm involved in a situation of corruption at high levels. I have something I'd like to leave with you for safe keeping if you don't mind," he said.

"Should I refrain from asking what it is?" Harold asked

while observing a box under Frank's arm.

Harold was a battle-hardened former Marine who had landed on three different beaches in the island campaign across the South Pacific during the War, including Okinawa, Tarawa, and, as a captain, had led a company of Marines during the first wave to hit the beach at Iwo Jima. Needless to say, Harold had seen every kind of human debauchery known to mankind. He was the kind of man who just wasn't afraid of anything. He had already been to hell. To Harold, even on a very bad day, life was good for him. Frank knew that if he could trust anyone to hold on to the original tapes, it would be Harold.

Inside the small box tucked under his left arm were the original tapes he had stolen. He had finally finished duplicating the tapes and had left the duplicates at his apartment. He figured if he were robbed, it would be much better for the duplicates to be taken instead of the originals. Prosecutors would have a difficult time making their case with duplicate tapes of the hard evidence.

Frank also included two envelopes inside the box with the tapes: one with Harold's name on it and one that said *For Elizabeth Gardener's eyes only*. Inside the envelope marked *Harold Gersen* was information on how to contact Elizabeth Gardener and instructions to give her the contents of the box. Inside the envelope marked for Elizabeth was a set of instructions that went into detail about what she should do in case he ended up on the wrong end of things.

Harold poured himself a cup of coffee and leaned back in his chair and waited to hear what Frank was about to say. He knew this was not going to be good, but he was determined to help his friend in his time of need.

"So, what's going on over at the Capitol that's got you running for the hills?" he asked.

"Well, Harold, I've got myself in a real mess. I'm not prepared to reveal any details at this time, but I've been involved in a bit of wrongdoing," he said wearily. "I have hard evidence that will bring down a very powerful senator and probably send him to prison. I'm sure you know that when someone of great stature on the Hill is humbled, everyone in his world goes down with him. It's just the way the political game is played. Never offend or expose wrongdoing by a powerful politician, or it will end very badly for you," Frank said with a quiet voice.

Harold had never seen his friend like this. He knew there had to be more to it than Frank simply crossing over to the other side. Moving away from duty and honor was simply not the Frank Rubenstein that he knew.

"So what does he have on you, Frank?" Harold asked in a matter of fact manner.

Frank thought for a moment at how intuitive both Harold Gersen and Elizabeth Gardener, who were strangers to each other, had instinctively known the reason he had gone to the dark side of Washington. That told Frank that at least two people in this town believed in him. That little revelation gave him the motivation to admit to himself that there was no use in trying to sugarcoat the situation, so he just decided to come clean with the former Marine captain sitting across from him.

Harold had already figured out that Frank had somehow

stumbled along his road on Capitol Hill and now needed to clear his conscience. He was not prepared to make a negative judgment of his longtime friend, so he just sat quietly while Frank gave him a brief overview of his involvement in the bribery scheme that Senator Whelan was operating. After Frank had finished, Harold asked how he could help.

"I have hard evidence here that will bring the senator down. I have reason to believe that my life may be in danger, and I want this evidence to be preserved in case anything happens to me," Frank said while placing the box containing the tapes on Harold's desk in front of him. "Inside the box is an envelope with your name on it. Please follow the instructions therein if anything happens to me."

Harold took a long moment to look at the box before he touched it or said anything. Finally, he picked it up, stepped over to his safe, and began to spin the combination dial on the door. "I'll look after this for you, Frank," Harold said as he placed the box inside the safe. "I will never open the box unless the unspeakable happens. Let's just hope it doesn't come to that. No one on this earth will ever know that I have this unless you tell him or her," he said in a stern voice.

Frank was both relieved and sad that he had to reveal his plight to a man whom he had always respected so much. Likewise, Harold had gained from Frank's revelation a higher level of admiration for his college friend for what he was about to do. As he stood at the cash register and watched Frank walking across the parking lot to his car with some of that familiar swagger missing, the thought came to him that Frank would do the right thing in the end. Harold had known Frank too long to believe otherwise. He just wished there was more he could do to help, but Frank was right. When the explosion detonated he, Harold, needed to be far out of range, or his family could suffer grave consequences for something they had nothing to do with. Powerful people were viciously protective of their station within the structure, and the center of world power was no place for a guy like Harold whose only connection to that power was about to go down for allowing an evil man to blackmail him. Harold felt helpless as he watched his friend drive away.

****

"I'll have a glass of your most popular red wine," David Squire said as the waiter approached his table. "You're pretty busy for this time of day, aren't you?"

"Oh, there's not really much lull in the action throughout the day around here," the waiter replied with a smile. "Drinks and deals. That seems to always be the order of business. Am I to assume you're not from the Washington area, sir?" the waiter asked.

"No, I'm from Chicago," David said.

"Well, we're glad to have you. Martin's Tavern has been a mainstay for all the principal players in Washington since 1933. President John F. Kennedy Proposed to his girlfriend, Jacqueline Bouvier, right over there in booth number three. We now call that the 'Proposal Booth,' and Vice President Lyndon Johnson's favorite booth is number twenty-four. He sat there many times as a senator while schmoozing his colleagues into seeing things his way on various legislative bills. It could be argued that I have one of the most interesting jobs in Washington outside of politics," he said laughing. "I hear just enough bits and pieces of the wrangling between legislative players that I could write a book on persuasive techniques."

"You should try that," David said with a smile.

After the waiter had left his table, David glanced around the dining room and saw a couple of congressmen that he recognized from TV news reports.

It must really be wicked to have no soul, he thought. *Just sit around and negotiate deals that will affect the lives of every American. Then when the law you've helped write creates more problems than it solves, you just deny any wrongdoing until the story becomes old news. Sooner or later the people that sent you here will forget that you raised their taxes and gave them nothing in return.*

"It's Bordeaux from 1961. A good year," the waiter said as he poured the wine.

"Thank you," David said as the waiter turned to attend to another table.

He was on a mission now, and it was going to be a waiting game for the next hour or so. He had decided it was time that he met this guy, Frank Rubenstein. Walt had briefed David on all of Frank's daily habits and hangouts. David had decided this was as good a place as any to begin his pursuit of this Mr. Rubenstein.

After a few minutes of reading the *Washington Post,* David looked up from the newspaper just in time to see Frank Rubenstein step through the front door. He was slowly looking around as if to see if he knew anyone in the crowded room. With all the tables and booths taken, Frank took a seat on a stool at the bar.

After David had studied the photograph given to him by Walt, he determined that it was, no doubt, Frank Rubenstein sitting at the bar. He stood up, got his half-full glass of wine, walked slowly over to the bar, and stood in front of a stool next to Frank.

"Hi, is this stool taken?" David asked with a warm smile.

"No, I'm just hanging out for a little while. I left the office early today and decided to drop by. This is a favorite hangout for a few congressional staffers who come here to wind down," Frank said.

"My name is David Squire," David said with a smile.

"Frank Rubenstein. Pleased to meet you," Frank said.

"You work for an elected official?" David asked.

"Yes, I'm an aide to Senator Whelan. Pretty grueling job sometimes, but I enjoy it," Frank said.

David was somewhat surprised at Frank's openness and warm, friendly manner. He was expecting Frank to be a much more reserved individual. The thought occurred to him that if a person is going to excel in this town, he just about has to have an unrestrained personality, or he'll get eaten alive by the culture.

"Senator Whelan? Isn't he from South Carolina?" David asked.

"Yes, he's the Senior Senator from South Carolina after incumbent Senator Mabank died right before the election of

1954. Former South Carolina Governor, Strom Thurmond, was elected as a write-in candidate that year, and is now the junior senator," Frank said. "Senator Whelan has been in the Senate since 1950."

"You don't speak with a southern drawl. You're not from South Carolina, are you?" David half asked, and half stated.

"No, I'm from Pennsylvania."

"Really? Big city, or country boy?"

"Country boy. I was raised outside a small town called McCary. My brother and I loved to ride horses through the countryside pretending to be real cowboys," Frank said with a smile.

Over the years when David was stalking a suspect, he had developed a keen sense of exactly when to move to the next level in the game. He strongly felt that now was the time to jump in with both feet. The target had warmed up to him much faster than he had expected, and David could see that he was ready for the ride down deceit lane, so he took the proverbial swing.

"I served in the Army during the War with a guy named Rubenstein. Aaron Rubenstein. McCary sounds like what I remember he once told me was the name of his hometown," David said.

Amazed at the coincidence, Frank was taken aback for a brief moment. "Where did you serve?"

"North Africa, Italy, D-day landing in Normandy, and my unit, The Big Red One, fought all the way across Europe to the German Fatherland, as the Krauts called it," David said.

"My brother was in the Big Red One and since you served with an Aaron Rubenstein, I'll have to ask him if he knows you. How may I reach you when I find out?" Frank asked with enthusiasm.

"I'll be here about this time of day for the next few days. My business in Washington won't be done for another week or so," David said, faking enthusiasm. "I'm anxious to know if it's your brother I served with. Maybe I'll see you here in a couple of days."

As David was getting up to leave, Frank asked him to write down his name and his military particulars such as Brigade, Regiment, Battalion, and so forth. David wrote down all of the above on a napkin right down to the exact company and platoon that he knew Frank's brother had served in. Frank also asked David where he was from. David told him Chicago. He did not tell Frank that he was originally from Arkansas.

As soon as Frank's brother told him he had served with no such person named David Squire during the War, the situation was going to get very interesting. David had told Frank the concocted story about serving with his brother to let Frank know that he had him under the microscope. It was an old trick that sometimes made it easier to flush out the prey if he knew that a detective was on to him.

Many times over the years David used similar falsehoods like this. He had always marveled at how unnerved people would become and how cooperative they would suddenly be when they were confronted with the reality that an investigator knew all about their family and friends who live in other cities and other states. In about two days, David expected Frank Rubenstein to become very easy to see things his way. Time would tell.

CHAPTER 7

"Bayless Farms, may I help you?" Sarah Jennings asked as she answered the phone.

"Good morning Miss Sarah. How's my pretty little friend doing this morning?" Thad McRae asked in his usual flirtatious tone.

"I'm doing fine," Sarah said with a smile.

"I hear there's a cold front coming through this weekend. I need a pretty girl to snuggle up with at the Razorback game. You wouldn't happen to know anyone who might be interested, would you?" Thad asked.

"Well, now, I just can't think of a single person, but if I come up with any names, I'll let you know," Sarah said with laughter.

Sarah Jennings and Thad McRae had been buddies since childhood. They started and finished all twelve grades of school together and had dated a few times until they mutually decided a romance just wasn't right for either of them. They had always remained close pals, however. Shortly after Sarah and her husband moved to Arkansas, Thad also moved to a neighboring county and opened a law practice. Sarah had often jokingly accused him of chasing her all the way to Arkansas. He had been a pallbearer at her husband's funeral after the tragic accident that took his life.

"Well, if I'm not getting anywhere here, you might as well pass me through to Clyde," he said with a fake despair in his voice.

"Sure, hold on," Sarah said smiling as she placed him on hold and buzzed Clyde.

The phone call from Thad McRae was an ugly reminder of a very depressing discovery she had made a couple of years ago when Thad mentioned to Sarah over dinner that he was doing some legal work for Clyde Bayless involving business contracts. Sarah had told him confidentially that she loathed Clyde and was going to one day see him come tumbling down for what he had done to her. She remembered that Thad sat across the table from her with a look of disbelief. He was representing a man who had inflicted harm onto one of his closest lifelong friends.

She had encouraged Thad to continue representing Clyde and not to worry about her personal grievance against him. That evening they made a pact to never let anyone in her community know that they were close friends. Sarah knew that Clyde Bayless would discontinue using Thad if he knew they were friends. Clyde did not trust anyone—not even a sworn officer of the court, so Thad and Sarah just thought it was best to keep their friendship a secret.

"Hello," Clyde said.

"Good morning Clyde, Thad McRae here. In response to your request to start taking inventory of the equipment on the Carter farm, I think it would be fine to start anytime you're ready. You will, of course, need permission from Joe Carter. After all, you haven't yet taken legal possession of the assets, and although you're probably going to soon after I get the legal petition filed, I highly suggest that you get his permission before you take the inventory."

"Thank you, Thad. I'll keep that in mind when we go to record the serial numbers," Clyde said with a bit of carefree flare in his voice. "I'll be in touch," he said as he hung up the phone.

Clyde wanted to expedite the foreclosure as soon as possible because Joe Carter didn't have much longer to live, according to the information he had obtained from Joe's doctor. Clyde just didn't want the delays that an estate settlement might cause for him to take possession of the Carter farm. He didn't have anything personal against Millie Carter, but he also had no sympathy for her because she was married to an old nemesis of his. The bottom line now was that Clyde had to get everything legally in place so that the day the judge ruled in his favor, he could approach Joe Carter face to face and kick him off the land. Clyde was relishing the thought of that. He had always despised Joe Carter and his two-bit friend, David Squire, and this was going to be fun.

A few more years and Bayless Farms would own twice the land as any other landowner in the county. How sweet it is, he thought as he unsealed the wrapper and toyed with an unlit cigar. *How sweet it is, indeed.*

****

It was almost nine a.m. as Billy Bayless rolled over and looked at the clock.

Dang, I slept through the alarm again, he thought. *Daddy's gonna be grumpy at me for this.*

Just as he was about to get out of bed, the phone rang.

"Where are you?" Clyde asked.

"Uh....uh....I'm on my way. I got sidetracked here with something this morning. I'll be down in a few minutes," Billy said nervously.

"Okay, make it snappy," Clyde said with a bit of irritation.

"I will," Billy said.

Billy Bayless was a classic example of the expression "Born with a silver spoon in his mouth." He had never experienced a need or desire that went unmet. If there was ever any such thing as a carbon copy of someone, it was Billy Bayless. He was exactly like his father, Clyde Bayless, in every way except for one. Clyde Bayless was not lazy. In fact, he would work many extra hours to figure out how to get the upper hand on whomever he was dealing with.

Billy, on the other hand, figured the world owed him a living. He figured it was his place in life to have money, leisure time, all the girls he wanted, and nice cars. He had floated through the University of Arkansas not because he was a genius, but because he had money to pay others to take tests for him in the courses at which he was weak. He had always viewed it as a favor to the guys taking his tests for him. He figured it was a quick way for them to make money. After all, they were usually from working class families who were struggling to send their kids to college. It was all part of being privileged. While he was a freshman and driving a brand new convertible, most of his classmates were walking or riding a bicycle to class.

Billy Bayless had always viewed himself as just a little better than those he grew up with. For that reason, from the first grade all the way to graduation, not even one of his classmates liked him. He had no friends. It had made him lonely and bitter to have been born to be short in physical stature like his father. He never understood that it wasn't because he was short that no one liked him. It was because he looked down his nose at everyone around him. He even looked down on most of his teachers. He figured they were just barely skimming by on a teacher's salary and would never really amount to anything. He had no idea of the positive impact a teacher could have had on his life if he had just come down from his throne. None of the teachers really blamed Billy for his self-centered attitude. They all just figured the apple didn't fall far from the tree. Nurture simply could not have outweighed nature with him. Just a snobbish kid who was convinced that everyone in his world was beneath him.

Clyde was on the phone when Billy came through the door. He glanced up at Billy and quickly decided that he had just gotten out of bed. After he had finished his conversation, he shot Billy a stern look but decided not to mention his tardiness.

"I have something I want you to do. I want you to go out to the Carter farm and inventory all the equipment on this list," he said as he handed Billy a list of equipment with serial numbers. "Make sure that all the equipment matches these serial numbers."

"Does Joe Carter know I'm coming?" Billy asked. "If we're about to foreclose on his farm, he may not be in the best of moods, and I don't want him giving me any grief," he said.

"He won't give you any grief, Billy. He knows we're foreclosing, and I'm sure he realizes he's in no position to start trouble for Bayless Farms this late in the process," Clyde said.

With that bit of assurance, Billy took the list and drove to the Carter farm confident that he would get what he needed in a little while. As he turned off the road and into the driveway in front of Joe and Millie Carter's house, he quickly observed that both the truck and car were gone. He drove along the lane beside the house to the shop area out back. After a moment of sitting in his car and thinking about whether or not he should go inside Joe Carter's tractor shed without informing him, he decided to just get what he came after. He figured if he hurried, he could have everything on the list checked off before Joe or Millie returned.

He was on the last five or six pieces of equipment when he heard a vehicle coming down the gravel road. As he looked up, his worst anxiety was realized. Joe had seen Billy's Jaguar convertible from the road, so when he turned into the driveway, he drove on around to the shop area where Billy was standing with an uncomfortable look on his face.

Getting out of his truck, Joe took a quick look around to see who might be with Billy. After concluding that he was alone, Joe walked over to Billy stopping about three feet in front of him. Joe's six-foot frame towered over Billy.

"What are you doing here, young man?" Joe asked with a strong, deliberate voice. "Didn't you see that nobody was home?"

"My daddy told me to come out here and check these serial

numbers of all the equipment on this list," Billy said with a noticeable shake in his voice.

"Let me see that list," Joe said while staring straight into Billy's eyes like a Bengal tiger just before it tears the head off its prey.

With a trembling hand, Billy stepped forward and handed Joe the equipment list. Joe did not look at the list. He maintained the piercing stare right through the eyes and out the back of Billy's head as he neatly folded up the paper and placed it inside his shirt pocket. He slowly, and with authority, stepped in closer to Billy—so close in fact that he could *feel* the fear coming from Billy, and for the first time in weeks, he felt in control. It felt good. He was feeling like a man again.

"You go tell your daddy that I said he can inventory my equipment when it belongs to him. I've already made the point clear to him. He can do whatever he wants to with my assets as soon as they belong to him, but I better not catch anybody else representing Bayless Farms on my property unless they have a court order," Joe said as he stood toe to toe and nose to nose with the petrified young man.

"Yessir," Billy managed to squeak out as he stepped around Joe and quickly made his way to his Jaguar. Joe did not take his eyes off Billy until he was out of the driveway and onto the gravel road speeding back toward town.

That's when he saw the movement out of the corner of his eye. She was leaning against a support post on the back porch with a half-smile and a look of sheer pride on her gorgeous face. Her long wavy hair was slowly moving back and forth across her shoulders in the gentle breeze.

During the altercation, neither man had noticed that Millie had arrived and had walked through the house and onto the back porch. Joe had once again reminded Millie why she loved him so. He was the quintessential man's, man. His quiet demeanor was never, ever to be mistaken for weakness. For a moment, she was reminded again of the first time he had stood up for her on the school bus so many years ago.

Joe slowly made his way to the porch where Millie was still leaning against the post; he climbed the three steps and walked over to where she was standing. He moved closer and kissed her on the forehead while at the same time wrapping his arms around her and giving her a long, gentle hug. She had always been his girl, and it was times like this that he appreciated her the most. She seemed to always know when to be still in the middle of the storm. She was his angel, and he was determined to be her hero until he took his last breath.

"Should I even ask what that was all about?" Millie asked quietly while resting her head on his shoulder.

"More of the same," Joe said.

Joe's thoughts were heavy in his heart right now. *If David doesn't come through for me soon, I don't know what I'll do. Millie doesn't deserve this.*

Millie sensed the heaviness of his thoughts by the change in his breathing, so she just held him softly.

Sometimes silence is more precious than any spoken word when two people love each other, she thought.

****

Clyde was about to call Whelan when the door swung open, and Billy came in with a look of terror on his face. "He threw me off the farm," Billy said almost shouting. "I was afraid he was going to jump on me. He got right up in my face, Daddy, and told me he better not ever catch anybody from Bayless Farms on his property again until we take possession."

Clyde was livid that Joe Carter would talk to his boy like that. "I'll take care of it," he told Billy. "You just go on about your duties."

After Billy had left, Clyde pondered on how he should handle this insult to his family. *Nobody insults the Bayless family like this and gets away with it,* he thought. *Nobody!*

There was no doubt in his mind what he really wanted to do. He wanted to go out to the Carter farm with a short joint of two-inch pump pipe and just beat Joe Carter until he got tired of swinging the pipe. However, there was only one problem with that idea. Clyde was not foolish enough to go by himself, and he did not know a single man who would be willing to go with him. Every man in the country would decline his offer for the same reason. Fear. Joe Carter was known far and wide as a man that should not be goaded into anger, so Clyde decided to just let it pass for now. He could not remember the last time he had been this angry.

I'll get him. It's just a matter of a few more days, and when I do, it's going to be sweet watching him humbled, he thought as he picked up the phone to call Whelan.

CHAPTER 8

Elizabeth Gardener had been taking calls for Senator Whelan all morning and had just about given up on finishing the letter that Senator Whelan had dictated to her the afternoon before. She was about to take a break when the senator came through the door separating their offices.

"Elizabeth, I need for you to call this guy and have him send over a couple of men to help me move a few things out of my closet," he said as he handed her a card with a mover's name and phone number. "Also, he will need to bring some packing boxes for long term storage.

"When do you want them to be here?" Elizabeth asked.

"Friday. The Senate is not scheduled to be in session then, and that would give me time to get my closet cleaned out," Whelan said.

"Yes, sir. I'll get to it as soon as I finish this letter," she said as she resumed typing.

Whelan stepped back through the door, walked over to the closet, and spun the combination. As he was pondering on how he was going to organize the packing of the tapes, it caught his eye—a gap in the line of tapes on the top shelf. Whelan stared at the open area where at least four or five were missing. He was stunned.

No one has the combination to this lock but me, he thought.

A quick examination determined that the door hinges had not been disturbed, and the lock hasp had not been damaged.

How could anyone have opened this door? he wondered.

After examining the door, Whelan went back to the shelf and looked at the date on the left of the gap and then the one on the right of the gap. From this, he determined that five tapes were missing from April through August 1963.

Whelan was a master of anything that had to do with deceptively meandrous behavior, and he knew immediately that someone was after those specific tapes because of the incriminating conversations they contained. He went back to his desk and thought about the events of the past few weeks. He remembered the last time he opened the door—the day before he left for South America. Then it hit him like a bolt of lightning. One time, the door had been left unlocked for about a half hour or so while he visited another senator down the hall. That was also the day before he left on his trip to South America.

Whelan sat there for a few minutes thinking how he should approach Elizabeth about the events of that day. He had always admired her work ethic and proficiency at her job. Likewise, he had observed that she was fiercely loyal to him. If he told her to inform a colleague of his whereabouts at any given time, he knew she would do so—even if she knew it was a blatant lie. She just answered all questions presented to her exactly as he had asked her to do. Simply put, she had never questioned him when he asked her to do something, and he was quite sure she would not lie to him, especially when it came to something as important as the missing tapes. For that reason, Senator Whelan decided to talk to her using a non-confrontational approach.

Elizabeth was about to make the phone call to the movers when Senator Whelan's door opened, and he came into her office. With a look that told Elizabeth, he was upset, maybe even afraid, he walked over to her desk and sat down across from her. He leaned back, allowing his head to rest on the wall.

"Elizabeth, I'm missing something from my office. I need your help in figuring out how it might have disappeared," he said.

"What's missing?" she asked.

Whelan was careful to use the right words and voice inflection so as not to suggest that she was involved in the theft, but he did not trust anyone, and although he liked her, he did not trust her either.

"Someone went into my closet where I keep personal things...and removed some things," he said, looking straight into her eyes as he spoke.

Elizabeth immediately remembered the day Frank went into his office and came out with a paper bag. She knew she had to make her reply look convincing, so she put on her best-puzzled face.

"I thought that closet was locked at all times, Senator. Aren't you the only person that has the combination to the lock?" she asked.

"Yes, but there's one day right before I left for South America that I was down the hall in a meeting with another senator. After I had come back, I noticed that I had left the door unlocked and it was cracked open. I think I may have been distracted by a phone call or something and forgot to lock it before I left for the meeting. A few minutes ago, when I realized that something was missing, I examined the door and the lock clasp. There was no damage to either. Since I'm the only person with the combination to the lock, the theft had to take place while I was in that meeting down the hall," he said, with his eyes affixed on hers. "Think hard, Elizabeth. Did anyone go in my office that day while I was out?" he asked.

"That was two weeks ago, Senator, I'll have to think about it. My first thought is the answer is no," she said with as much smoothness as she could muster.

"No one? Not anyone on the staff? Didn't you tell me that Frank Rubenstein came to see me while I was out? Now, I realize it was two weeks ago, but think about it. Did Frank go into my office?" He asked while piercing her with his stare.

"No, I don't think so. In fact, I'm sure he didn't, Senator. Why on earth would Frank Rubenstein be interested in anything in your closet? I've had many dealings with him for the past few years, and I do not think he's a thief. There has to be another explanation for this, Senator Whelan. There just has to be," she said.

Convinced for now that she was telling the truth, Whelan stood up, thanked her, and went back to his office. There he sat for another half hour racking his brain to try to figure out who could have stolen the tapes.

Elizabeth stared at her typewriter for a full five minutes until she could breathe again. She knew what she had to do now. She reached for her Rolodex.

"Frank Rubenstein," the voice on the other end of the line said.

"Frank, we have to talk. Can you meet me for lunch?" she asked with as much poise as she could assemble.

Frank knew his friend well, and he immediately knew that something was wrong. "Sure, where do you want to meet?" he asked.

"Meet me at the Old Anglers Inn in Potomac Maryland," she said. "I'm taking the afternoon off, so whatever time is okay with you is fine with me."

"I'll be there at one o'clock," Frank said.

Whelan sat at his desk thinking about how anyone could have come into his office right under his executive secretary's nose and stolen the tapes out of his closet.

That's impossible. There's no way someone could have come into my office and figured out the combination of my Sargent and Greenleaf padlock. It just couldn't have happened. The thief either knew the combination and was allowed to enter my office while I was in South America, or was allowed inside the day I forgot to lock the closet for a few minutes while I was out of the office, he thought. *All of this points directly at Elizabeth Gardener.*

Whelan decided to pursue other avenues first. He knew he was in a bad spot. Washington was one giant glass house, and everything that happened was scrutinized by a rabid press corps. If he caused a ruckus within his own staff, the press would not leave it alone until they extracted every story-worthy thing they could from the event.

Frank was standing next to the hostess at the Old Anglers Inn when Elizabeth walked through the door. She was fifteen minutes early, and he was already there.

The hostess seated them at a window overlooking the patio and asked what they would like to drink. Elizabeth ordered a double martini. Frank ordered tea. She gave them their menus and left their table.

"What's wrong, Elizabeth?" Frank asked. "You just ordered a double Martini. I've never seen you drink alcohol. Something bad has happened, hasn't it?"

"Yes, Senator Whelan discovered something missing out of his office closet—the one he keeps locked. He asked me if you had gone inside his office the day before he left for his trip to South America. I told him you had not. I don't know if he believed me, but he's sure someone went into his office that day because he has one of those high-security combination locks on the closet door. He's sure no one could have figured out the combination. In other words, Frank, Whelan has already narrowed down the focus of his investigation to two people— you and me. I have no idea what was in that paper bag that day after you came out of his office, but whatever it was, it's got Senator Whelan very nervous.

"I do not know if I can hold up to high-pressure interrogation, Frank. I'm just a secretary. I'm trying to figure out which way to go with this thing. At this point, I can say that I thought about it and finally remembered you went in his office briefly. I believe I can convince him that I didn't lie to him when he asked me this morning, and I told him no."

Seeing fear all over her, Frank decided he should deflect the punishment away from Elizabeth and just take the hit. He felt sure he could stand up to any interrogation that Whelan could administer.

Looking into her worried eyes, he said firmly, "That may be the safest thing for you, Elizabeth. When you get back to work tomorrow morning, just tell him you thought about it all night and decided that I did, indeed, go into his office. Just explain to him that Friday was an incredibly busy day, and when he originally asked about it, you didn't remember."

"I've thought about doing just that, but every time I almost decide to do it, I can't seem to bring myself to leave you hanging in the wind like that," Elizabeth said.

"Don't worry about me. This whole, rotten mess is of my own doing. I could have just allowed the Senator to hold my past mistake over my head and therefore never run for public office. Whelan is very good at keeping his hand on the pulse of those around him, however. He knew that I had a great desire to be a Senator from Pennsylvania, and he waited until the right time to inform me that he had the goods on me. Then he proceeded to involve me in a small one-time scheme to 'pocket a few extra bucks' to use his jargon. I relented, and now, two and a half years later, I'm up to my elbows in this mess. As I told you a couple of weeks ago, the only way out is to come clean about the bribery scheme, and maybe I can bring Whelan down with me."

The two friends decided to relax as best as they could and

just enjoy their lunch. It was clear to both of them that there would not be too many more lunch dates like this one, so they just had small talk and even shared a couple of laughs.

After lunch, Frank walked Elizabeth to her car, and they exchanged a few words before she drove away. As she was getting onto the street, Senator Whelan along with his friend and colleague, Senator Mike Mansfield, turned off the same street. Whelan recognized Elizabeth's car. When he and Senator Mansfield exited his Mercedes, Whelan noticed another car exiting the parking lot. He was sure it was Frank Rubenstein's Ford Sedan. Immediately, his suspicion clock hit midnight. Common sense told him that there was no way that Frank and Elizabeth were at this restaurant unless they were meeting to discuss something important. Although it was only a few miles from Capitol Hill, staff members rarely drove this distance for lunch.

They're here discussing the missing tapes from my closet, he thought. *Why else would they be here? It's too far to drive during lunch for staff members. They don't have that much time.*

The late lunch with Senator Mansfield lasted through most of the afternoon, and when he finally got back to his office, Whelan decided to call his special investigator. As he thumbed through his address book, he thought about how he was going to get his man to approach the investigation. The one thing he did not need was for a private detective to bully his way around the Senate office building. When he found the number, he reached for the phone.

"Walters investigations. How may I help you?" Evelyn

Byrd asked as she answered.

"Good afternoon; this is Senator Duff Whelan. I need to talk to Haunce Walters, please," Whelan said emphasizing his Southern charm.

Evelyn knew the name well, so she wasted no time passing him through to her boss.

"This is Haunce Walters," Haunce said as he answered the phone with his usual gruff, scratchy voice.

"Good afternoon; Whelan here," he said. "I have something to discuss with you. Can you meet me at the usual place tomorrow morning around ten o'clock?"

"I'll be there," Haunce said and hung up the phone.

Whelan always admired the way Haunce Walters never looked up to any man. He had just snubbed a United States Senator by not attempting to engage him in conversation. Whelan was used to everybody he came in contact with treating him like he was Elvis Presley or some other rock and roll star.

Whelan was aware that he was dealing with a dangerous man and that there were limits of what he would ask Haunce to do during an investigation. Haunce killed a guy once while on an investigation for Whelan; he had to pay off a couple police officers to keep Haunce out of jail and sweep the killing under the rug.

Haunce Walters had been raised in an abusive home. His father was an alcoholic who abused his wife and children. Haunce was the oldest of four children and often had to stand as their protector between them and his father; therefore, he usually took the worst of the beatings. It left an indelible dark mark of absolute fearlessness on his emotions that had both served him well and had provided a good plan for the dirtiness of life that he was to encounter throughout his career.

Whelan had used him on many covert investigations over the years when he needed to get the dirt on an opponent. More than once, Haunce had come through with exactly the right information that Whelan needed to bend someone over the barrel and pressure him into seeing things his way.

Frank Rubenstein was a classic example of the ruthlessness of the Whelan/Haunce Walters dirt machine. Whelan had sent Haunce to Frank's hometown to find leverage on Frank.

Haunce discovered an incident involving a twenty-four-year-old Frank Rubenstein and a sixteen-year-old girl. Frank had gone to the parents and apologized profusely insisting that he thought she was twenty-one. The parents of the girl accepted his apology and did not press charges. They told no one of the incident. Shortly after the affair, the family moved out of state.

Eventually, Haunce found the family. Haunce interviewed the girl, who was then twenty-eight years old. After giving the girl some money, she revealed that she had a twelve-year-old son and that Frank was the father. Frank knew nothing about the existence of the boy.

Whelan had hit the jackpot.

Whelan was sitting in his Mercedes in the parking lot of the Rock Creek Park near the Maryland state line. He pulled out a Cohiba cigar straight from Castro's personal stash and bit the end of it. He and Castro both loved their Cohiba, the brand of royalty in Cuba. It was not sold to the public but instead was reserved for members of Castro's inner circle and diplomatic delegates from other countries.

Whelan had gained a few brownie points with Castro when he fought against economic sanctions that were to be imposed on the island nation. Although he had lost the fight, his flailing rhetoric on the Senate floor to show mercy on the innocent Cuban people impressed Castro. Two weeks after the legislative battle was over, a package arrived from Cuba with a note praising him "for his gallantry against the imperialists," personally signed by Castro himself. That was the first time Whelan had ever tasted a Cohiba cigar.

Whelan heard a car pulling up beside him. The driver got out, opened the passenger side door of Whelan's Mercedes, and sat down next to him.

"Good morning Duff," Haunce said.

Haunce always prided himself on being on a first-name basis with whomever he was working. He had done investigations for many Congressmen and Senators over the years and had concluded that all of them were just alike. They sold themselves to the highest bidders on a daily basis. He had even pondered on writing a book to expose their dirty deals but had decided against it.

"What can I do for you today?" he asked.

Observing caution in his presentation, Whelan told him the story about the missing tapes and that he did not believe anyone could have broken the combination on the high-security lock on his closet door. He explained to Haunce that he figured it had to be an inside job since the lock and door hinges were not damaged. Haunce asked him if he had any suspects, and Whelan gave him the names of his secretary, Elizabeth Gardener and a legal aide, Frank Rubenstein.

The two men talked for a while longer on how the investigation would have to be very discreet and how important it was not to allow the two subjects to know they were under investigation. Haunce agreed that he should move with caution and promised to do so. After Haunce and Whelan had talked it over and had figured out a preliminary strategy, Haunce got back into his car and left.

****

"What do you mean he did not serve with you?" Frank asked incredulously.

"There was no David Squire in my company during the War," Aaron Rubenstein said to his brother. "What's going on, Frank? Do you think this guy's up to something?"

"I can't answer that, but I guarantee I'll find out," Frank said.

"Well, just watch your back, little brother," Aaron said.

"I will," Frank said as he hung up the phone.

What is this guy up to? How did he know my hometown and my family? What does he want from me? Frank thought.

Frank may have been a fool for allowing Whelan to blackmail him into being part of his bribery scheme, but he was not stupid. He knew this guy, David Squire, was attempting to gain leverage on him for some seedy reason. He didn't know what it pertained to, but he had seen enough shady characters in Washington to know when someone was pulling a fast one. No one would go through all the trouble to find out about a lowly legal aide to a powerful United States Senator just for a few free tickets to the World Series or some other sporting event.

No, this is heavyweight stuff. Someone is after something big, and I'm going to find out what it is before I say another single word to this Squire character, Frank thought.

After thinking about all the possible scenarios, he decided to just confront David Squire and demand to know what he was up to. The one thing in his life he did not need right now was for some clown to attempt extortion against him.

David Squire was sitting in booth number three, also known as the "Proposal Booth," in Martin's Tavern at precisely four forty-five. Frank Rubenstein had asked for a meeting there at Five fifteen, but David had arrived early so they could have a booth for privacy. When the waiter asked if he'd like to sit in number three, David accepted the offer. He thought it might be quite fitting for him and Frank to be sitting in the same booth where John F. Kennedy had proposed to his girlfriend. After all, Frank and David would be in life changing negotiations that afternoon, so why not sit in the historical booth? Of course, their little meeting was not likely to be all that friendly. David had deliberately lied to Frank in order to catch him off guard. He was sure his tactic had worked because when Frank called David, he was not friendly. His tone of voice was cold, and he was short and to the point. That's exactly what David wanted to hear. Frank was nervous and was going to be easier to manage when they met.

Just as David had figured, Frank was early. At exactly five

o'clock, Frank walked through the door and saw David in the booth waiting.

Making his way over to the booth Frank said, "Good afternoon. I see you chose a nice booth."

"Yes, I figured if the President can make big deals in this booth, then so can I," David said in a no nonsense voice.

"Okay, Mr. Squire, why don't we just get right to the point. First off, I do not take kindly to someone who misrepresents himself to me so you can start by telling me why you lied to me," Frank said with a dose of repugnance as he sat down.

"I lied to you to get your attention, Frank," David said. "I'm a private investigator here on a mission, and I'm on a short leash of time. I'm just doing what investigators do. Following one lead until it takes me to another. Many times, it takes weeks of going down rabbit trails to get where I need to be, but this time the trail was straight and narrow and led directly to you, Frank. In fact, I got here in almost record time, quite honestly."

"And what kind of investigation are you conducting, Mr. Squire?" Frank asked.

"Well, first of all, you can cut the 'Mr. Squire' crap. David will do fine. We're both grown men of about the same age, and we've both been down life's path, Frank. I have your military record. I know where you've been and what you've done. You may call me David because I'm not here to harm you or cause grief of any kind unless you choose not to cooperate with me. Do you understand?" David asked while looking directly into Frank's eyes.

David's intense stare was working its magic. Frank's eyes

were projecting an ever-so-small amount of stress—the kind of stress that's caused by deep fear. David knew that now was the time to pour the fuel to the fire.

"So tell me, Frank, Just exactly where do you fit into this little money trafficking scheme from Arkansas to Washington?" David asked.

Arkansas! So that's where the money source is, Frank thought. *This guy knows things about Whelan's deal that I don't even know.*

Frank knew that playing dumb with Squire at this point would be total nonsense. It was obvious that if David's investigation had led straight to him, then he knew that Frank was deeply involved.

"So what do you have on me, David?" Frank asked in a relaxed manner.

"We know that you're involved in a movement of dirty money," David said cautiously.

Noticing the reference to 'we,' Frank asked, "And how did the trail lead you to me?"

"Well, if you're going to navigate a river, the best way to do so is to start at the source, and just ride the current to wherever it takes you. It brought me here, Frank. Right here at this booth, of all places, where our president proposed marriage to his girlfriend. Right here where our very own version of Camelot was born. Now you need to fill me in on the details, Frank. You need to tell me the rest of the story because, as I said, I don't have much time,"

"I might cooperate, but first I want to know what

organization you're representing and what is their motive?" Frank asked.

"That's a very good question. I am not representing an organization. I'm representing an individual, whose name I am not prepared to reveal to you. Our motive is not greed or the blackmailing of any high-powered Senator, or any other elected official. This is purely personal and has nothing whatsoever to do with Washington politics except for the fact that the trail has led me here. It's actually much more basic than that. We're after the guy on the Arkansas end of this thing. We don't care about you or the leader of this little two-bit scheme. We wouldn't even care to know who's on this end of the deal, except we have to know. We can't put our guy over the barrel and get what we need from him until we know what he's involved in. We think that the two ends know who each other are, but we think you probably do not know who's at the source of the money trail," David said.

"It's going to take a minute to absorb all of this, so let me see if I understand you correctly. You want to know this end because you do not know, and you have to find out so you can blackmail the guy on the other end for money. In other words, you want to a piece of the action down in Arkansas," Frank said.

"No, that's not at all what I want. I do not care two hoots in hell about your payoff scheme, and we do not want any piece of the action. You see, the guy on the other end has something we want very badly. He snookered my client out of the thing that he has, and we cannot get it back using the legal process. Besides, there's no time for that. My client is very ill and cannot fight the guy in court who stole the item in question from him. We stumbled upon the evidence quite by accident that eventually led me to you. Will you cooperate with me on this, Frank?" David asked.

"So, you're not the average run-of-the-mill scam artist. You just want to retrieve an item or items from the guy on the Arkansas end. Items that have nothing to do with the operation I'm involved in. Right?" Frank asked.

"Right. That's all we're after. Give me what I want. Again, I need the name of the ultimate recipient of the money, and you have my word of honor that you will never hear from me or any of my friends again."

Frank could not believe what he was hearing. He was actually being given a gift that just may help him out of this mess.

If I give the tapes to this guy, and if I can get him to blackmail Whelan, then the entire scheme will end immediately, and no one gets hurt. Not me, not Elizabeth, and not Whelan. And Whelan will be forced to stop blackmailing me. I can move on with my life and maybe finally have some peace, Frank thought, almost giddy.

"I will cooperate with you, David. I've been at odds with my very soul over this since the beginning. I was about to blow the lid on the whole operation when you entered the scene," Frank said, with relief in his voice.

"May I ask a question just as a matter of curiosity?" David asked.

"Sure."

"We've done an exhaustive investigation of all the known characters, and of all the men involved, you're the least likely to ever be tangled up in a mess like this. So, may I guess? The guy at the top of this scam has something on you, doesn't he?" David asked.

This guy is good, Frank thought. "Yes. You're spot-on, David. You're very good at your job. As for me, I just lost my way, I guess. So, here goes. Senator Whelan from South Carolina is my boss. He has something on me that could ruin me politically. He knows I have aspirations to, one day, be a Senator from my home state of Pennsylvania. When I joined his staff, he knew I was a young idealist, and he knew I had my eye on eventually entering the fray. So, being the pond scum that he is, he got the goods on my involvement with an under aged young lady. I thought she was much older than she was, but that's beside the point. I was never charged with the incident, and the whole thing was dropped. The local people in the community didn't even have firsthand information about it—only rumors. Whelan's investigators somehow got hard evidence of the affair, so he blackmailed me into running this scam for him. I could have declined but have chosen not to.

"I'm no better than Whelan, David. I'm just another misguided soul who came to Washington with a desire to make a difference for the better and ended up here with you. And with a lot of hard evidence that would bring down the world of one of the most powerful United States Senators in history," Frank said, sadly.

"We all make bad judgment calls now and then, Frank.

Don't be so hard on yourself," David said.

"I have a proposition for you. If I give you hard evidence I have that would put Whelan away, would you consider blackmailing him into stopping this scam?" Frank asked.

David sat quietly for a moment while he collected his thoughts and weighed his options. Then he spoke. "So, you want me to get down in the dirt against a powerful United States Senator by holding hard evidence over his head to get him to cease his little scheme. Simply put, you want out, and this is the best way for you to accomplish that?" David asked.

"That is correct," Frank said while staring back at David.

David had very good instincts and was skilled at negotiating with a scared cat, so he knew what he was going to have to do now. He knew that Frank was about to walk and let the chips fall where they may if he didn't agree to his offer.

"I will do it. Yes, I will do it, and I will leave your name out of it altogether if possible. I have no quarrel with you, Frank, so I have no reason to hurt you. It appears that you've done enough of that to yourself," David said.

The relief that rushed over Frank was indescribable. He had finally found a possible way out of this awful mess.

"Before we go any further, I need all your personal information. I want to do a background check on you. I want to know firsthand who you really are," Frank said.

"Not a problem. I'll give you all you'll need," David said.

David handed Frank an envelope containing everything he needed to check out his legitimacy, including a Polaroid photo of his Illinois driver's license, and his Illinois Private

Investigator's license. Frank was slightly taken aback that David already had all that information for him.

A shrewd investigator, Frank thought. *This guy knows how to place his opponent in the corner. I just hope he checks out okay. I would love to see him jam this whole rotten deal down Whelan's throat.* "You came prepared, didn't you?" Frank asked David.

"Yes I did," David said with a smile. "I'm on a time sensitive mission here, Frank, so I decided to just go for the throat when the trail ended with you. Nothing personal. In another time and under different circumstances, you and I could be friends. Otherwise, without your help, I cannot get to the end of the money trail. And without that, I cannot force the crook on the Arkansas end to give my client what he needs. When can you have the evidence for me?" David asked.

"I can have it in your hands in a day or two," Frank said.

"Great. Be in touch," David said as he got up to leave. "Oh, and tell the sheriff I said hello."

"The sheriff?" Frank asked.

"Yes, your brother, Sheriff Aaron Rubenstein," David said as he turned and walked away.

Frank had not told David that his brother was the county sheriff back home. *A very good detective, indeed,* Frank thought, with a smile. *If he checks out to be legitimate, I think we can do business. It's going to be amusing to watch the all-powerful and mighty Senator Whelan halt his little enterprise under duress. I can just see the wheels turning in that crooked head of his when he's confronted with the fact that someone anonymous has the goods to bury his political empire. Now if I can just keep Elizabeth and myself safe for a few more days...*

CHAPTER 9

President John F. Kennedy was hosting a bipartisan meeting on health care for the aged when Kenneth O'Donnell, his Chief of Staff, pulled him aside and informed him that the Attorney General needed to meet with him. President Kennedy said his goodbyes and made his way out of the meeting room and back to the Oval Office. President Kennedy always made time for his younger brother Robert F. Kennedy, who had been his Attorney General since taking office in January of 1961. He did not show favor to his brother but always took the time to meet with him because the President knew that if Bobby, as the family called him, asked to see him without getting an appointment ahead of time, then it was important. The two brothers were always in harmony when it came to the nation's business. Sibling rivalry did not exist in the Kennedy Whitehouse.

He was barely back at his desk when his private secretary, Evelyn Lincoln, buzzed him on the intercom to inform him that the Attorney General had arrived. The President asked her to usher him in.

"Good morning, Mr. President," the Attorney General said.

"Good morning, Bobby," the President said. "What brings you over here on such short notice?"

"Well, Mr. President, it seems that we may have a bit of a

problem concerning the defense industry. I've learned that there are some pretty strong insinuations floating around. Some of my staff believes there may be corruption in the defense industry involving contractors and at least one Senator," Bobby said.

"What kind of corruption?" The President asked.

"Bribery. It seems that an upper-level manager for an aircraft manufacturer in Georgia has been charged with a relatively minor crime involving a paperwork problem. He's probably looking at a year of incarceration, so he decided to mention to the federal prosecutor handling his case that he had information about a much larger crime. He said he had knowledge about certain colleagues in his company paying off someone in Washington for favors on contracts. It appears that it may be bid rigging, but we're not sure of that yet. I felt like I needed to inform you, Mr. President, that there's no telling whom this might involve. I need your support before I move forward," the Attorney General said.

President Kennedy leaned back in his chair and thought about what a scandal might do to the political landscape on Capitol Hill. Then, as was indicative of his character, he looked at his brother and said, "Go get the crooks, Bobby, just like you've been doing with organized crime. Bring them down. I don't care who's guilty; just get them."

"Yes sir, Mr. President," the Attorney General said as he turned to leave.

"One more thing, Bobby," President Kennedy said. "Tell Mr. Hoover I said I want this expedited immediately."

"I will," Bobby said as he disappeared through the door.

****

As always, FBI director, J. Edger Hoover was in the outer office of Attorney General, Robert F. Kennedy, fifteen minutes early. He always made it a point to be punctual and had only been late once in his career for a meeting with any high-level government official.

J. Edgar Hoover was the first and only director of the Federal Bureau of Investigation, after being appointed by President Franklin Roosevelt in 1935. Hoover was known to be a stickler for details and had managed to keep subordinates petrified of him. FBI agents were not the only ones who were afraid of Hoover. He had amassed a mountain of files on every senator and every congressman for almost three decades. If he needed to intimidate a legislator, all he had to do was leak information from their file to a member of their staff. Almost every Senator and Congressman had skeletons in his closet, and the FBI director had the good stuff on every last one of them. He also had huge files on every president since Roosevelt— and that included John F. Kennedy and his brother, the Attorney General.

"Good morning, Mr. Attorney General," Hoover said as he entered Bobby Kennedy's office.

"Good morning. Glad you could come on such short notice," Bobby said.

"My pleasure, Mr. Attorney General," the FBI director said.

Hoover was never one for small talk. He didn't suffer politicians very well and only tolerated them because it was part of his job.

Bobby Kennedy knew that little personality characteristic of the Director, so he got right to the point. "The President has asked me to investigate a matter concerning an alarming accusation made by a suspect in a criminal case in Georgia," the Attorney General said. "If it's true, then some politicians may be taking money under the table."

"How did you hear about this?" Hoover asked.

"It doesn't matter how I know, Mr. Director; it only matters that I'm aware of the case. Why do you ask?" Attorney General Kennedy asked.

Hoover did not like a politician to condescend upon him, and he especially did not like it coming from a lightweight lawyer who had never tried a case of any kind in a court of law. Little Bobby Kennedy was the Attorney General of the United States for one reason—Joseph Kennedy had forced the hand of his son, the President, to appoint his little brother to the post. Nevertheless, as a committed bureaucrat, he would respect the office of the Attorney General no matter who held the position.

"Because I'm aware of the accusation by the defendant in that case in Georgia. I was briefed on it a couple of days ago. We're gathering evidence now on the Georgia end, and our preliminary plan is to put a couple of senators under surveillance," the Director said.

"You already have names?"

"No, but we have a couple of obvious targets who are on the right Senate Committee to gain the most from this kind of thing."

"Well, Mr. Hoover, just use great caution. That's all I ask. I really don't care to be hearing from some angry senator threatening to complain to the press that I'm trying to destroy his career with false charges." Bobby said. "Meanwhile the President wants this handled as quickly as possible."

"The perpetrators will not know a single thing about it until it's time to move in and make the necessary arrests. By then, you'll already have a full detailed report," Hoover said.

"Thank you," the Attorney General said as he got up to usher the Director to the door.

"I'll keep you up to speed on everything," the FBI Director said as he turned to leave.

****

Back at the Bureau, Hoover summoned Bill Caplan into his office. Agent Caplan was in charge of special investigations for the Washington Bureau.

"Agent Caplan, I have an investigation of a very sensitive nature I need you to conduct. I just left the Attorney General's office whereby we discussed a possible bribery case involving defense contractors and politicians."

The Director spent the next few minutes briefing Agent Caplan on the events in Georgia. The two men discussed ways to go about the investigation to keep it secret. They decided the best approach would be to wiretap possible targets for any suspicious phone activity. Of course, they would not bother to get a court order. That would be a matter of public record, and they could not allow anyone involved to know what they were up to.

"Do you have a starting point, Mr. Director? I mean who do you want me to target first?" Agent Caplan asked.

"I think we should start with Senator Benjamin Duff Whelan. He's the chairman of the Senate Committee on Armed Services, and if anybody in the pipeline were in a position to gain the most from a bribery scam from defense contractors, it would be him. Besides, he's always conducted himself a little too close to the edges in my opinion. We almost had him a few years ago on a little thing that wouldn't have amounted to much legally but would have probably destroyed his career. I really have no problem destroying the career of a politician for wrongdoing, but we just couldn't quite come up with the evidence we needed. He had an iron fist around the neck of the main witness, and we eventually had to back off. Eventually, the whole thing was dropped.

"I need your best man on this one, Agent Caplan. We do not need any leaks. And we certainly do not need any high and mighty politician thinking we're spying on him," Hoover said. "Especially one that we almost had over the barrel once before."

"I have the right guy in mind. His name is Agent Buck Huston. He's been in the Washington Bureau for a few years, and you probably didn't know it, but he was on the Whelan case that you just referred to. He knows Senator Whelan well, and I think he still carries a bit of anger over the way the senator dismissed him throughout the investigation. Agent Huston knew that Whelan was guilty but simply could not get the key witness to agree to testify against him," Agent Caplan said.

"Then he's the one I want. Bring him in immediately and

brief him on what we know. Then I want to meet with the two of you," the Director said.

Agents James Buckner "Buck" Huston and Bill A. Caplan had been good friends for many years. During the war, they had worked on a team of FBI agents that busted a German spy ring sending messages to submarines off the coast of Florida. Since the war, they had both worked their way up through the ranks of the agency and were now working at the Washington Headquarters.

"Good afternoon," Buck said as Bill's secretary ushered Buck into his office. "Tell me you have a good one for me. I'm tired of working on that boring Kentucky corruption case."

"As a matter of fact, I do," Bill said. "Pour yourself a cup of coffee and sit down. You're going to like this one."

Bill briefed Buck on the situation in Georgia and got him up to speed on all the players down south. But he saved the best for last.

"Our first key target is none other than Senator Duff Whelan," Bill said.

Buck, who was stirring the sugar in his coffee, stopped dead still and just stared at his friend. Bill stared back at him with a faint smile. "So how do we approach this?" Buck asked.

Bill and Buck spent the next hour or so discussing different approaches to the investigation. Although they didn't decide on a strategy, they did both agree that Senator Whelan's phone lines needed to be tapped. The two men were sad to see that a representative of the people, a United States senator, might be involved in a bribery scandal, but both were actually a bit happy that the culprit might be Whelan.

CHAPTER 10

Clyde Bayless was at his desk reading the Arkansas Democrat-Gazette and chatting with a couple of farmers that were in his stable of hangers-on when Sarah Jennings knocked on his door and stuck her head inside.

"Joe Carter is here to see you," she said.

Clyde knew this was going to be a bit testy, so he told her to hold on for a moment. After she had closed the door, he told the two men that this was not going to be a very nice exchange between himself and Joe, and he would appreciate it if they would hang around.

He had barely finished telling the two men about the problem when the door swung open, and Joe Carter walked in.

"We need to talk," Joe said.

"Well, we're kind of in the middle of somethi..."

"I don't care; this is more important. As for these two big-shot wannabes, they'll just have to wait their turn," Joe said with a stern voice.

"Okay, Joe, What can I do for you?" Clyde asked with a bit of shake in his voice.

"Yesterday you sent your little boy out to my farm to intrude on my space. I didn't appreciate that. Tell me it won't happen again, Clyde. Tell me you will do what I already told you that you could do—that you can sit in the swing on my front porch and drive my tractors after they belong to you. Tell me that right now, Clyde, so I won't have to bend that crooked little nose of yours back toward the other side," Joe said.

The reference to Clyde's crooked nose was a harsh reminder to him that Joe had broken his nose when they were teenagers over a deal whereby Clyde had sold Joe a small wooden boat. Clyde's father found out about the deal and wouldn't allow him to go through with the sale. Clyde had always figured he didn't have the same set of responsibilities as everyone else, so he just attempted to keep the fifteen dollars that Joe had given him for the boat. The argument that ensued ended with a broken nose for Clyde and a mortal fear of Joe Carter ever since. Joe had always laughed with his friends about how Clyde's broken nose was worth ten times the price of the boat.

"I will honor your request, Joe," Clyde said.

"It's not a request, Clyde. It's an order. Do not come back to my farm until it belongs to you," Joe said as he turned to leave.

Outside Clyde's office door, Sarah Jennings had heard the entire exchange. Joe had not bothered to close the door when he entered Clyde's office, so Sarah took advantage of it by easing over near the doorway. As he walked past her, Joe noticed the faint, mischievous smirk on her face. With a thin smile and a wink, Joe made his way to the exit door.

Clyde was still shocked as he asked the two men to excuse themselves because he had to make a phone call. After they had left, he picked up the phone and dialed the number. As Thad McRae's secretary answered the phone and Clyde asked to speak to him, Sarah was placing a stack of invoices on his desk. As she turned to leave his office, she heard Clyde ask for Thad.

"Mister Clyde Bayless is on line one. Says it's urgent," Thad McRae's secretary said.

"Good morning, Clyde," Thad said.

"How much longer do you think it's gonna be until we can move on this Joe Carter thing? I'm having a lot of resistance from him, and I just want to finish it up," Clyde said.

"I've got all the documents together, and now it's just a matter of getting before the judge. I think I can get us a court date within a very short time. The docket is not even half full right now, so let me see what I can do, and I'll get back with you," Thad said.

"Thank you. I'll be waiting," Clyde said as he hung up the phone.

****

Sarah Jennings had left a message for Thad McRae to call her as close to five-thirty as possible. As usual, Thad was not late. The phone rang at precisely half past five.

"Good afternoon to my pretty friend," Thad said after she answered.

"Good afternoon to you, too. I won't keep you because I'm sure you have things to do, but I really do need to see you tonight if possible," Sarah said.

"When and where my love? Is everything okay?" Thad asked.

"Not really. Can we just talk about it tonight? You can come over, and I'll fix you dinner. Would that be okay?" Sarah asked.

"Splendid. I always enjoy the company of a gorgeous woman over dinner," he said with a smile. "Do I need to bring anything?"

"No, just be here at around seven," Sarah said.

"I'll see you then," Thad said as he hung up.

After hanging up, Sarah got busy making her special spaghetti casserole. She was just about finished when a knock at the door told Sarah it was seven o'clock. Thad had always been punctual since they were kids.

"Good evening," Sarah said as she opened the door.

"Good evening. How's my girl doing?" Thad asked.

"I'm fine."

The two friends sat in the living room and talked for a little while until the casserole was done. Sarah was aware of Thad's likes and dislikes in food, and she knew he liked red wine with his dinner so she had a bottle ready for him. He once said it was a family tradition. His grandmother was Italian and believed that a little wine was good for the stomach, so he always had a glass with dinner.

At dinner, Sarah and Thad exchanged small talk until Thad's curiosity got the best of him.

"So, what's on your mind, Sarah?" He asked.

"You and I have been friends since we were children, Thad. You know I would never ask you to do something unethical, or that may cause you to lose a client, but I have a request that you may have to decline. If you say no, I will understand," she said quietly.

Sensing that his childhood friend was in a very bad way,

Thad was careful to choose his words. "How may I help you, little Sarah-from-the-third-grade?" he asked with a soft, gentle voice.

"It's a rather long story, so I'll make it short and get right to the point," Sarah said. "A couple of close friends of mine borrowed a large sum of money a few years ago from an individual who tricked them into allowing him to place a mortgage on everything they own. They thought they were mortgaging their farm equipment only, but he slipped their farmland in on the deal at the end of the transaction, and they didn't catch it. By the time they realized it, the statute of limitations to file a lawsuit for the fraud had passed, and their attorney told them they had no legal recourse. Since then they have fallen on hard times and have been unable to pay back the money. He's now foreclosing on the property, and they are losing everything," Sarah said.

"That's a horrible thing, Sarah," Thad said. "At what stage is the foreclosure?" He asked.

Sarah looked at her friend for a long moment. Finally, she said, "You tell me, Thad. You're the attorney handling the case for the plaintiff."

Thad just stared speechless at Sarah for a moment. After collecting his thoughts, he asked, "Are you talking about the Joe Carter farm?"

"Yes."

"I'm shocked. Are you telling me that Clyde Bayless tricked Joe Carter into giving him a mortgage on everything he owned without his knowledge?" he asked.

"Yes. Joe Carter is not stupid. He had no idea that Clyde would do such a thing. They grew up together, and although they weren't friends, they were both local boys all of their lives, so Joe just simply did not have a clue that Clyde was doing that to him until three and a half years later. By then, it was too late to file a complaint," Sarah said.

Thad was having a hard time comprehending what he was hearing. He had suspected that Clyde was a bit hard-nosed in his business dealings, but had no idea he was an outright crook.

"So, what is this unethical thing that you're about to ask me to do?" he asked.

"Only to drag your feet in implementing the proceedings for a few days. We have a friend involved in this thing. He's an investigator. He believes he can get leverage over Clyde that may resolve the whole ordeal for Joe and Millie," she said.

Thad thought about what she was saying for a moment. He finally decided she wasn't really asking too much. He would only have to make it appear that he couldn't get a court date as soon as he had told Clyde that he could.

"Okay, Sarah. I'll do this for you, but you have to give me your solemn promise that you will never ever say a single word about this to anyone in this community. Not even Joe Carter or his wife," he said with a stern look. "This is, indeed, unethical, but it's not illegal for me to do what you're asking. Lawyers drag their feet all the time when they're not prepared to fight a case in court. Meanwhile, this delicious special spaghetti casserole couldn't actually be used in a court of law as a payoff for me to stall my client on a case I'm handling for him."

"Oh, thank you," Sarah said with tears in her eyes. "I can't tell you any details right now, but our friend is close to something big that may give Joe and Millie the leverage they need to secure the deed to their farm. He just needs a little more time. Maybe a week or two."

"I will slow down the process for you, but it's against all the rules of good client representation to do this kind of thing. As bad as I feel for Joe Carter and his wife, I have a client to represent, and I have to be on the case until it's finished," he said.

"Thank you, Thad. I will forever owe you," she said.

After they had said their goodbyes, Sarah cleaned up the kitchen and went to bed knowing Joe and Millie would have at least a one-week reprieve from Clyde Bayless' hideous actions.

CHAPTER 11

Elizabeth Gardener sat silently as Frank Rubenstein revealed things about his past that she had not known. The crisp, cool breeze and the familiar dusty smell of falling leaves as the trees retreated to dormancy was a friendly reminder that autumn had arrived.

Frank had asked Elizabeth to meet him in Lincoln Park at two-thirty. She had been waiting on a bench near the monument of Abraham Lincoln when he arrived. The two of them had been sharing small talk for about a half hour when Frank decided it was time to tell Elizabeth the rest of the story about his past shortcomings so she wouldn't have questions when all hell broke loose if he was forced to go public with the information he possessed. He wanted her to know what Whelan had on him.

As Elizabeth listened, Frank talked about the young girl back in his hometown. He explained how she had told him that she was twenty-one years old and how her father had confronted him about seeing her. He had no way of knowing she was only sixteen. She looked like a grown woman and acted like one, so he just never questioned her when she lied about her age. Frank told Elizabeth that after the incident, the family moved to another state and did not pursue charges against him.

"I realize you probably think less of me now, Lizzy, but it's important that you know the rest of the story behind my involvement with Whelan and his scheme," he said.

Looking into the sad eyes of her friend, Elizabeth took a deep breath and released it slowly. "I do not think less of you, Frank. I've already told you that. You're the good guy in this mess. You're going to make amends for your lack of judgment. When this ordeal is over, you will be known by the world as the man I know you to be—honest, forthright, and a man, who in the end, did the right thing. It's one thing to make a mistake but yet another to simply, without any moral bearing whatsoever, take the muddy trail through a hog pen of human debris like Senator Whelan has chosen to do," she said.

"I'll take that as a small bit of support," Frank said.

"You're very observant, Frank," she said. "For me to no longer want you in my world, you would have to do a whole lot more than compromising your dignity to save your family from the embarrassment that would be heaped upon you."

Elizabeth had secretly loved Frank for years but had never found the right opportunity to show him. As they stood up from the park bench to leave, she leaned into him, put her arms around the back of his neck, and kissed him gently. As she backed away, Frank grabbed her, pulled her close to his chest, and kissed her long and softly. They stood in the shadow of the Lincoln Monument and held each other without speaking a word. Both were keenly aware that the world as they knew it was about to come tumbling down around them, and there was no way to predict how either of them would endure once the media show started.

At the very least, Frank knew that his time was up as a

Capitol Hill aide to any senator or congressman. He was also fully aware that his dream of a career in politics no longer existed. All he had left was his friend, Lizzy. Knowing that she was in his corner made him feel much stronger about his decision.

They looked into each other's eyes one last time before saying their goodbyes. Finally, Frank got into his car and drove away. He was off that afternoon, but Elizabeth had to go back to work. Frank had asked her to meet him at his apartment, but she was unable to do so because she had unfinished work on her desk that was on a deadline. For the first time since she had known Frank, she allowed herself to wish that she could have followed him home.

Oh well, maybe another time, she thought as she watched his car disappear around a curve.

Elizabeth got into her car and drove back to work with Frank heavy on her mind. She was both worried for him and proud of him for doing the right thing.

****

Haunce Walters sat in his late model sedan across the street from Frank Rubenstein's residence waiting for his men to complete their search of Frank's apartment. The afternoon sun was filtering through the trees and providing just enough rays to keep the inside of the car warm on the cool November afternoon and to provide Haunce with enough light to read his latest piece of entertainment, Joseph Heller's *Catch-22*.

Haunce was a complicated man. To those who hired him, he was just another goon wearing a nice suit, but he was actually a very literate man. After the war, he had earned both a Bachelor's and Master's Degree in English from the College of William and Mary, and had read all the Twentieth Century classics by authors such as F. Scott Fitzgerald, John Steinbeck, and Ernest Hemingway. Haunce, like Hemingway, fought depression every day of his life, and like the famous author, he turned to alcohol to ease the pain. Those around him only knew that he was a man with a short fuse and no conscience. They did not know the other, softer side because he would never let anyone inside. He lived a life of total isolation from the rest of the world, including those who were around him every day.

Across the street, Haunce's men were about five minutes into the ransacking of Frank Rubenstein's apartment when a man pulled into a parking place in front of the building and got out of his car. Haunce instantly recognized the man as Frank Rubenstein.

Uh oh. We've been made, he thought. *He's arrived an hour and a half early. This is going to get sticky very quickly.*

Haunce put his novel down, jumped out of the car, and quickly made his way across the street and into the building. He discreetly followed fifteen feet behind Frank.

Inside Frank's second floor apartment, Benny Flaigo and Alfonse Giovetti were tearing up the place. They had just finished wrecking the living room when Flaigo heard a disturbance in the hallway outside the apartment. He motioned for Giovetti to be still. It was obvious that someone was about to enter. Flaigo jumped behind the door as it was opening.

As soon as Frank opened the door, he knew something was

wrong. The sofa cushions were turned upside down, and the clear glass jar of chocolate treats his roommate, Jay Booker, kept on the coffee table was broken, and Hersey's Kisses were scattered everywhere. He instantly decided to run, but it was too late. As he began turning, a strong force behind him pushed him into the room and onto the floor.

When he came to his senses, a stunned Frank looked directly into the fiercely violent eyes of Haunce Walters.

"Good afternoon, Frank," Haunce said. "Get up and sit on the sofa here. I have a few questions for you."

Frank pulled himself up, picked up one of the cushions from the floor, put it back in its place on the sofa, and sat down as the three men surrounded him.

"I'm sure you know why we're here, so why don't you just give me what I want so I can be on my way," Haunce said.

"What exactly is that?" Frank asked.

"Oh come now, Frank. You're wasting my time and yours. From the looks of things around here, you have quite a mess to clean up, so why don't you just hand them over so you can get to it?" Haunce half asked, and half demanded.

"Again, what do you want me to hand over?" Frank asked while staring directly at Haunce.

"The tapes, of course. We know you have them, so to keep from getting the rest of this neat little apartment torn apart, just hand them over," Haunce demanded.

"I don't have any…"

Flaigo, who was standing behind Frank, hit him across the right ear with a sock filled with a half dozen golf balls that he often carried as a weapon. The sting was deep and intense.

"Now, I'm going to ask once again. Where are the tapes? I don't want to hurt you, and you don't want to get hurt, Frank. Just hand them over, and we'll be on our way. After we're gone, if you get right to it, you'll get this place cleaned up before your roomy gets home," Haunce said.

Frank was not stupid. He knew that he would not be alive to see Jay arrive. He knew that Haunce Walters was going to kill him. It was, after all, his style. He didn't know what kind of cover story they would come up with, but he knew Whelan had too many friends in high places to let the death of a staff member get in the way of even one of his objectives. The only thing that was keeping him alive was that Haunce wanted the tapes and wanted to get them the easy way. The curtain was coming down fast, and his thoughts were of how he had outsmarted the all-powerful Whelan. His friend, Harold Gersen, had the original tapes locked away in his safe at his hardware store, so Frank knew it didn't matter what happened to him. He knew that Harold would do as instructed in the note he left inside the package with the tapes.

In spite of his predicament, Frank found himself laughing, quietly at first because he knew that Whelan was going down for his murder. Suddenly the world seemed a lot smaller to him. The high and mighty Senator Whelan was just a little man after all, and the rest of the world was going to watch as he burned for what he was about to do to Frank.

If he were lucky, Frank thought, Haunce would not ask if there were any copies. He figured they were in a hurry because the longer they hung around, the more likely they were to be seen by neighbors.

As Flaigo and Giovetti continued to tear the bedrooms apart, he could no longer contain the silent laughter. It began as a chuckle and then a little louder until Frank was laughing aloud straight into the face of death itself. The more he laughed, the angrier the three men got. At one point Frank was laughing so loud that Flaigo took a double swing back and forth with his golf ball sock at the expense of both of Frank's ears. It didn't stop the laughter, however. Frank knew he was going to die as soon as they found the tapes.

Finally, out of anger, Flaigo grabbed the laundry basket full of clothes and flung it across the kitchen. That's when the tapes slid out of the basket and onto the floor. All three men stopped and stared at the tapes for a long moment. Frank stopped laughing and looked right into the piercing eyes of Haunce Walters who was still standing over him on the sofa.

His silence only lasted for a short beat before he started laughing again. He knew he was going to die, but he also knew that in the end, he was going to get the last laugh, and oddly, he just decided to do it now. So he laughed and laughed...and then it was over. Flaigo took a butcher knife from the kitchen and jabbed Frank from the side where the neck met the shoulders. He was dead instantly.

****

As Haunce was getting into his car, Flaigo stopped him and handed him an envelope.

"I found this on his desk. I took a quick look inside

the envelope and decided to keep it. Looks like a private investigator's ID and some personal information. Looks like he's from Chicago," Flaigo said.

"Thanks. Good work. You need to go get cleaned up. You have blood on your trousers. Then come on back to the office. We have to discuss this situation," Haunce said.

"Will do," Flaigo said as he turned and walked toward his car.

CHAPTER 12

Harold Gersen had allowed Jay Booker to have the rest of the afternoon off. It was three p.m., and he had decided to go out to Fort Marcy Park to enjoy the cool autumn afternoon. The leaves were a magnificent multitude of colors, and the smell reminded him of a home in Pennsylvania in the fall.

Jay had been working for Harold since he began renting a room from Frank Rubenstein two years ago, and he was gradually getting used to city life. Every now and then, however, he just needed to see some countryside. So on that beautiful November afternoon, he sat in his car and watched the occasional squirrel as it took nuts from the oak trees and buried them to be used later for winter food.

After listening to music on the radio and having a couple of beers, Jay decided he should be getting on home. It was four-thirty, and the traffic would be heavy soon, so he started the engine and drove back toward his apartment a few miles away.

****

Back in his office, Haunce Walters pondered the elimination of Frank Rubenstein. He had taken a calculated risk and lost the gamble. Frank was not supposed to be at home that early in the afternoon. Therefore, Haunce did what he knew to do. He took out a key witness before he had a chance to talk to the FBI, but it was not just *any* witness. Frank Rubenstein was an aide to a powerful U.S. senator, and the police might conduct a deeper investigation than normal.

Whelan had assured him that Frank would not be at home. Whelan had been wrong. He was unaware that Frank was taking the afternoon off and had no idea he would surprise Haunce and his men.

Haunce wasted no time making the senator aware of what had happened. He picked up the phone and dialed Whelan.

"This is Senator Whelan," Duff said.

"We got the goods but ran into a serious problem," Haunce said. "Meet me in twenty minutes at the usual place."

"What happened?" Whelan asked.

"We need to talk, so just be there in twenty," Haunce said as he hung up the phone.

Whelan had always known Haunce to be rough around the edges, but he knew by the tension in his voice that something awful had gone down. He immediately buzzed Elizabeth Gardener and told her he would be out of the office for a while.

As Haunce slid into the seat next to Whelan, the senator could see that the conversation was going to be tense.

"We had to kill him, Senator," Haunce said.

"You what?" Whelan shrieked.

"Settle down, Whelan. I said we *had* to kill him. He came in while we were sorting through his things and it left us no choice. He knew me, Whelan. He would have squawked to the cops, and that would not be good for me—and it would not be good for you either. I am not going down for you or any other crooked politician. I'll do your dirty work as long as you pay me well, but just remember not to ever trust me if I get in big time trouble while working for you. I'll rat you out in a heartbeat," Haunce practically barked. "You told me he wouldn't be there. You said he wouldn't be leaving the office until five, at least. When he showed up, we had no choice but to take him out. I would have thought you would, at least, have control of when your staff is off duty."

Whelan just sat there, stunned. When he had regained his composure, he asked, "What do you think we should do now?"

"I don't care what you do now, Senator. Just make damn sure you leave me out of it," Haunce said as he got out of Whelan's car. "Don't forget what I said, Whelan. I meant every word of it. By the way, I have the merchandise in my car. I'll get it."

Haunce reached inside his car, pulled out a paper bag containing the tapes, and threw it on the front seat of Whelan's car. The cold stare in his eyes told Whelan that he meant business. A tiny chill went up his back as he watched Haunce drive away.

After Haunce had left, Whelan sat there staring at the scenery in the park as he tried to figure out what to do. He knew if he was going to get through this mess, he had to talk to his man in the police department. Time was of the essence now.

At a pay phone a few parking spaces from his car, Whelan made contact with his friend, Captain Danny Evans of the Metropolitan Police Department.

"Good afternoon, Danny, Whelan here. I have something of urgency to speak with you about. May I see you immediately?" Whelan asked.

"Sure, where are you?"

"I'm in Rock Creek Park in the same parking lot where we last met," Whelan said.

"I'll be there in fifteen minutes, Senator," Evans said.

Danny Evans had helped Whelan on many occasions when things got out of hand, or when he just needed a little favor from time to time. Evans had made more than one incident go away for Whelan over the years including the last time Haunce Walters screwed up and killed someone.

Whelan had always paid Captain Evans well for his favors. In fact, Whelan had a simple rule when he needed to use one of his operatives. Pay them well. That way, they were as immersed in the illegal activity as he was. If they betrayed him, he would simply return the favor with one thousand percent more force.

Danny Evans pulled up to the curb in the same parking space Haunce Walters had occupied a few minutes before. Whelan was sitting in his Mercedes with the windows down smoking a Cohiba.

"Good afternoon, Senator," Danny said.

"I wish I could say it's a good afternoon, Captain," Whelan said.

"So, what's going on?" Danny asked.

"It seems that I have a real problem on my hands. I lost an aide about an hour and a half ago, and I have to figure out what to do about it,"

"What do you mean when you say you lost an aide?" Danny asked.

"I mean a certain private investigator that we both know

made another mistake, and now I have to fix it," Whelan said.

"Would Haunce Walters be a good guess?" Danny asked.

"Yes."

"Would this happen to have anything to do with one Frank Rubenstein?" Danny asked.

"How did you know that?" Whelan asked.

"Because we got the call just as I was leaving the office a few minutes ago. His roommate called the MPD and told us that he had come home and found Frank dead on the sofa from a knife wound to the neck," Danny said.

"Listen, Captain, we have to figure out a way to fix this thing. Maybe you can frame the roommate for this. Maybe we could accuse them both of being queers, or something," Whelan said. "Anyway you look at it, we have to separate Haunce Walters and me from this thing."

"Okay, I'll see what I can do. I'll be in touch as soon as possible. I better get down there right now so I can be in on the initial investigation," he said.

"You do have my private office number and my home number, don't you?" Whelan asked.

"Yes," Danny said as he got out of Whelan's car.

After Danny Evans had left, Whelan sat there for a few minutes. As he gazed at the colorful autumn scenery in front of him, he thought about Frank Rubenstein. Whelan was never sympathetic toward anyone, especially someone who tried to smear him. As far as he was concerned, Frank Rubenstein deserved what he got.

****

When Captain Danny Evans arrived at the crime scene, investigating officers were busy collecting evidence. The police photographer was taking pictures of every detail inside Frank Rubenstein's apartment.

Danny was pleased to see that the detective in charge of the investigation was Gerry O'Malley, a good friend of his. The two of them had arranged for the last murder case involving Haunce Walters and Whelan to go away.

"Good afternoon, O'Malley. What do we have here?" Danny asked.

"Well, we don't know any details yet, but it appears that either a fight ensued inside the apartment or someone was looking for something, and Mr. Rubenstein surprised them and was killed as a result," Gerry O'Malley said.

"You said 'he surprised them.' How do you know it was more than one perp?"

"Because the victim was sitting on the sofa while being stabbed in the side of the neck from behind. No man will allow that to happen, so there had to have been more than one perp," O'Malley said.

"You and I need to talk, Gerry," Danny said.

"Okay, but I have my hands a bit full right now. How about in an hour or so?"

"No, we have to talk right now," Danny said.

Gerry O'Malley stopped what he was doing and ushered Danny outside the apartment into the hall where they could have some privacy.

"So what gives, Captain?" Gerry asked.

"It seems that we have a very sensitive situation here. I just had a meeting with a certain senator that you and I both know very well. He informed me that we need to take care of this the same way we took care of the last problem of this sort that he got himself involved in," Danny said.

Gerry just stared at Danny. "Don't tell me. Let me guess. This Walters character was doing some clandestine work for the heretofore unnamed senator, and the situation went south. A fight ensued, and now we have a dead man on our hands," Gerry said.

"You're a very observant man, my fine Irish friend," Danny said.

"So, before I make a move on this thing I want to know how, when, and how much I'm going to be compensated for my help," Gerry said.

"That should be the least of your worries right now, Gerry. I believe I can squeeze twice as much out of him as we did last time. This one seems to be more urgent. The senator evidently has his fingerprints all over it because he spoke to me with a much more sense of urgency," Danny said.

"Okay, I'll do it," Gerry said.

"Good. So what do we have so far?" Danny asked. "And who discovered the body?"

"His roommate."

"Where is he now?" Danny asked.

"He's in the dining room sitting at the table," Gerry said. "He hasn't been much help. Said he came home, and when he opened the door, this is what he found."

"Okay, let's start with him," Danny said.

For the next hour, Danny Evans interviewed Jay Booker. He found out that Jay had been at Fort Marcy Park since 3:00 p.m. He also found out one other very useful piece of information. Jay Booker had seen no one at the park that afternoon, and to his knowledge, no one had seen him. In other words, there were no witnesses as to his whereabouts at the time of the murder, which could be a significant tidbit that could fit a plausible theory of Jay Booker's guilt of the murder.

From the beginning, the police Captain realized that Jay Booker was not a very bright young man. In fact, it was clear that he had a mild mental deficiency. Now, if he could figure out a way to place the blame for Frank Rubenstein's death at the feet of Jay Booker, then the case would be solved, and he and Gerry O'Malley could collect a nice little pile of cash from Whelan, just in time for the holidays.

****

David Squire had been sitting at the bar in Martin's Tavern for over an hour, and Frank Rubenstein had not arrived. The investigator in him suggested that something had gone wrong—maybe even terribly wrong. He had learned over the years to trust his intuition, but he was giving the present situation the benefit of the doubt. After all, Frank did work for a United States senator, and he understood that there might have been urgent business at the office.

Finally, after two hours, David decided that Frank wasn't coming, so he stood up, paid his tab, and left. He figured Frank would either contact him the next day with the evidence or would contact him to tell him he is not interested in dealing with an outsider like David.

****

Danny Evans and Gerry O'Malley were very good interrogators. If a suspect were guilty, they would get the truth out of him. Sometimes if a suspect needed to be guilty, even if he weren't, Danny and Gerry would get the confession out of him.

Danny was an all-around nasty cop. He had done some dirty things to suspects in the past, and more than a few innocent citizens had served time for something they had nothing to do with. His primary objective was to get the case file off his desk as quickly as possible, and tonight was going to be no different. He picked up the phone and buzzed the sergeant in charge of the jail.

"Sergeant, send the prisoner back to interrogation room number three," he said.

"Will do, Captain," the sergeant said.

Sergeant Gene Waldrop had been in charge of the jail for years and was good friends with Danny and Gerry. He had helped them through so-called "tough" situations from time to time over the years. Usually, when they were receiving orders from someone in power who wanted a perpetrator, better known as a victim, to confess to a crime he may or may not have committed, they called on the help of their reliable jailer friend, Gene Waldrop.

After Sergeant Waldrop had escorted Jay Booker to the interrogation room where Danny and Gerry were waiting, the two police officers wasted no time drilling him. When questioning a prisoner, the plan was always to use the old time-honored Mutt and Jeff routine. It was a classic "good guy/ bad guy" act usually involving only two police officers. Gerry played Mutt, the bad guy, and Danny played Jeff, the good guy in their little mind game with the prisoner. Law enforcement officers everywhere had used the technique for many years to get a prisoner emotionally rattled during questioning. They had refined their technique so well that they often took bets between the two of them as to how quickly they could get a prisoner to talk. All of this, of course, was before the prisoner was allowed to see an attorney—even if he had asked for one.

Most of the time the average, uneducated, criminal did not know his constitutional rights such as access to an attorney before being interrogated.

That was the case with their victim, Jay Booker. Both Captain Danny Evans and Lieutenant Gerry O'Malley knew the exculpatory evidence at the scene was overwhelmingly in favor of Booker's innocence. The only thing they had in their favor was their ability to twist him around and turn him every which way but loose until they got a signed confession from him.

"Mr. Booker, you said you came home from the park and discovered the body of your roommate, Mr. Rubenstein lying on the floor," Gerry said.

"Yes, that's right," Jay said.

"Now, you said you were at the park from around midafternoon until you came home. Am I correct in understanding your earlier statement while we were at the apartment?" Gerry asked.

"Yes, that's where I was," Jay said.

"Did you have a good relationship with Mr. Rubenstein?"

"Yes, he was nice to me. I came here from Pennsylvania, and he took me in and helped me get a job," Jay said.

"How did he help you get a job? Did he know the guy you work for?"

"Yes, I think they were friends from college, or the military, or something," Jay said.

While Gerry was asking questions, Danny made notes. He knew they had to get a lot of basic knowledge before they could begin to tighten the rope around the victim's neck.

"So, the owner of the hardware store and your roommate were good friends?" O'Malley asked.

"Yes."

"Did he know that you and Frank Rubenstein were homosexual lovers?" Gerry asked Jay with a piercing stare into the eyes of the prisoner.

"What? I'm not….he's not…we are not homosexuals, officer. Where did you get that idea?" Jay asked.

"Because we believe that the two of you were. Think about it, Mr. Booker. Your roommate was forty-two years old and had never been married. Neither are you. We think the two of you were lovers. Plain and simple. What we think is that we have an open and shut case here. One queer gets jealous of the other queer, and the fight that ensues ends up in murder. Captain Evans and I see it all the time. You see, we see all the sludge in the city. All the bad, and not much good. The captain and I live in a different world from all the rest of you. We've known for some time that Frank Rubenstein was a queer. His boss, Senator Whelan, made us aware of that a few years ago involving another case whereby Frank Rubenstein was caught on a seedy side of town with another man in a, shall I say, compromising position. Now, do you understand how I can conclude that you and Rubenstein were just a couple of queers who got into a fight and you won? It could have been worse, you know. It could have been you down at the morgue on the slab, and him sitting in that chair answering the same questions," Gerry said with a glare.

"I have no idea what you're talking about, officer. Frank Rubenstein was not a queer, as far as I know, and neither am I," he said emphatically.

That was the last time Jay Booker said a single thing during the entire interrogation from an offensive stance. Every question he answered while being denied a restroom break for the next six hours was from the standpoint of a cornered mouse that was about to be devoured by a hungry snake.

Sometimes, during Gerry's unrelenting aggressiveness Danny tempered the conversation with occasional "intervening" on Jay Booker's behalf just long enough to convince the weakened, confused, victim that he should cooperate with Lieutenant O'Malley so they could all get some rest.

The two officers knew that Frank Rubenstein was not a homosexual. Whelan had never told Danny Evans any such thing. They made it all up for the expres purpose of choking the guilty confession out of their victim. They only cared about the nice little pile of cash they were both earning.

By one-thirty A.M., the two officers had obtained their signed confession from Jay Booker. There was only one thing left that Jay Booker had to be 'persuaded' to do. He wrote and sign a document apologizing for all the pain he had caused the family of Frank Rubenstein and his own family. Then, of course, there was only one more piece that needed to be in place for this thing to end the way their customer, the senator, wanted it to. Jay Booker had to be forever silenced. It would have to be arranged for another prisoner to kill him in his cell.

Danny called Gene Waldrop and asked him to place Jay in a cell with a known violent criminal. Sergeant Waldrop escorted Jay to a cell with Harold Washington. Harold had been picked up about the same time as Jay and was heavily intoxicated. He had been in a fight with his girlfriend and her brother, whereby Harold had shot her brother twice in the head. Waldrop told Danny that he didn't seem to care that he had just murdered a man. He just wanted to take a nap. He was already asleep. It was exactly the setup the two officers wanted.

Gerry and Danny went to an all-night diner down the street from the police station and discussed what they would do next. Or, more specifically, who was going to do the deed. After twenty minutes, Gerry said he would take care of the final task, but that he wanted a huge payoff. Danny said it would be huge, so Gerry took the job.

****

Twenty minutes later, Gerry was fumbling through a wall cabinet at the back of his garage. After moving several bottles around, he eventually retrieved a small bottle of chloroform and a cotton rag. In another small cabinet, he retrieved a large sheet of wax paper. He folded the paper and put it inside his shirt right behind his belt.

It was almost 4:00 a.m. as he made the fifteen-minute drive back to the police station. Thankfully, Gene was still on duty and asked no questions when Gerry asked to see the prisoner. He escorted Gerry to the cell where Jay Booker and Harold Washington were both sleeping. He opened the door, and Gerry stepped inside. Sergeant Waldrop closed the door and locked it behind Gerry.

"I'll be right down the corridor. Just call me when you're done," he said.

"Will do," Gerry said.

After the jailer stepped around the corner, Gerry quickly took out the bottle of chloroform, poured some on the cotton rag, and gently placed it over the mouth and nose of Harold. After a short, weak struggle, the prisoner was sleeping deeply again. Gerry then turned his attention to Jay Booker. He quickly poured more chloroform onto the rag and placed it over the victim's nose and mouth. The plan was a simple one. Just blame Harold Washington when officers discover Booker's body at breakfast time. With Harold Washington's record, it would be easy to blame him and make it stick.

After Gerry was sure that Jay was out cold, he placed his hands around his throat and pressed until long after he was sure that Jay Booker was no longer breathing. He placed his ear to Jay's heart, and after a full minute of no heartbeat, he was satisfied that Jay Booker was dead.

He then pulled the wax paper out from behind his shirt and wrapped the cotton rag inside it to contain the faint smell of the chloroform. He gently slid the wax paper covered rag back down inside the back of his pants under his jacket.

He called out to Gene Waldrop who was talking through the cell bars to another prisoner down the corridor. Sergeant Waldrop came back and opened the door. A quick look inside the cell and the jailer made the comment that Jay Booker must not have awakened.

Gerry chuckled and said, "Yeah, I think he had a very tiring night down in room number three. He woke up for a moment or two, but I couldn't get him to respond very well, so I just gave it up. I was trying to get his mother's phone number so we could call her in a couple of hours."

After leaving the station, Gerry called Danny at home and told him everything was taken care of and that he needed to meet with the employer immediately. Danny agreed and said he would take care of it before noon.

As he hung up the phone, Danny walked through the back door of his house and onto the back porch. The sky was faint with daylight, so he decided to make a pot of coffee and stay up. He figured he would call Whelan in an hour and arrange to meet him at the park for the money. He knew Whelan would squawk at the fee, but he also knew he would pay it because there was simply too much at stake.

CHAPTER 13

Senator Whelan had just arrived at his office when his private line rang.

"Senator Whelan here," he said.

"Good morning, Senator, the project is complete. We need to meet as soon as possible to finish the transaction. I've been up all night, so I need to get a little sleep," Captain Danny Evans said.

"Okay, meet me at the same place in 20 minutes," Whelan said.

"Will do, Senator. Oh, by the way, bring your roll," Danny said as he hung up the phone.

Bring my roll? Whelan Thought. *That can only mean one thing. This is going to cost a lot more than I expected.*

Twenty minutes later, Whelan pulled into a parking space immediately to the left of Danny in Rock Creek Park. After he had parked, Danny got out of his car and slid into the passenger seat next to Whelan. On the seat between the two men was an attaché case.

Times like this, Whelan felt vulnerable. He did not like feeling this way because he was not in control of the situation. Today, however, he had to concede any semblance of power over the business at hand, so he decided to get right to the point. The last thing he wanted was to get into an argument with a cop who could bury him in a mountain of criminal charges.

"How much?" Whelan asked.

"Twelve thousand. Five for my friend, five for me, and two for our jailer friend," Danny said nonchalantly.

"That's a lot of money, Danny," Whelan said.

"Yes it is, but it was a huge task, Senator. It took us all night and the employment of our jailer friend to arrange the proper location for the victim," Danny said.

"So, am I to assume you eliminated the roommate?"

"Yes."

"I don't want to know the details. I just want to know this one thing. Is there any chance that this is going to go the wrong direction for us?" Whelan asked.

"No, Jay Booker signed a confession stating that he killed Frank Rubenstein because of jealousy, and then before he could recant, he was murdered by his cellmate who was already agitated from an earlier murder of his girlfriend's brother. His cellmate was the only person who could have killed him because he was the only person who was in the cell with him from the time Jay Booker was placed there until his death by strangulation a few hours later," Danny explained. "An airtight open and shut case, Senator."

Whelan took a draw from his cigar and slowly forced a billowing cloud of thick smoke from his mouth as he thought about the situation. Finally, without a word, he reached for the attaché case, opened it, and counted out twelve thousand dollars in hundred dollar bills. The amount was extraordinarily excessive in his opinion, but he had no choice. Haunce had screwed up a simple burglary and had caused a chain reaction that, for now, seemed to be at its end.

****

David Squire had been to a café on the corner for breakfast and had returned to his room and called his office manager, Madge Bellows. She had briefed him on what was happening within his organization and how his investigators were advancing on various cases. Satisfied that everything was okay in his Chicago office, David decided to read the morning paper before attempting to find Frank Rubenstein. It had been very puzzling to him as to why Frank did not meet him at the restaurant as planned.

As he unfolded the paper, the headline hit him like a freight train. *Aide to Senator Whelan Murdered.*

The headline glared at him for a full ten seconds before he was able to read the story. That's when his worst fears were realized. Frank Rubenstein was murdered, and his roommate was being held for questioning. It was believed that the two were homosexual lovers and that an argument had escalated into a physical confrontation, whereby Jay Booker, Frank's roommate had taken a butcher knife from the kitchen, sneaked up behind him, and stabbed Frank Rubenstein in the side of the neck as he sat on his sofa.

David immediately picked up the phone and called Walt Austin. Walt was with a client at the moment, so David asked the receptionist to have Walt call him as soon as he could.

While waiting for Walt's call, David leaned back in his chair and thought about everything Frank had said to him in their last meeting at Martin's Tavern. Frank was at the end of his rope and was about to give up his freedom and everything else he owned to bring down Whelan. David had no doubt that Frank had known the odds of not surviving and was willing to take the risk. His death had changed everything.

David knew that he had to get the evidence from Frank's apartment before Whelan got there if he was going to be able to place both the senator *and* Clyde Bayless over the barrel and squeeze Clyde until he coughed up what David wanted.

The ringing phone broke David's thoughts.

"Good morning, Major," Walt Austin said.

"Good morning, Walt. A terrible thing happened last night that has thrown a monkey wrench into the gears of our plan," David said.

"I'm aware of that, Major. When I saw it in the paper this morning, I immediately dispatched one of my investigators who has a close relationship with a female officer that works at the downtown police station. We thought maybe we could possibly get access to the so-called murderer. We were too late. He was murdered in his cell last night, but not before he signed a written confession that he killed Frank Rubenstein in a jealous rage," Walt said.

"This is not adding up, Walt. This smells like a setup—a first class frame," David said.

"My thoughts exactly," Walt said.

"I had a strong feeling this guy was in trouble when he failed to show up at Martin's Tavern yesterday afternoon as planned. You and I need to meet right now, if possible," David said.

"Sure, come on over," Walt said.

"I'll be there in twenty minutes," David said as he hung up.

One hour later, David was sitting across the desk from Walt. The two men had been discussing how to proceed. The dilemma in which they had found themselves was clearly a major setback to their mission.

"I believe the best thing, for now, is to put out a couple of feelers in the right places," Walt said. "I'll get my man that has the female contact inside the police department to see if he can find out who the players were within the department. If we knew who Jay Booker's arresting officers were, we would at least have a starting place."

"Agreed," David said. "There's one thing for certain, Walt. This Whelan character is not your average, old fashion crooked politician. He's worse than just dirty. Likewise, little Clyde Bayless on the other end of the money pipeline is in way over his head. He's a bonafide chicken, and I would bet everything I own that he didn't bargain for all this killing."

The two men discussed all their options for the next thirty minutes until they were satisfied that the Metropolitan Police Department was the next place to go for answers. Approaching a powerful United States Senator at this stage of the investigation was simply not the right course of action. They knew they had to keep stirring the pot if they were going to get answers, and right now, the Police Department was the most logical place to do that.

The killing of Frank Rubenstein was a bad and possibly

explosive, thing to happen. They knew they had to make the right people nervous so that someone might talk.

Time was running out, and he knew that he desperately needed a solid lead. He needed something, *anything*. Maybe someone's arm to twist, or a snitch that needed money for a bottle of wine.

"Our lead is out there, Walt," David said. "I'll find it. I have to. Joe Carter is my oldest friend, and I will not let him down."

Walt knew David meant what he said. Many times in hostile occupied France during the war, Walt had seen Major Squire pull tricks out of the bag when it appeared that all was lost. Walt had seen the same look in his commanding officer's eyes time and time again. He had no doubt that Major David Squire would win this fight.

****

"No one will ever make me believe that Frank Rubenstein was a homosexual," Elizabeth Gardener said to Senator Whelan through tears. "He was all man. He was a very decent man, Senator. If his roommate killed him like they're saying, then it certainly wasn't because of a fight between two homosexuals."

Senator Whelan sat quietly across the desk from his executive secretary, as she held on to her composure while she talked about the loss of her friend. Whelan had not realized the extent of the friendship between Elizabeth Gardener and Frank Rubenstein until then. He had just assumed they were casual friends. Now he was beginning to wonder if Elizabeth had lied to him about Frank entering his office that day when his closet door had been left open.

As she sat there talking about the gentlemanly ways of her friend, Whelan thought, *she may have been covering for him, but it doesn't matter now. He's dead, and I have the evidence he took from me.*

After a few more minutes of listening to Elizabeth weep, Whelan realized there was nothing much he could do to make her feel better, so he decided to go back to his office and get some work done.

Back at his desk, Whelan decided to place the tapes back in their original places in his private closet. He reached for the paper bag containing the tapes that Haunce had given him.

Haunce Walters may be a brute, but he delivered the goods. He retrieved the tapes from Frank Rubenstein's apartment and secured my place near the head of the table inside the most elite power structure the world has ever known, he thought. *Now all I have to do is look sad for the camera during the inevitable network interviews that are sure to follow.*

That's when it hit him. After removing the first tape from the paper bag, he immediately saw that it was not his tape. The reel box was the wrong brand. He had always used one brand of audiotape because of its reputation for making high-quality recordings. This was clearly a different brand. Scrambling through the rest of the tapes, he realized they, too, were the wrong brand.

After exchanging the tape that was installed onto the recorder with one of the tapes from the paper bag, his worst fears were realized. They were duplicates. They were not blank.

Whelan had learned long ago never to make a decision from his emotions. So, back at his desk, he sat there for a while and pulled a few long drags on his Cuban cigar. After thinking things through, he decided that Elizabeth Gardener was somehow involved in the theft of the tapes.

Pressing the intercom button he asked, "Elizabeth, could you come in here, please?"

"Yes sir, I'll be right there," she answered.

With pad and pen in hand, Elizabeth took a seat in the chair next to the wall where she always sat while taking dictation from the senator.

"Elizabeth, I know this is a sad time for you, and the timing might be a bit off, but there's something I need to put to rest," he said.

Elizabeth knew what was coming now. Whelan was going to drill her about whatever was in that brown paper bag that Frank had retrieved from his office.

With as much calm as she could muster, she asked, "What is it, Senator?"

"I want you to, once again, think back to the day I was down the hall. Did Frank go into my office?" he asked.

Elizabeth sat stoically and stared at the floor in front of her. Finally, after thirty seconds, she raised her head and looked straight into the eyes of the man she knew was responsible for the death of her friend. With a look of total disconnect, she said, "I've been thinking about that for the last couple of days, and I think I remember him going into your office for a brief moment. I was distracted by a phone call from Senator Russell

Long's secretary concerning the budget for next year. I had my back to your door and thought he was waiting for me to get off the phone. When I turned back around, I thought I noticed that he was closing the door behind him. I can't say that he was actually in your office. Finally, he laid a folder of legal documents on my desk that he had for you. I was still engaged in the phone conversation, and he hung around until I got off. Our conversation was such that it did not cross my mind that he may have gone into your office."

Whelan's sense of sniffing out a story invention was telling him that she was lying, although she wasn't showing it. She was actually very calm, *too calm* in her delivery of the little story about the phone call. Now was the time to find out if she had been lying to him about the burglary. He wanted a confession out of her if she was guilty. He needed to find out if she was involved in some sort of conspiracy with Frank, and if anyone else was involved. It may be ugly, but he *had* to know the whole truth involving the missing tapes. He had to know who had possession of the originals and if Elizabeth knew anything about it. So he decided to squeeze her.

"You know more than you're telling me, Elizabeth," Whelan said with a cold stare.

"I do *not* know more than I'm telling you, senator," Elizabeth said with equal intensity.

Elizabeth had been raised by parents who were born in the nineteenth century. Her father had fought in the trenches of France during World War I. They had taught her the difference between good and evil and how to deal with the latter when confronted with it. She was not about to back down from this monster that had taken the life of a man who was very dear to her.

"I think you do," Whelan said.

"I really don't care what you think, Senator. If you don't like the quality of my work here or don't like my forthright answer to a direct question, then you can remove me from your payroll. Otherwise, do not *ever* question my integrity again," she said with a piercing glare. "Now, I need to take the rest of the day off. I'm in a bad way. Frank Rubenstein was a good friend of mine. I don't think I would get much work done today."

Whelan did not believe Elizabeth Gardener, but he was surprised at the tenacity in her voice as she spoke, unafraid of him. She had shown no fear of what might happen if he caught her lying.

"Now may I go, Senator?" She asked calmly.

Whelan knew she was not going to budge from her story no matter how intense the interrogation got, so he decided to let her off for a day or two. Maybe she would come to her senses and realize that the big loser in this situation was going to be the person in possession of the missing tapes.

"Why don't you take off the rest of the week and get yourself together. I think you need to know, however, that this thing is not over, Elizabeth. I will get to the bottom of what happened to the items that were stolen from my office. It makes no difference who it affects or how the chips may happen to fall. I will get the answer," he said.

Without a word, Elizabeth just stared at Whelan for a few

seconds. She was not afraid of this low-life and was not going to give him the pleasure of thinking she was. She made up her mind right there that she would give her all to avenging the death of her friend at the hands of this self-described king of the Washington political mountain. Nothing was going to stop her now. She arose from her chair and left without saying a word.

After Elizabeth was gone, Whelan reached for his phone and dialed a number.

"Walters Investigations," the secretary on the other end said.

"I need to talk to Haunce. This is Whelan," he said.

"One moment."

"Haunce here," Haunce Walters said in his usual gruff voice.

"We need to talk right now. Meet me at the same place in twenty minutes," Duff said.

"Will do," Haunce said as he hung up the phone.

Twenty minutes later, Whelan was sitting in his Mercedes next to Haunce Walters. "We've got a big problem, Haunce. The tapes you retrieved from Rubenstein's apartment were not the originals. They were duplicates," he said.

"Well, let's get one thing straight, Senator. *You* have a big problem. I do not. I did what you asked me. I delivered tapes that you told me were in his apartment," Haunce said.

"Okay, I have a problem, then. I need your help to find the originals. Are you interested?" Whelan asked.

"Yes, I will help you, senator. I just didn't like the suggestion that I didn't deliver what you asked," Haunce said.

"I think I may know where they are, but I'm not sure," Whelan said.

"Okay, just give me the address, and I'll go get them for you," Haunce said.

Whelan explained to Haunce all about the relationship between Elizabeth Gardener and Frank Rubenstein. He told Haunce that it was a high likelihood that she had the original tapes somewhere in her apartment. He informed Haunce that he would need to stake out the apartment to make sure she was not there. He explained that she had the rest of the week off and would likely be there quite a bit. Whelan did not want to have to explain the murder of another staff member to the news media and police. That would be entirely too much heat, so he warned Haunce to make sure she was not at home when they searched her apartment.

"Not a problem, Senator," Haunce said.

"Good because I can't keep covering up for your mistakes, Haunce," Whelan said.

"What's the address? I'll take care of this. You'll be proud of me, Whelan," Haunce said.

Whelan immediately felt the intensity of Haunce's stare and the implication that he would do it his way no matter what Whelan had to say. He gave Elizabeth Gardener's address to Haunce as the detective got out of the car.

"By the way, Duff, there is one more thing I forgot to mention to you earlier. We found an envelope in the apartment containing the name and address of a man from Chicago. He's a private detective. In light of all that's happened here, I think we should check it out," Haunce said.

"What was the name?" Whelan asked.

Removing the envelope from his jacket pocket, Haunce read the name aloud, "David Squire. The notes inside the envelope contain all his personal information. Maybe Rubenstein had hired this Squire guy to help him in whatever he was about to do with the stolen tapes from your office."

"Check him out, and if he's anywhere in the D. C. area, put a tail on him. I want to know what he's up to," Whelan said.

"Will do," Haunce said as he got into his car and drove away.

After he was gone, Duff mulled about what had occurred the last two days. First, there was the murder of a staff member and then the murder of another innocent victim to cover up the first murder. And now there was the revelation of this Chicago private detective.

Why was Frank Rubenstein in contact with a private investigator? What could this guy know about all of this? Where is this going to end? I can't believe my career and my very life have come down to this one thing—having to depend on a murderer to keep me out of a long stretch in a federal prison.

CHAPTER 14

FBI Director, J. Edgar Hoover was in deep thought reading a field report when his secretary buzzed him.

"Yes?" He asked.

"Agent Bill Caplan is here to see you, sir.

"Send him in," he said.

Bill entered the director's office and stood quietly near the door until Mr. Hoover spoke. Because Hoover did not like it when an agent entered his office and began chattering, he had a standing rule that when an agent entered his office, he was always to stand quietly until the director spoke to him.

"Good afternoon Agent Caplan. What do you have for me?" he asked.

"Well sir, an interesting thing happened last night that may have a connection to the Senator Whelan case. It seems that one of his top aides was murdered in his apartment. The Metropolitan Police arrested and obtained a confession from his roommate," Agent Caplan said.

"Okay, so what is it about this murder that may have something to do with our investigation of Senator Whelan?" Hoover asked.

"The police department has released to the press that the two men were homosexual lovers. They're saying that the two got into a lover's quarrel and the roommate stabbed the aide, one Frank Rubenstein, in the side of the neck. He later confessed to the crime. The strange thing about this is that when we investigated Whelan a few years ago, we did a thorough background check on his entire staff. Mr. Director, Frank Rubenstein was not a homosexual. A couple of our agents actually became friends with him over the years. I've talked to both of the agents, and they tell me there is no way that Frank Rubenstein is a homosexual," Agent Caplan said.

"Interesting. Now, tie this together with our Whelan investigation for me," Hoover said.

"Everything we have, other than the normal sexual orientation of Frank Rubenstein, is strictly circumstantial at this point. One of our agents who was a friend of Rubenstein's told me that Frank had mentioned to him just a few days ago that he had something very important that he may soon be sharing with him. The agent told me that Frank seemed to be a bit disturbed as if he were about to unload something heavy on him," Agent Caplan said.

Hoover leaned back in his chair and thought about it for a moment. "So what is your plan of action concerning this?"

"Well, sir, the two police officers that interrogated Rubenstein's roommate have been on our radar for a few years now. We've looked at them pretty hard on several occasions concerning racketeering accusations by prisoners at the city jail. When you put that piece of information together with the ludicrous charges of homosexual behavior by both dead men, it has raised the eyebrows of every agent assigned to the Whelan investigation," Caplan said.

"Good work, agent Caplan," Hoover said. "I think you should take a look at the murder and subsequent death of the roommate at the city jail. Just be discreet about it. Again, we don't want Senator Whelan to know we have him in our sights. Not yet, anyway. We'll save that little revelation until it's time to put him on the hot seat."

"Yes sir, Mr. Director. We will move with caution," Agent Caplan said as he was leaving.

****

David Squire and Walt Austin had spent most of the morning discussing all the options and different directions they should take in the investigation. Finally, they agreed that they should tap the phone lines at Whelan's office.

Walt and David knew that they were about to embark on a very shady thing, indeed. To tap into a Capitol Hill telephone line legally required a court order from a federal judge. Walt had never before ordered the illegal tapping of a telephone system. He had always worked within the law on such matters, and usually, company owners were the ones that asked him to bug their own telephone systems.

This was different, however, and Walt was willing to do whatever it took to help David get what he needed to wrap the case. Walt briefed David on some of the more sinister things Whelan was rumored to have been involved in during his Senate tenure. He also informed him about Whelan's shady private investigator, Haunce Walters, who had been linked to more than one death of subjects he had been investigating. Walt warned David to watch his back at all times concerning Haunce Walters.

Walt introduced David to Clarence Grafton, a fine investigator with many skills. Walt asked him to go with David to the basement of the capitol building to make the tap. Walt issued the two men fake work suits that looked exactly like the real telephone company repair uniforms. With the help of a friend of Walt's on the Capitol security force, they managed to get a repair pass to go inside the secured basement area where the bank of phone wires was located that led to the various offices throughout the building.

Clarence Grafton had worked for the telephone company for ten years after the war until he got bored with the quiet life of a civilian communications worker. In 1955, he had gone to work for Walt where he had been called on to do all the wire-tapping whenever a client needed it. This was, however, going to be the biggest task he had been asked to do since he came to work for Walt. On top of that, he and David would both end up behind bars if they got caught.

The two men walked along the corridors of the Capitol building and eventually into the basement area where the phone wire bank was located. David was amazed at the thousands and thousands of wires leading from the trunk line into the building and dispersing in hundreds of directions to the various offices throughout the building. He had never thought about the complexity of a telephone system in a large building.

"How are you going to find the correct line that goes to Senator Whelan's office?" David asked.

"With the help of this," Clarence said as he removed a rather large schematic from his pocket.

"Where did you get that?" David asked.

"Might be better if you don't ask," Clarence said as he began to study the schematic.

The two men worked on tracing the phone line to Whelan's office for about two hours before they finally found the correct wires. From that point, it only took a few minutes to connect all the wires to another, unused wire that could be utilized to attach a tape recorder at a remote location.

CHAPTER 15

The sun was just beginning to rise over the eastern horizon as Aaron Rubenstein made his way back to his hotel room after having breakfast down the street. The crisp morning air accompanied by a slow breeze accentuated the smells of Washington. Aaron had visited his brother a couple of times while he worked here but never at this time of year.

On this morning, however, he was in no mood to see the sites or try out any new restaurants. He was here for one thing only—to make arrangements to take Frank back to Pennsylvania for burial in the Rubenstein family plot in their hometown cemetery.

Although Rubenstein was generally thought of as a Jewish name, Aaron and Frank's parents had raised them as Catholics. Their father, Joseph Rubenstein, was a Jewish immigrant from Germany who had fled the unbelievably inflationary economy of his homeland in 1919 right after The Great War. He stowed away on a cargo ship at the port city of Bremerhaven, and after getting caught halfway across the Atlantic, he was allowed by the good graces of a sympathetic captain to work with the rest of the crew for his food and a bed. After he arrived at Ellis Island in New York Harbor, he quickly found work as a house painter. His boss liked him because of his work ethic, and eventually, he had Joseph running a crew.

City life did not agree with Joseph Rubenstein, however, so he drifted west to the Allegheny Mountains of Pennsylvania. There, he met Eleanor O'Casey, a devout Catholic, and second generation American whose grandfather had emigrated from Ireland in the nineteenth century. The two were immediately enamored with each other and were married within six months. Joseph Rubenstein converted to Catholicism soon after, and the couple raised two sons, Aaron, and Frank.

This morning was going to be a busy yet sad day for Aaron. He and Frank were close, and now he was going to have to arrange the transport of his brother's body home and make the funeral arrangements with the family priest, Father O'Hara. Aaron's parents were getting on into years, and they simply did not have the emotional strength to handle such a traumatic thing.

To make matters worse, Aaron had read the morning paper that stated his brother was a homosexual and that the murder was a result of a lover's quarrel. That accusation alone had burned Aaron to the very marrow of his bones. He immediately knew that something was awry with this whole investigation. He vowed to come back and clear his brother's name of such a hideous accusation—but not today. He had things to do, starting with meeting an attorney and going to Frank's apartment.

Aaron had to see the crime scene for himself. As the sheriff of a Pennsylvania county, he had been involved in many investigations of all kinds over his eighteen-year law enforcement career. He knew if he could just see the undisturbed crime scene, he could get a better picture of what may have happened.

****

William St. John was reading a court document from a trial he had recently been involved in when his intercom buzzed.

"There's a Mister Aaron Rubenstein here to see you," the secretary said.

"Send him in."

The door opened and St. John's secretary ushered Aaron Rubenstein into Williams St John's office.

"Good morning, Mr. Rubenstein," William said.

"Good morning," Aaron said.

"First off, I'd like to give you my deepest sympathies for your loss," William said. "There is simply no good way to describe a situation like this one, so I'll just say I'm sorry for your loss."

"Thank you," Aaron said. "You're the first person I've talked to here in Washington, so I'm going to start by telling you emphatically that my brother's murder was a lot more than just two queers getting into a lover's quarrel. I knew both of the men all of their lives. The young man, Jay Booker, was not a homosexual, and neither was my brother. This thing stinks like dead fish. I'm not speaking to you as a man who has lost his only brother. I'm speaking to you as a Sheriff who keeps the peace in a county of ninety-eight thousand citizens. This is a cover up, William."

William sat there quietly. Finally, he spoke. "Mr. Rubenstein, if you say this is not what it seems, I believe you. There is one thing, however, that you have to understand. I cannot get involved in a murder case involving a top aide to a powerful United States senator. I have made arrangements for you and me to meet at your brother's place. I think we will have a fair amount of time to look around the apartment since the police have pretty much concluded their investigation."

"Good. When do we start?" Aaron asked.

"Right now if you wish."

I'm ready," Aaron said.

The two men drove to Frank's apartment and obtained a key from the manager of the building. Upon entering the living room, it was immediately clear to Aaron that the place had been torn up—but not in a fit of rage. Looking through the eyes of an investigator, Aaron took notice of every little thing in the living room. He observed that the photo of his brother and the President had not been disturbed along with everything else on the mantel. Basic investigating dictates that in a lovers quarrel, the first things to be destroyed are items that are precious to the lovers. Aaron knew that Frank cherished the photo of himself and President John F. Kennedy.

This was not a fight between lovers, he thought. *This is exactly what I knew it was from the beginning—a murder by someone with connections. They even managed to kill Jay Booker in his jail cell after they beat a false confession out of him. This was a job perpetrated by someone who was looking for something. Frank surprised them, and they killed him.*

The two men had walked through the house for fifteen minutes as Aaron keenly observed everything that had been disturbed when they heard a soft knock at the door. They had left the door slightly ajar when they entered so friends of Frank or Jay who wanted to stop by could see that someone was there.

Aaron went to the door and opened it just enough to look into the hallway. He had investigated enough murders and accidents during his career to know not to expose too much of the crime scene to the eyes of someone who may have an emotional bond with the deceased. A pretty, blue-eyed brunette of about thirty years old stood in the hall staring back at him.

Aaron instinctively knew who it was. "You're Elizabeth Gardener, aren't you?" he asked.

"Why, yes…I…I…How did you…." She stopped herself in the middle of her question after seeing the strong physical resemblance to Frank.

Seeing that she was about to lose her composure, Aaron stepped forward, placed his arms around Elizabeth, and gave her a long hug. She began to weep as he held her. It was all he could do to keep his own composure, but the veteran sheriff managed to hold onto his emotions. It was clear to him that she had lost a dear friend in his brother.

"I just wanted to come by and see if anyone was here. I want very badly to have something of Frank's. He was a very close friend of mine," she said.

"I know. Frank and I never kept any secrets from each other. He told me not too long ago that you worked in his office. He said you were the kind of girl that could make a man happy forever. My brother was secretly in love with you, Elizabeth. He was never very good at expressing his feelings like most people," Aaron said softly.

That's when Elizabeth lost it. She openly cried for several

minutes before regaining her poise. Their feelings had been mutual, but until recently, she was unable to even admit it to herself. The thought of her meeting with him at the park a few minutes before he was killed reminded her that it had been the closest thing she would ever have to actually go on a date with him. The way he gently held her in his arms as he kissed her before he left made her feel so alive—more so than she had ever felt. For a young, virtuous woman who had never known a man in the biblical sense, it was the single most thrilling moment of her life—and now he was gone forever.

Her prince in shining armor was brutally murdered on the orders of her very own boss. She knew it as well as she knew her own name. As she stood leaning against the wall while Aaron held her hand, she solemnly vowed that she would get the sub-human who did this terrible thing.

"May I see the inside of the apartment? I would very much like to have a little something to keep as a memento," she asked.

"It's not a pretty sight, Elizabeth. I'm not sure you should do that," Aaron said.

"Young lady, I do not believe you should go in there," William St. John interrupted.

He had been standing in the hallway during the entire exchange and had garnered enough information to know that this murder was not what the papers were reporting. As an attorney who had seen many underhanded dealings, including a couple of murders, he decided it was time for him to make his exit. He simply did not want to know any more than he already knew.

"Sheriff, I think I'm going to be on my way now. I wish you the best, and I'm very sorry for the loss of your brother. Miss Gardener, I'm sorry you lost your friend, and I wish you the best, too," William said as he turned to leave.

"Thank you, Counselor," Aaron said.

Turning to Elizabeth, Aaron was about to coax her into not going inside until he saw the hard, determined look in her eyes. He knew it would be useless and downright mean for him to deny this lady one last look at the memories of Frank.

"You want to go inside?" he asked.

"Yes," she said.

"Okay, but you have to understand it's not just a messy house. It's the scene of a murder whereby the perpetrators tore up the place...and there's blood. Can you handle it?" he asked.

"Yes."

"Wait right here. I'll be back in a moment," he said.

He went inside and closed the door behind him. In the laundry room, he found two sheets in a neat stack of linens. He went back to the living room and covered the blood on the sofa and the floor.

Back in the hallway, Aaron took Elizabeth by the hand and led her into the apartment. As she slowly made her way around the living room, she tried to learn what she did not know about Frank's life. She wanted to *feel* how he lived his private life. She stopped at the mantel and gazed for a long time at the photo of Frank and the President. She turned around and looked at Aaron.

"You can have it," he said before she could speak.

Aaron knew what she had been doing as they slowly walked around the room. He knew she was absorbing things about the life of his brother that she had never had the privilege of witnessing for herself, and when she stood gazing at the photo, he knew it belonged to her.

"Oh, thank you," she said. "I promise I'll hold it close to my heart."

"I know," he said quietly.

As they continued around the room to the sofa, she asked, "Why are the sheets on the sofa?"

Looking into her eyes, Aaron didn't really know how to say it. Finally, he decided that she was strong enough to handle it, so he just told her it was to cover up the blood. He told her she didn't need to see it.

"It's the blood of the only man I ever cared about. Besides, he died because he crossed the wrong man. I can handle it. Please remove the sheets," she said calmly.

Aaron had been in law enforcement long enough to recognize strength when he saw it. He reached down and gently removed the sheets. Elizabeth just stood stoically and stared at the bloodstains all over the sofa and floor.

Watching her closely as she observed without emotion, the revelation came to him that she would have been the perfect woman for his brother. Frank needed a strong woman, and this lady certainly fit the bill.

"We should go now, don't you think?" he asked.

"Yes, I guess so," she said quietly.

As they opened the door to leave, Aaron noticed a man

coming toward them from down the hall. As he got closer, Aaron took Elizabeth by the arm and gently moved her to a position behind him.

"Hi, are you police officers?" David Squire asked.

"No, this was my brother's apartment," Aaron said.

Noticing a strong family resemblance David said, "You must be Sheriff Aaron Rubenstein from Pennsylvania."

"I am, and who might you be?" Aaron asked, a bit puzzled.

"I knew your brother for a short time. I'm a private investigator. Frank and I were working on something together. My name is David Squire."

"So, you're a private investigator?" Aaron asked.

"Yes, your brother and I were working on something very big. I can explain, but first I'd like to tell you how sorry I am at your loss," David said.

"Thank you for that, but I have a simple question for you," Aaron said. "Why did you lie to my brother about serving in the same unit with me during the War?"

David looked at Aaron for a quick moment so that he may get some feel for his attitude. Finally, he said, "My apologies for lying to Frank about knowing you during the War. I told him that for a simple reason—to get his attention. I was pretty sure he wouldn't cooperate with me on what I'm investigating unless I made him think I was running a scam of some sort. My tactic worked. He and I had two long conversations, and he was very helpful to my investigation. He was about to put me in a position to help him out of a very bad situation, but before he could give me what I needed to help him, he was murdered. I'm pretty sure I know who's behind this, but I'm at a total loss if I can't find the missing piece of evidence he had for me. I thought if I could take a look around inside the apartment, I might just get lucky and find it."

"I'm not prepared to let a total stranger go inside of my brother's apartment and look through his things. I'm sure you understand. Besides, he's dead now, so it doesn't matter anymore, does it," Aaron said.

"I agree wholeheartedly. I really don't think here, outside your brother's apartment, is the place to discuss with you what I need to tell you. May I invite you and the young lady for a cup of coffee?" David asked.

"I don't think that's a very good idea," Aaron said. "My brother's gone, and I just want to go make arrangements to have his body transported back to Pennsylvania for burial. Now if you will excuse…"

"I want to know what you have to say," Elizabeth interrupted.

Her comment caught both men off guard. Finally, Aaron spoke up. "What do you expect to learn from this, Elizabeth?"

"I knew of something that was tearing at Frank's heart. He told me all about it. I want to know what this man has to say. We'll never know the real truth unless we hear what Mr. Squire has to say," she said with determination in her voice.

"Okay, we accept your offer; lead the way," Aaron said, as he turned to lock Frank's door.

At a diner two blocks down the street, they ordered coffee and engaged in small talk until they were served. After the waitress left, David began the conversation by briefing them as to why he was in Washington in the first place.

"I have an old friend back home that has been scammed by a wealthy, local man. In short, Clyde Bayless loaned my friend Joe Carter money to operate his farm. Then, he snookered Joe into mortgaging all his land on the deal a few years ago. By the time Joe realized what Clyde had done to him, the statute of limitations had expired, so he had no legal recourse. By then, he was in trouble financially because of commodity prices among other factors.

"Clyde is now foreclosing on Joe and his wife, Millie, and is only waiting for the legal documents to be signed. To make matters worse, Joe is dying of cancer. I'm trying to save his land that was mortgaged under false pretense so that Millie will not be homeless after he's gone.

"A third party who works as a secretary for Clyde Bayless gave me a solid lead on a money scam that led me straight to your brother. I know you loved your brother, but because he was being blackmailed for a mistake he made years ago, he found himself up to his eyeballs in the trafficking of dirty money from Clyde Bayless to a United States Senator—one Benjamin Duff Whelan.

"In our last meeting, he told me he had hard evidence that would implicate his boss, Senator Whelan, as the mastermind behind the scam. He assured me the evidence would prove Whelan's guilt beyond any shadow of a doubt.

"And then his life was brutally taken. The newspapers are reporting statements from anonymous sources that Frank and his roommate, Jay Booker were lovers and that Jay Booker had killed Frank in a lover's quarrel."

"That's a damn lie," Elizabeth blurted out. "I'm sorry for my language, Mr. Squire," she said. "Frank was *not* Jay Booker's lover.

"I know that," David said. "Everything that's happened in the last thirty-six hours has been an orchestrated effort to smear the reputations of two perfectly normal, hardworking men. It made no difference about the dignity of the victims and their families. The men who were behind this horrible series of events clearly care about one thing only—money.

"A wise detective always follows the money. In this case, it brought me to the feet of Senator Whelan. The dilemma I'm in now is that I don't have the evidence that Frank had in his apartment," David said.

"Exactly what are you looking for, David?" Aaron asked.

"That's just it. I do not know. I'm sure I would if I saw it, but your brother never told me, Sheriff," David said.

"Well, I can tell you that it's not in the apartment," Aaron said. "I examined the crime scene very carefully. The perpetrators were clearly looking for something, and they found it, or it wasn't there. It was easy to figure that out by the way they ransacked the whole apartment. In light of what you've said here, assuming you're telling the truth, I believe the murder was by design or at least the cover up is. They, no doubt, found what they were looking for."

"He's telling the truth, Aaron," Elizabeth said softly. "Frank recently revealed to me everything that Mr. Squire has said here. He was being blackmailed by our boss and was ready to get out of the situation no matter where the chips fell for him. Frank was a good man. He was a man of honor. I was there when Frank stole items from Senator Whelan's office while the senator was in a meeting down the hall. He stole these items out of the senator's private closet. Senator Whelan had accidentally left the door unlocked, and Frank went inside and took the items."

"What did he take from the senator?" David asked.

"That's the sixty-four-thousand-dollar question, Mr. Squire. He did not tell me, and I did not ask. The only thing I know is that he left with a rather large paper bag with items from the closet. In a couple of subsequent conversations, Frank told me everything he had done, and why. He was ready to take his medicine with federal prosecutors. He said he could no longer participate in the trafficking of dirty money. I warned him that he could end up dead over this, and he said, 'so be it,'" she said as she began to weep.

They sat there for a while longer as David and Aaron discussed possible directions they could pursue. Finally, after thirty minutes of bantering back and forth, Aaron announced he had to go. He had to meet with D. C. police officials to arrange for Frank's body to be shipped home. Aaron gave David his home number and the Sheriff's department number back in Pennsylvania in case there was anything David needed to ask him. Likewise, David gave Aaron his hotel room number and advised him that he checked his messages with the front desk regularly.

After Aaron had left, David and Elizabeth sat and talked for a long time. Because David knew that Elizabeth could shed light on the situation, probably without even realizing it, he engaged her in conversation about her job and how business was conducted in the Senate office.

Eventually, she mentioned a conversation she overheard while inside a small storage room between her office and Senator Whelan's. The conversation had been between Senator Whelan and a man named Haunce. From the conversation, she determined that Haunce was a bad character. She had heard rumblings around the office that Whelan had a private investigator brute he used from time to time. There were even unsubstantiated rumors of a situation whereby Senator Whelan's private investigator was the perpetrator in a murder. Elizabeth had never met him and had never taken a call from him.

"Senator Whelan has a private line that does not go through my office. It's direct from his office to the outside of the Senate building, so I've never talked to that guy," she said.

"Walters. His name is Haunce Walters," David said.

"How do you know that?" Elizabeth asked.

"I have an old friend that has an investigations business here. He told me about Haunce Walters. You're right, my friend said he was a bad character and warned me to steer clear of him if possible," David said.

"You have a friend here in the Washington area that's in the investigation business?" She asked.

"Yes, we served in the same unit in the OSS during the war. He's helping me with this case," David said.

"So, you didn't just walk into this thing blind?" she asked.

"No, I did not. My buddy is well established here and knows a lot of people in politics. He knows many of the perimeter players as well and has been a huge help for me on this thing," he said.

"That's good to know. This town has a way of swallowing up outsiders. You could get hurt very badly if you don't have connections," Elizabeth said.

"What we have to find out now is what evidence Frank had against Whelan. I'm going to meet with my investigator friend in a little while. We'll discuss the situation and go from there. A lot of people have a vested interest in the outcome of this. On our side alone, there are six different individuals, including myself, with six distinctly different motives for justice. My old friend in Arkansas, the victim of the original crime, needs to reclaim the deed to his farm that was stolen from him through deception.

"The lady who works for the perpetrator there, and who, through a stroke of luck, found the piece of evidence that could bury him along with Senator Whelan, has her own motive involving deep revenge for what the perpetrator did to her in a separate incident.

"Then there's my investigator friend here. He feels like he owes his life to the victim back home because he saved the life of my friend here behind enemy lines during the War.

"Of course, there's Aaron Rubenstein. He lost his brother, and his brother's name is being inexplicably smeared. He wants his brother's name cleared.

"And there is you. This whole horrific ordeal has to be very mind-numbing for you. You were in love with Frank, and now he's forever gone. His life was stolen from him by a crooked scoundrel that has no regard for the preciousness of life itself.

"Finally, there is me. I have loved my friend back home like a brother since we were small boys. We grew up on neighboring farms. Our mothers were French immigrants brought home from the Great War with our dads. As chance would have it, both families settled in the same community.

"In short, Elizabeth, I went into this thing not giving two hoots in hell about Senator Whelan's involvement in a money scam. I only wanted leverage for my old friend back home so that he may regain the deeds to his land. It seems that the deeper this investigation leads me into the abyss, the more determined I've become to bring all of them down. I barely knew Frank, but I knew immediately that he was a man of strong character who made a mistake.

"I guess the bottom line is this, Elizabeth. My primary goal is to get Joe's deed for him, but I cannot sit idly by and see so many other good people hurt without doing something about it if I can get the goods on the bad guys. I will not give up until every piece of scum is scooped up and brought to justice," he said.

Realizing that she was looking into the eyes of an infinitely dangerous man, Elizabeth felt both adoration for all he was risking for a friend and fear of the powers he was about to take on.

"I need to get back to my apartment. I have a few things to

do, and then I need to run some errands," Elizabeth said.

"Okay, I have your phone number, and you have mine. If you run across any new information, please let me know. I'll pick up the tab for the coffee," he said as they stood up.

"Thank you," she said as she turned to leave.

As David was at the cash register paying the tab, a man walked past him and out the door without paying. He thought it was a bit odd but didn't think much of it.

What he didn't know was that the man was Benny Flaigo, the man who had stabbed Frank in the neck as he sat on his sofa. Alfonse Giovetti still sat in a booth adjacent to where David and the others had sat. The two men had been watching Frank Rubenstein's apartment and had followed David and the two others to the diner.

Flaigo and Giovetti were following Haunce Walters's orders to put a tail on anyone who entered Frank Rubenstein's apartment.

Giovetti decided it was time to pay the tab for him and Flaigo so he could immediately fall in behind David. He got up and made his way to the cash register where he waited right behind David. Maybe he had the original tapes they were looking for—or maybe the girl had them. Either way, they had to find out for sure.

As he stood behind David, Giovetti, who was just over six feet, examined David from head to toe.

David finished paying his bill, turned, and within thirty seconds, he was around the corner walking at a good clip down the sidewalk.

As David walked along, he pondered on what his possible next move might be. He wasn't sure which way to go, but he did know he had a very short window of time on both ends. Clyde Bayless was doing all he could to get the foreclosure expedited, and Whelan was doing all he could to stop any snooping around by outsiders.

CHAPTER 16

"Senator Whelan," Duff said as he answered the phone.

"Duff," Haunce Walters said. "Just want to give you a heads up on where we are with our surveillance. We observed three subjects this morning having coffee in a diner—two men and one woman. One of the men had a strong family resemblance to Frank Rubenstein. We figure he's probably here to claim the body of his brother or some such reason. The other man matches the photo on the private investigator's license we found in Rubenstein's apartment. His name is David Squire from Chicago. I could send a man there and snoop around if you'd like. We might be able to find out why he's here. Might go a long way to understanding what his connection is to Rubenstein. There's got to be a strong reason why he came all the way here from Chicago to get involved in this matter.

"As for the female, it's your girl, Elizabeth Gardener. We've got a tail on her right now. We're watching her every move. If we see her carrying anything that looks like it might be the tapes, we'll just do a quick purse snatching on the street."

"Do not harm her if possible," Whelan said. "I do *not* need any more killings on my staff. This has become too sensitive for me to take any more unnecessary chances."

"We will do our best to prevent any more violence,"

Haunce said. "What do you want to do about sending a man to Chicago to see what he can dig up on this guy, Squire?" He asked.

"I think we need to hold off on going to Chicago for right now. If this thing gets more complicated, we'll send somebody then," Whelan said. "Meanwhile, I want you to do a complete background check on him. I want to know whether he's a Cubs or White Sox fan and how many games he went to for the last ten years. Don't miss a single thing about who this man is, Haunce."

"Okay, we'll get right on it," Haunce said as he hung up.

****

Agent Buck Huston and Carl Honeywell walked through the Senate Office Building and made their way to the entrance to the basement where the telephone lines entered from the trunk line under the street. They wore fake telephone jumpsuits and carried fake phone company documentation to gain entry to the secured area. When Buck gave the guard the fake work order, he examined it for a moment and then gave both men a skeptical look. He told them to wait while he made a call. He disappeared for a couple of minutes, and when he returned, he told the men they had been approved to work on the phone lines.

"I was beginning to think that Bill Caplan had screwed up the arrangements for us to gain access," Buck said to Carl after they were out of sight of the guard.

"I think that clear polish on your fingernails made him suspicious, or maybe it was that Mississippi accent," Carl snickered.

Taken aback for a moment, Buck finally got the joke. "You saying I don't look like a telephone repair man?" He asked, laughing.

"That's about it, Agent Huston," Carl said.

Carl Honeywell had tapped more telephone lines, both legally and illegally, for the FBI than any actual telephone employee had ever thought about doing. He had been in the basement of the Senate Office Building more times than Telephone Company workers. Most of the time the guards recognized him as an actual employee of the telephone company and didn't even ask for identification. He was top notch and had never let the Bureau down on an important wiretap.

Today would prove to be a bit different from any normal tap, however. When he and Buck arrived at the bank of wires, Carl immediately realized there was already a wiretap on one of the Senate offices. He decided to see who was giving up their office secrets so he clipped his headphones to the wires and waited for it to ring. It didn't take long.

"Good afternoon; Senator Whelan's office," the receptionist said.

Carl couldn't believe his ears.

"Someone has already done all the hard work for us, Buck," he said.

"What do you mean?" Buck asked.

"I mean that Senator Whelan is already being tapped."

"What? We need to call Bill Caplan before we do anything," Buck said.

As he waited for Carl to find an unused wire to hook up a

special telephone for them to call the office, he began to think about all the possibilities. He couldn't come up with a single theory as to who it could be unless it was a political enemy to Senator Whelan.

After Carl had found a clear wire, Buck dialed Bill Caplan's number.

"Agent Caplan," Bill said.

"Bill, this is Buck. We're in the Senate basement. Someone is already tapping Senator Whelan's phone lines. What do you think we should do?" Buck asked.

The two men discussed the situation and finally decided to just pull one of the clips off the wire and make it look like it fell off. Then they could post a man near the entrance with a camera and take photos of everyone coming and going into the basement area. Sooner or later, the people responsible for the wiretap were sure to come back.

They also decided to notify the Capitol Police as to what they were observing. Every time someone went into the basement, they would be photographed going and coming. The Capitol Police would agree to allow everyone who claimed to be a telephone repairman passage into the basement.

****

"Hello," Elizabeth Gardener said as she answered the phone.

"Miss Gardener, I'm Harold Gersen, an old friend of Frank Rubenstein's. I own Gersen's Hardware at the corner of M Street and North Capitol. May I have a moment of your time?" Harold asked.

"Yes you may," Elizabeth said.

"A few days ago Frank was in my store and left something here for you," he said.

Elizabeth was astonished. She could not believe that Frank had left something at a hardware store for her.

"Okay, shall I come down and pick it up?" she asked.

"Yes, I'll have it here for you anytime you're ready. We're open from seven in the morning until six in the afternoon Monday through Saturday," he said.

"I'll be there in a little while," Elizabeth said as she hung up.

****

"Harold Gersen was at the cash register giving a customer her change when Elizabeth walked through the door.

"May I help you?" he asked.

"Yes sir, I'm looking for Mister Harold Gersen. He's expecting me," she said.

"I am he, and you must be Miss Elizabeth Gardener," he said with a smile.

"Yes sir, I am," she said.

"Follow me. I have something for you," he said.

In his private area inside his office above the warehouse, Harold stepped over to the cabinet and retrieved a clean cup from the rack next to the coffee machine.

"Coffee?" he asked.

"No, thank you," she said.

"You might as well, Miss Gardener; we're probably going to be here for a little while. I have some things I need to talk to you about," he said.

Elizabeth would normally have been a little uncomfortable at a stranger saying something like that, but in light of all that had happened the previous two days, she was numb to almost anything.

"Okay, I'll take mine black, no sugar," she said.

After he had handed her the coffee, Harold stepped over to his safe and unlocked the door. Reaching inside, he retrieved the box that Frank Rubenstein had given him for safekeeping. He set the box between Elizabeth and him in the middle of the small dining table. She stared at it without saying a word as Harold poured himself a cup of coffee.

"Frank Rubenstein was a good friend of mine. His roommate worked for me. The kid had a mild developmental deficiency and was slow to catch on, but he was a hard worker. Always on time, and never missed work," Harold said. "I have no idea what you know about Frank's private life, but unless you tell me something different from what I already believe, and are prepared to back up what you say, then I'm emphatically going to say right here and now that Frank Rubenstein was not a homosexual. He just wasn't. I knew him well."

Elizabeth could feel the lump swelling in her throat as she listened to this stranger make such strong, positive statements about her friend. She knew this meeting was going to be emotional and she just decided not to fight it.

"Frank was the most gentle man I've ever known outside my own father. He was my friend from the very first time I met him a few years ago. We both worked for Senator Whelan and had lunch many times. We used to sit for hours and talk about how the political game always seemed to consume even the most idealistic of men who embraced it.

"As for Frank's sexuality, we were not intimate, but I would bet my very life on what you just said. He was not a homosexual, and I believe he was murdered by someone else who holds a position of great power in this town. That awful accusation was pinned on him in the cruelest of ways. He's gone and cannot defend himself, but I can," she said through her tears.

"This could be very dangerous for you, Miss Gardener," Harold said.

"I don't care," she said as she stared right into Harold's eyes.

Harold saw a determination in this young woman that he hadn't often seen in a lady this young. He sat there for a moment pondering on what he should do now. He knew if he gave her the box, she could very well get herself killed. After a moment of reflection, he decided that this was what Frank had asked him to do.

Shoving the box across the table to her, Harold said, "Miss Gardener, the contents of this box could get you killed. I do not know what the box contains, but Frank left it with me a couple of days ago and told me to give it to you if anything tragic happened to him. That alone tells me that what's inside this box is very dangerous for whomever has possession of it. Accept it at your own risk. A grave risk, I might add."

Elizabeth began to open the box when Harold stopped her.

"Please do not open it here, Miss Gardener," he said. "It's best that I don't know what's in it. I'm not a coward, and I'm not afraid of dying. I've already been to hell in the South Pacific during the war. Nothing scares me, ma'am. It's just that when I was in the Marines, I was only nineteen years old and had no wife and children to think about. If whoever comes after you concerning the contents of that box knows that I am privy to what it contains, they will leave my wife and children without a husband and father. I owe it to them to be responsible to my obligations as the patriarch of my family. Dying when it can be prevented is not responsible behavior, Miss Gardener. Are you willing to take that chance?"

"Yes, Mister Gersen, I am. If it's the last thing I do on this Earth, I will clear the name of my friend," she said.

"Very well. Good luck to you," he said. "One more thing, Miss Gardener. I truly admire your tenacity. I just pray that you'll be okay in the end."

"Mister Gersen, my uncle, was in the Marines during the War, and I know what you faced on a daily basis. I know the hell you lived through as well as anyone who never was actually there. My uncle fights the shell shock every day of his life. You did your duty, and now it's time for me to do mine. This was placed in my lap by a dear friend, and I swear to all that is in heaven, I will not let Frank down," Elizabeth said as she arose to leave.

She turned and made her way down the stairs and back through the store to her car outside. Parked a few spaces away, Benny Flaigo was waiting when she came out of the hardware store and got into her car. He started his engine, and when she pulled out of the parking lot and onto the street, he did the same, following about a half block behind her. He had noticed the box in her hand.

****

David and Walt were having coffee at Walt's favorite short-order diner down the street from his office when their waitress came over and announced to Walt that he had a phone call from his office. He thanked her and made his way to the telephone near the end of the counter.

"This is Walt," he said.

"Walt, this is Clarence. We've lost the tap," he said. "I was listening to an interesting conversation between Senator Whelan and some guy with a southern accent when the line went blank."

"I'll be right over," Walt said as he hung up.

Back at the table, Walt told David what had happened and that they needed to be back at the office. They paid their tab and left.

Unknown to the two men, Alfonse Giovetti had been sitting in the booth behind David. He had recognized Walt Austin and had done his best to hear what David and Walt had been discussing. He was sure that he had heard Walt mention something about a tap that had become disconnected.

Giovetti was not the sharpest pencil in the pack, but even he could figure out that Walt Austin was watching and listening to Whelan. After all, this David Squire fella had been showing up everywhere about the murder of Frank Rubenstein.

Back at the office, Walt and David sat down with Clarence to discuss what telephone conversations he had recorded of Whelan.

"Tell us about the conversation you were listening to when the line went dead," Walt said.

"Senator Whelan used the man's initials to address him. He called him *JC*. He asked this JC if he knew David Squire. When JC said he did, Whelan told him that this Squire guy is snooping around into the senator's business," Clarence said.

David knew immediately the name of the man Clarence was talking about—Jasper Clyde Bayless, the little punk from the schoolyard who always tried to get all the other kids to address him as *JC*.

"What was his reaction after Whelan told him I was snooping around in his business?" David asked.

"That's when we lost the connection. I heard him say 'This could be…' and then the line went dead," Clarence said.

Turning to Walt, David said, "We need to fix this right now. I need to know what Clyde's pulse is at the moment."

After Walt and Clarence had talked it over for a couple of minutes, they decided it would be better to fix it right now. They needed to get on tape every conversation Whelan had concerning David and Walt.

"Major, I don't believe I have to tell you that you're in a bad spot here. They're going to throw everything they possibly can at you. These are dangerous people, and they will not hesitate to run over you to get what they want," Walt said.

"So am I. Dangerous, that is," David said.

A thin smile slowly crept over Walt's face, and David knew that his old friend understood that he was not going to run now. He was in too deeply to turn back. The next few days were going to be critical on both ends of the money trail, and David was very aware that everything had to fall into place or the whole investigation would come crashing down around him.

****

Agent Charlie Johnston was wandering around the Senate Building near the basement entrance attempting to look like a tourist. His assignment was to watch for men entering the basement area where the telephone lines entered the building. Buck had placed Agent Johnston on the stakeout because of his record of collecting solid photographic data of subjects the FBI were watching.

The FBI had no idea who might be behind the wiretapping of Whelan's phone lines, but Buck was determined to find out. If it were the Soviets, then the FBI had to know. If it was a political enemy trying to gain information on Whelan so he could use it against him, then Buck was actually okay with that. On a personal level, he didn't care what kind of secrets Whelan lost to his political opponents. He needed to be held at bay for what he was doing to the taxpayers. Buck knew, however, that he was bound by duty to stop any illegal wiretapping by anyone, no matter who it was.

He was well aware that his own wiretap attempt on Whelan was unlawful because he had no court ordered warrant. He found it ironic and hypocritical that he was committing an illegal act that he was about to arrest someone else for engaging in. The only reason the FBI could get away with that sort of outright criminal, albeit relatively minor, activity was that the Director had thick files on everyone in government from law enforcement to the President. No one was ever going to complain about the Bureau listening to a crooked senator as he made sleazy deals on the phone. Everyone knew that national security matters were never discussed on the telephone, and such conversation always took place behind closed, soundproof doors. That's why Buck had concluded that this was probably not a Soviet undertaking but rather a political enemy. Nevertheless, he needed to know, so he had assigned Agent Charlie Johnston to the job of photographing the perpetrators of the wiretap.

Agent Johnston did not have to wait long. Only a couple hours had passed when two men dressed in telephone jumpsuits appeared from around the corner and were walking toward the guard in charge of access to the basement area. Quickly and without drawing attention to himself, he aimed his camera and began shooting photos of the two men. When he had taken at least two dozen photos, he unassumingly turned and made his way out of the building.

Back at FBI headquarters, a dozen agents were sitting around a long conference table examining the photos that Agent Charlie Johnston had taken.

"Take a very close look, gentlemen. We need to make these guys. If you see any resemblance to any man you've ever met, then tell me.

"The shorter one is Clarence Grafton," Agent Jason Martin said. "I came across him several times when I was working a case a couple of years ago. From what I could determine, he was an honest, hardworking investigator. He was investigating a man who was trying to stiff his estranged wife during divorce proceedings, and I was after the same guy for another reason. He works for Walt Austin over at *Austin Investigations*."

"Does anyone know the other guy in the photos?" Buck asked.

When no one spoke up, Buck decided to place Walt Austin's office under surveillance and see if his agents could get a name for the other man. He decided to allow them to keep the wiretap on Senator Whelan's office without arresting them. He ordered his technical men to go back to the basement and run a piggyback wiretap right over the top of Walt Austin's tap. That way they would have the same information that Austin had concerning Whelan's behavior.

In the meantime, Buck needed to know what Walt Austin was up to. This was very out of character for Walt. Buck was a very straight-laced investigator. He knew that Walt was too, so he decided to give him the benefit of the doubt. It must be something *huge* for him to compromise his company and his entire career as a private investigator. That, alone, was the reason Buck was going to turn his head for the time being.

CHAPTER 17

Whelan was talking to Elizabeth's temporary replacement when his special phone line rang. Excusing himself, he stepped back through his office door and closed it behind him.

"Senator Whelan," he said as he answered.

"Duff, this is Haunce. I've got a full report on the subject you asked about yesterday afternoon. I can be at the usual place in fifteen minutes," Haunce said.

"Okay, I'll be there," Whelan said.

After telling his temporary secretary that he would be gone for a little while, Whelan left for Rock Creek Park.

When Whelan got to the park, Haunce was already there. Whelan pulled into the parking place next to Haunce and unlocked his passenger door. When Haunce got in, he handed Whelan a file folder that contained several pages of material on David Squire—everything from growing up on a farm to his career as a private investigator.

"I think that gives a good overview of who this guy is," Haunce said. "We know where he grew up, and we know where he lives now. We even know the name of his wife, who has been dead for several years."

"It seems to be very thorough. Good job, Haunce. When the time is right, maybe we can use this," Whelan said.

"Good," Haunce said as he was getting out of Whelan's car.

Back at his office, Whelan looked over the report Haunce had put together. Noticing the correct grammar usage, and the way the words all flowed properly, he wondered who wrote the report. He was sure an illiterate monster like Haunce Walters didn't write it. Whelan pored over the details of the report, and in doing so discovered one disturbing fact that jumped off the page at him. David Squire was born and raised in the same small farming community as Clyde Bayless. Whelan was stunned.

Whelan had survived for years in a game where the stakes were very high. The center of world power had a set of rules that were very different from those for common folk across the country. Whelan had always thought of himself as a top player of the game, and surviving meant he had a keen sixth sense along with a deep distrust for just about everybody. The possibility of Clyde Bayless double-crossing him was very disturbing, however. Clyde was at the top of his list of trustworthiness. That's why he picked him to run the other end of the money trail. Clyde had always been a loyal trooper and had helped Whelan on several deals over the years. Nevertheless, the evidence of a connection between Clyde and David Squire was overwhelming, and he had to follow the truth wherever it led.

He picked up the phone and dialed Clyde's number. "Good afternoon, JC," Whelan said as Clyde Bayless answered the phone. "How's everything down in the country?"

"Everything's going well. I think I'm going to have a meeting with one of our investors in a day or two. I'll be keeping you posted. How's everything in the Capitol?" Clyde asked.

"Well, JC, things are getting a bit sticky up here. Do you

know a man named David Squire?" Whelan asked.

How could Duff know David Squire? Clyde thought. *There is no logical connection between them.* He was beginning to get nervous.

"Yes, I do. How do you know him?" Clyde asked.

"Well, he's been nosing around in some business up here that has to do with some delicate matters. I put my investigator onto him, and he has dug up some interesting facts about this Squire fella. He's found out that Squire is from your hometown, and, according to birth records, he's the same age as you. So, I need to know who this guy is working for. Would he by any chance be working for you?" Whelan asked with an authoritative tone.

"Of course he's not working for me," Clyde exclaimed. "I've known him all my life, but we've never been friends. He's a guy from the other side of the tracks—grew up on a small farm. After the War and after his parents died, he sold the property and moved to Chicago. Hadn't seen him in fifteen years until a few days ago when he was here visiting another schoolmate. I don't know what he's up to, Whelan, but I guarantee it isn't good."

"Well, I already know that by the company he's been keeping," Whelan said. "He's been investigating a man who worked for me, and if he isn't working for you, then he's working *against* you. How could he possibly know a connection between you and me?"

"I have no idea," Clyde said wearily.

"Think hard, JC. There's got to be someone that's a mutual

acquaintance or maybe someone that works for you. There is only one way he could connect you to me, and that's if he knows someone who knows you and also probably knows me. And, by the way, that someone is more than likely an employee of yours. It's probably someone who sees you every day—and he or she probably has a grudge against you, and is aiming to settle the score," Whelan said.

Then it hit Clyde like a bolt of lightning. *Sarah Jennings. She could have a motive against me for what happened a few years ago, and she might know David. Whether or not she's the culprit, I'll figure out a way to squeeze her. I'll find out,* he thought.

"I'll give it some thought, and get back with you tomorrow," Clyde told Whelan.

"Okay, just be on high alert," Whelan said as he hung up.

Clyde was terrified that David may be on to him and Whelan, but he knew he had to remain calm; therefore, he decided to think about it for an hour or so before making a move.

Thinking back on the events of the last few days, Clyde tried to put together a scenario that would place his secretary, Sarah Jennings, into a friendship, or at least an acquaintance with David Squire. To his knowledge, David had not been in Arkansas for maybe a decade. He was sure that Sarah had probably never met him until he was visiting a week ago. He thought about the possibility of her meeting David at his office that day.

Then he remembered overhearing two of the office girls chatting on the day he had been in the office. Sallie McLaren and Elaine Holt were laughing about something, and he may have heard David and Sarah's name mentioned in the same sentence.

Sallie had come to Clyde several times to tell him about things going on in his office. She was a young, ambitious girl who had come from nothing, and she was hungry for more out of life. Clyde had discreetly made her his official snitch for all things office related, often giving her a few dollars for her observations. Of course, he always made the gifts straight from his pocket so there would be no record of it.

After considerable thought, Clyde decided to bring Sallie into his office and see what she had to say about a possible introduction between David and Sarah last week. At the water fountain just outside his door, Clyde caught Sallie's eye and gave her a subtle nod to follow him.

With his office door closed behind them, Clyde said, "I noticed something last week while an old schoolmate friend of mine was here that sort of caught my interest. I was wondering if you could help me with this for a moment. My old friend was a fella named David Squire. Did I hear him talking to Sarah out in the main office area after my meeting with him?"

"Oh, yes sir, she introduced herself to him. She stopped him on his way out after he met with you. Elaine told me that she saw Sarah give him a note from the palm of her hand. I thought she was kidding, but Elaine insisted that she saw it. She stared right through him as they talked. We couldn't hear what they were saying, but I could see that she liked his looks. I assumed that she passed him her phone number because he's so handsome," she said with a smile.

"Well," Clyde said with a chuckle. "I was thinking the same thing, but I just wanted to know if I was the only one in the office that thought it. I don't like to get involved with gossip, but I just think it's rather amusing that she was attracted to him. I have known him all my life and have never thought of him as being a particularly nice guy."

After Sallie had left his office, Clyde sat back down at his desk and thought hard about the past week's events. The longer he sat there, the more he believed that Sarah was up to something with David. He now believed it all started there in his office with the passing of that note. Clyde believed she already knew something before she even met David. What he couldn't figure out was *how* she could know about anything between him and Whelan. He was sure that no one knew about his black record book. As that thought crossed his mind, he automatically felt under the bottom of his middle desk drawer. Satisfied that it was still where he had left it, he leaned back in his chair and began considering all the possibilities before him.

His gut was telling him that David's investigation began with whatever was on that note that Sarah gave him ten days ago in Clyde's own office. There had to be something profound in that note too because David stopped his own work in Chicago and went to Washington.

Clyde thought about the day he and James Benton encountered Sarah and her friend in Little Rock. He tried to remember everything said in the exchange between Sarah and James while they all stood on the sidewalk outside that shoe store. She had asked James several questions...

He sat there a while longer and pondered on what to do. Finally, he decided the best way to get a feel for the level of friendship between Sarah and David was simply to ask her. Buzzing her desk, Clyde asked Sarah to come into his office.

He knew he would have to choose his words carefully to not arouse suspicion. Sarah was a smart woman, and Clyde knew that. If he projected any concern about her knowing David, she would notice it.

"Sarah, you're friends with Joe and Millie Carter, aren't you?" he asked after she was seated.

"Yes sir, I am," she replied.

"I thought so. I'm sure you know that I'm foreclosing on their farm. I just want to let you know how sorry I am that I've had to do what I'm doing," he said. "I gave them plenty of time to pay what they owed me, but they never came up with the money, so I had to do what I did. I'm not the only owner of Bayless Farms Corporation. I have others to satisfy, so as much as I'd like to extend the time, I simply cannot. I hope you understand," he said with as much humility as he could project.

"I do understand, Mr. Bayless. Everyone has a responsibility to pay their debts, and since you hold the mortgage on their land, and they owe you, then you have to do whatever you can under the law to protect your investment," Sarah said as she stared right through little Clyde Bayless's eyes.

It was all she could do to hold the anger that was building inside of her—not because her two close friends were losing everything they owned to this tyrant, but because of the manner in which he did it. Nevertheless, she sat quietly and waited for him to respond to her statement.

"Well, I just wanted you to know that there is nothing personal about what I'm forced to do concerning the Carter farm," he said. "You may go now."

As she got up to leave, Clyde stopped her. "Oh, I've meant to ask you this. Have you ever had a chance to meet Joe's old friend, David Squire? He came by to see me about a week ago. We all grew up together. Do you know him?" he asked.

Clyde was doing it again. He was trying the impossible—to fool Sarah. She had made it her life's mission to observe his every move. Whenever he came out of his office for a soda, she knew he was going to do so, before he actually came through the door. Therefore, she *knew* he was up to something.

"Oh yes, you mean that tall, handsome man who came by last week?" She asked. "I don't believe I've ever met him. If I had known he was a friend of the Carters, I would have spoken to him."

Clyde knew that Sarah was lying. Sallie had already told him all about Sarah meeting David.

Wrong answer, he thought. *She and Squire are working together, and I have to find out what she knows.*

Clyde decided to call Whelan to discuss the possibilities of what David may know and to tell Whelan that James Benton, the courier from Washington, was the one who placed suspicion on the money scheme in the first place.

"Senator Whelan," Duff said.

"Whelan, this is JC. I have a theory as to why David Squire

is snooping around up there," Clyde said.

"Okay, I'm listening," Whelan said.

"I think your courier is the problem. He has a big mouth. It's a long story, but I'll just tell you the short version. I was in our usual location and had made contact with your guy when we inadvertently bumped into an employee of mine. I noticed that she was asking the courier a lot of questions, and they were the kind of questions that a southern lady would not ask a stranger. Nevertheless, your guy was eating it up. It seems that he fancies himself a lady's man, so he revealed entirely too much personal information to Sarah Jennings, an office worker for my company. The more she asked, the more he revealed. He even told her where he lived. That was insane," Clyde said.

"Why do you think this Sarah Jennings might have any interest in the courier?" Whelan asked.

"That's the part I'm not sure about, but I have a theory," Clyde said.

"What would that theory be, JC?" Whelan asked.

"I'm in the middle of a foreclosure down here involving a man and his wife who have been unable to pay me back. Sarah is a good friend of the couple that I'm foreclosing on. I think though I'm not positive, that the three of them share a mutual friend—David Squire.

"If that's true, then maybe they have hired Squire to see what he can dig up on me. I have no reason to believe they have any evidence of our deal. There's just no way Sarah could possibly know anything. The line that I'm talking to you on is not connected to any other phone in my office building. It's connected to a separate telephone device altogether, and that device is right here on my desk. Therefore, she could never have overheard a single phone conversation between you and me. I think they're grabbing at straws," Clyde said.

"Well, JC, it seems that you're wrong about that. My investigator is telling me that this Squire fella is meeting with some interesting people here. People who are intimately connected to a certain person that was an integral part of the operation, and is now no longer among the living," Whelan said. "This includes a brother to the deceased and a female employee here in my office. These are people who could possibly have known about our deal. This makes me nervous. There is only one reason Squire has ended up here in DC meeting with people with ties to our deal, and I think we both know why that is, don't we? It all points directly toward your end, JC," Whelan said.

"I'll get to the bottom of it within 48 hours. I guarantee it," Clyde said.

"I hope you do. We need to find out who knows what, and we need to eliminate all evidence leading to me. If it leads to me, then it leads to you. Do you understand what that means, JC? Why don't I just tell you? If I end up in the can over this thing, so do you," Whelan said. "Are you prepared for that?"

Swallowing hard, Clyde said, "It's not going to come to that. I will take care of this end. Just keep me informed as to what's happening there. I'll be in touch."

"Okay, I'm depending on you," Whelan said as he hung up.

Duff could feel the tear in the seam of his partner's

otherwise cocky persona. He knew that Clyde would not be able to withstand an FBI style interrogation. Whelan was becoming acutely aware that he was just going to have to get more involved in this mess and was going to have to do it very quickly or everybody was going down, including himself.

Clyde was now getting worried. Very worried. It had become evident that David knew more than he thought, and if he did, Clyde knew David would bend him over the barrel and squeeze the Carter deed out of him. He *knew* that David would blow the lid off everything if he had hard criminal evidence against him. He would expose everything if he didn't get his way. He was also sure that David couldn't care less about what happens in Washington and probably would not attempt to bring down a powerful United States Senator just to help a friend who was not connected to Washington politics.

As he sat there and thought about his conversation with Whelan, he thought back about everything and anything that could have happened in the last three years that could have made Sarah Jennings suspicious.

How could this have come to this point? Could Sarah be involved in something so big as to expose Whelan and me? And if she is, then why? Why would she care about what I'm doing outside my company? What motivates her? he asked himself.

Clyde sat staring at the occasional farmer driving by on the street outside his window as he meditated on Sarah Jennings' motive to harm him. He could only think of what happened a few years ago, but he had compensated her for damages, and she had seemed to let it go. If she had a vendetta against him, surely she would never have worked for him in the years since then. It had to be something else.

There was, however, the connection between Sarah's friends, Joe and Millie Carter, who were also friends with David. Could all four of them be friends? If that were the case, and even if they were determined to find something to use against him as leverage, they could not possibly know a single thing about his deal with Whelan.

Or could they? He thought.

Clyde wondered if Sarah had discovered his little black book. He thought about how the odds of that were overwhelmingly in favor of her *never* discovering it. She simply had no business fooling around under his desk because she did not do the cleaning of his office. The thought of her possibly finding his record book, however, created even more stress.

Clyde was getting paranoid, and when he got like that, he always had knee-jerk reactions to everything that seemed to be suspicious to him. Suddenly this sweet little deal between him and Whelan was beginning to have a bitter taste. He could not hold the thought in his head that he might end up in prison.

As he pondered on the events that were unfolding, he decided to check his record book. Once on the floor under his desk, he could see that the book was in its place exactly where he had left it the last time he removed it. He decided if Sarah was looking at the book that she probably would not put it back in the exact same place, so he decided to place pencil marks on the bottom of the desk drawer along with the outside edge of the book. However, before he marked the perimeter, he decided to take it from its position and write something inside on the page where his last entry was located. If Sarah came into his office without his knowledge and got the book, she would immediately know he was onto her antics. After writing a short note, he placed the book back in its location and made the pencil marks around the edges. If Sarah wanted to get into a cat and mouse game, he would gladly oblige her. She just didn't know who she was messing with.

After returning the book to its place under the desk drawer, Clyde reached for his briefcase and headed to the door. In the outer office, he announced to the office staff that he was leaving for the day as he stepped outside into the cool afternoon.

It was 5:30 when Sallie McLaren collected her things and left for the day. After Sallie had left, Sarah got the key to Clyde's office, entered, and quickly made her way to his desk. After crawling under the desk to retrieve the record book, she immediately noticed the pencil marks around the outside perimeter of the book.

When she opened the book to the last page of entries, the words hit her in the face like a freezing winter rain, sending a cold chill down her spine. In bold print, Clyde had written the words with his own hand: *"I'm on to you, Sarah."*

The words jumped off the page and slapped her across the jaw. She knew she was caught—or at least that Clyde was suspicious of her. She didn't know what he might do, but she was immediately reminded of what David had told her on her front porch during their first meeting. *"Do not underestimate a cornered rat. He's a dangerous little animal under the right circumstances."* The chill down her spine told her that David was right. Clyde Bayless may seem like a harmless little man with a huge ego, but he could be much more than that. She now understood what David meant—Clyde would be no different than any other cornered rat. He would bite whoever was the closest to him, and he would bite hard.

Sarah quickly placed the book back into its place exactly where she had found it and left Clyde's office. Back at her desk, she sat staring at a photo of her teenage daughter for a long moment. She swore to herself and to the memory of Joanie that she would stay the course. She would not, under any circumstances, waver from the path that had brought her this close to getting the revenge she so desperately craved.

CHAPTER 18

"**G**ood afternoon, Mr. Squire, I have a message for you from a Miss Gardener," the desk clerk said as he retrieved a message from the key bin, and gave it to David.

"Thank you," David said as he placed the message in his shirt pocket and headed for his room.

After seating himself in a chair next to his bed, he retrieved the note from his pocket and looked at it.

"Mr. Squire, I have some exciting news for you. Please call me immediately, Elizabeth."

David picked up the phone and asked the front desk to dial the number. Elizabeth was sitting next to the phone when he called and wasted no time answering. She got right to the point.

"I met with someone today who gave me the evidence you need to make all your problems go away," she said. "We need to meet immediately so I can pass this along to you."

"I'll be at the same diner as yesterday in twenty minutes," David said.

"I'll be there," Elizabeth said.

When David walked through the door of the diner, Elizabeth motioned to him from her booth next to the window near the back of the room. Making his way to her table, David did not notice the two men sitting two booths away from Elizabeth.

Benny Flaigo and Alfonse Giovetti had been taking turns

following and watching Elizabeth Gardener's every move all day long. Now that this Squire guy was meeting with the Gardener lady, things were looking up. Maybe she was going to give him the box she had carried into the diner. From where they were sitting, it was impossible to see what was going on in the booth with David Squire and Elizabeth Gardener, so they just decided to take notice of which one of them left the diner with the box. If Squire left with it, then it was surely the tapes. If the woman left with it, they would just tear up her apartment after she left next time. They would be watching every move she made, and as soon as she left, they would pounce on the apartment.

At the booth, David waved at a waitress and asked for coffee. The elated look in Elizabeth's eyes was unmistakable.

"That's a million dollar look you're sporting on that pretty little face of yours, Miss Elizabeth. So, go ahead and tell me what you have for me before you explode with excitement," David said with a smile.

"I have the five original tapes that Frank Rubenstein stole from Senator Whelan's office closet," she said with a giant smile. "Frank left these original tapes for me with an old friend in case something happened to him. The man called me earlier, and I went over and picked them up."

"Originals? So Whelan's men that killed Frank stole audiotapes from Frank's apartment? And they were not the originals. That can only mean one thing, Elizabeth. Whoever is in possession of those tapes is in a lot of danger. You better give them to me right now," David said.

Elizabeth handed the box containing the tapes to David. He took them out of the box and placed them under his coat inside his belt in different locations around his waist.

"How do you know these are the originals?" he asked.

"Because Frank left a detailed note as to what to do with them if anything happened to him," she said. "He did not specifically tell me to give them to you, probably because he had not yet met you when he stored them with his friend. But, he just told me in his note to be patient, and the right person at the right time would come along. I don't think he thought that person would appear so soon, Mr. Squire, but I have no doubt that you're that person."

"May I see the note?" David asked.

"No, you may not, Mr. Squire. A large portion of the note was personal and will forever be between Frank and me," she said.

As David gazed for a long beat at this young lady with the courage of a lion, he couldn't help thinking about what was going on inside her heart.

"That's okay, Miss Gardener, I don't have to see it. I just thought there might be something of importance that I might need to know," he said.

The two of them sat there for another twenty minutes discussing what she should do next. David advised her to go back to her apartment, collect some things, and leave town until this thing blows over.

After they decided the best course of action she should take for her own safety, they got up and made their way to the cash register. David paid the tab and went through the door and onto the sidewalk where Elizabeth was waiting. She carried the empty box that the tapes had been in. The two of them said goodbye and went separate ways.

Flaigo and Giovetti had watched the two as they had paid the tab. They noticed that Elizabeth still had the box she was carrying when she arrived at the diner. They decided to follow her and grab the box at the first opportunity.

After she left the diner, Elizabeth decided to stop at her bank and cash a check so she would have money to travel. As she grabbed her purse to get out of the car, she noticed the empty box that had contained the tapes, so she decided to discard it inside the bank.

Flaigo and Giovetti parked in a space near Elizabeth and watched as she got out of her car with the box. They figured it must contain the tapes, but they could not accost her in the parking lot of a bank.

Upon entering the bank, Elizabeth found the nearest trash can and dumped the box. The line at the teller was long, so she had to wait fifteen minutes to get her check cashed.

Flaigo and Giovetti were waiting when Elizabeth came out of the bank, and to their surprise, she was not carrying the box.

"She put it in her safety deposit box," Flaigo said. "Now what are we going to do?"

"We can just follow her to her apartment and call the boss then. He can tell us what to do," Giovetti said.

Outside her apartment, Giovetti sat in the car and watched Elizabeth Gardener's apartment while Flaigo called Haunce

Walters from a pay phone on the corner.

"Hey Boss, the girl went to the bank and went inside carrying the same box she had with her when she left Gersen's Hardware. When she came out, she did not have the box. What do you want us to do?" Flaigo asked.

Haunce thought about it for a moment. Finally, he said, "If she has put the tapes in a safety deposit box, then that's a little bit above our pay grade. We'll just have to let the senator take care of that himself. In the meantime, stick to her like glue. If she leaves, then follow her, and keep me posted as to where she goes and what she does."

"Will do," Flaigo said as he hung up.

After he had returned to the car, the two men resumed their surveillance of the apartment.

"You know what I think we should do?" Flaigo said.

"What?" Giovetti asked.

"We can't really just bull our way through her door and make her talk in this neighborhood. There are too many kids. We should just wait until she leaves, and when she stops, we can grab her, force her back into her car, and use our special technique to make her tell us where the tapes are. If they're safely at the bank, then we can discontinue this boring surveillance," Flaigo said.

Giovetti agreed, so they sat there with their windows down listening to the radio. After forty-five minutes, the door to Elizabeth Gardener's apartment opened, and she stepped outside carrying two suitcases. She made her way to her car, unlocked the trunk, put the two suitcases inside, and closed it.

"It looks like she's going to take a trip," Giovetti said.

"Yes, it does. Our orders are to follow her, no matter where she goes, so start the engine," Flaigo said.

Elizabeth went back inside for a brief moment and then came back, got into her car, and drove away, followed from a safe distance by the two men. After five miles, she pulled into a roadside motel. The two men parked their car a fair distance away and watched closely as she went inside to the front desk.

Elizabeth had decided to check in a motel for the evening because she did not want to be on the road at night. She was driving to South Carolina to stay a few days. Before she left her apartment, Elizabeth had called Frances Lansing, a childhood friend, and had asked if she could stay with her for a few days. She hated leaning on an old friend like this but knew that she could not go home. It would not be safe for her parents if she were to go there. She knew that no one in Washington knew her friend, so she was sure it would be ok to go to Frances's house.

"I need a room for tonight," Elizabeth said to the desk clerk.

"Okay, just fill out this registration form for me, and I'll see what we have available," the clerk said as he handed Elizabeth the form.

Elizabeth decided to register using a fake name so there would be no record of her staying there, so she chose Mary Barton as her assumed name. After filling out the registration form, she gave it back to the clerk, and he handed her the key to room 146.

"Room 146 is on the back side of the building near the far

end. It will be quiet back there, Miss Barton," he said. "My notes from the maid say she was short on towels when she cleaned the room, so I'll send some down in about thirty minutes."

"Thank you," Elizabeth said as she turned to walk away.

Back in her car, Elizabeth drove around the end of the building and toward the far end. She pulled up in front of room 146 and got out of the car. After unloading the suitcases and night case, she locked the door and decided to relax on the bed for a while.

She went to her purse and pulled out a 45 caliber automatic pistol that her father had given her for protection when she moved to Washington a few years ago. She turned the covers back and pushed the pistol under the pillow on the left side of the bed.

She kicked her shoes off, lay down on top of the covers, and began to recap the events of the day in her mind. The longer she stared at the ceiling, the heavier her eyes got until she finally began to drift off.

Outside parked next to Elizabeth's car, Flaigo and Giovetti were talking about how they might proceed. It was clear that she would not be leaving her room. They discussed the merits of forcing their way into her room and scaring her into telling them the truth about her stop at the bank earlier in the afternoon. If they forced her into telling them that she had left the tapes at the bank in her safety deposit box, then they could stop this twenty-four-hour surveillance. They knew she wanted to get out of town, and they were willing to oblige without hurting her.

"How we gonna get into her room?" Flaigo asked.

"Maybe we can say we're here with the pizza," Giovetti said.

"That won't work," Flaigo said. "She'll just tell us she didn't order a pizza. You have to remember, she's leaving town under a cloud and is probably suspicious of everything."

As the two men sat there trying to decide how they were going to get that door open, a motel employee turned the corner at the other end of the building carrying a small stack of towels. When the motel employee was about three rooms away, Flaigo quickly got out of the car.

On the sidewalk, he smiled at the young man and asked, "Which room are you going to?"

"I'm going to room 146," the man said.

"Great, we've been waiting for these towels," Flaigo said.

Reaching into his pocket, Flaigo pulled out a couple of dollars and gave them to the young man. "Here, take this for your trouble," he said.

"Thank you, sir," the young man said with a smile. "If there's anything else we can help you with just let us know."

"I will," Flaigo said.

When the young man was clearly around the corner at the other end of the building, Flaigo told Giovetti to follow him and make sure he was out of sight of the peephole in the door.

The knock on the door abruptly awakened Elizabeth just as she was slipping into a deep sleep.

"She asked, "Who is it?"

"Room Service, ma'am. We have your towels," Flaigo said.

Without another thought, Elizabeth got off the bed and opened the door. The two men quickly forced their way through the door as Flaigo pushed her down on the bed. Giovetti quickly slammed the door shut and locked it as Flaigo jumped on top of her and pressed one of the towels over her mouth so no one could hear her scream.

With the towel muffling her screams, Flaigo looked right into her eyes with a cold stare for a moment and then just told her to shut up, or he would kill her.

"We only want information, Miss Gardener. If you tell us what we want to know, we will let you be on your way. We have no reason to keep you from leaving town. We only want information that we know you possess," Flaigo said.

"If you start screaming when he takes that towel from your mouth, he will strangle the life out of you, Miss Gardener. My friend here is a very impatient man," Giovetti said.

With mortal fear in her eyes, Elizabeth nodded that she would not scream. Flaigo took the towel off her mouth and slowly got up and stood at the foot of the bed. That's when Elizabeth slowly and deliberately rolled over as if to attempt to sit on the side of the bed.

"Okay, I'll tell you what you want to know if I have the answers to your questions. I just want out of this town," she said as she slowly moved to the edge of the bed.

With Elizabeth's calm demeanor and voice of defeat, she made the two men believe they had her right where they wanted her—petrified with fear and unwilling to fight back. They were wrong. As she slowly swung her legs off the side of the bed, she intentionally pulled her dress about eight inches above her knees. The distraction worked perfectly. While the two men were gawking at her legs, she slipped her hand under the pillow and grabbed the 45 caliber automatic pistol.

Like a flash of lightening, she swung the pistol around and within three feet of Flaigo, had it pointed right at his head. With fire in her eyes, she said, "One move and I'll kill you, mister."

Benny Flaigo had seen a lot of things in his years working the streets for Haunce Walters, but he had never been beaten to the draw.

"Ok, Miss Gardener, You got us," he said as he stepped back and stood next to Giovetti.

"You're working for Senator Whelan, aren't you?" she asked.

"Well, I guess there's no reason to lie about it. Yes, our agency has been hired by the senator to take care of a little piece of business he's been forced to deal with lately," Flaigo said.

"And what kind of business is that?" Elizabeth asked while staring intensely at Flaigo.

"A little money situation. I really don't know the details. We weren't hired to ask too many questions as to what the deal involved. We were only hired to find something that our client badly needs," Flaigo said.

"You mean the tapes?" Elizabeth asked.

"Yes, exactly," Flaigo said.

Flaigo and Giovetti were not new to being on the wrong end of a bad situation. They had both been on the streets most of their lives and knew how to survive when the odds were against them. Flaigo figured the longer he kept Elizabeth Gardener engaged in conversation, the more likely he could find a weakness, but it was strongly evident that she was not nervous. She exhibited none of the symptoms of a coward. Her voice was calm and deliberate. The barrel of the gun pointed at him was not shaking like scared people when they know they're up against seasoned professionals.

"Which one of you killed Frank Rubenstein?" she asked calmly. "And who else was there when you did it?"

Stunned, Flaigo just looked at her. *How could she even know that we did that?* He thought. *This dame is onto us. This changes everything. Either we don't leave here alive, or she doesn't. It's as simple as that,* he thought.

Elizabeth had already determined that if she ever had the opportunity to get even with the perpetrators of Frank's death, she would do so without remorse.

"Answer me," Elizabeth said.

"Does it really matter who killed Frank, Miss Gardener?" Giovetti asked.

"I just want to know," she said. "And I want to know who was with you."

"Flaigo did it, Miss Gardener," Giovetti said calmly. "And our boss, Haunce Walters, was with us."

"How do I know you're not lying to me?" she asked.

"Because you're going to kill both of us anyway," he said with a resigned look.

"Did you kill him, Flaigo?" She asked.

"What if I did?" he asked as he glared at her. "If it hadn't been me, it would have been somebody else."

"I want to know his last words," she said. "I might spare the two of you if you tell me how he died."

Knowing that she was lying, Flaigo just answered the question. "He had no particular last words. For the previous five minutes, it was like he knew he was going to die, so he just started laughing. It was a soft chuckle at first, and then it got louder. He was genuinely happy about something. We couldn't figure out why. Do you have any idea, Miss Gardener, why Frank Rubenstein would laugh like that knowing he was about to die? Just laughing until I shoved that knife into his neck?" Flaigo asked.

Flaigo knew that if Elizabeth Gardener had any emotions at all, then telling her the gruesome details of Frank's last moments was the only way to find her weakness, thus giving the two men the only possibility of turning the situation around for them. He was mistaken.

When he finished, she looked at him calmly and said, "The reason Frank was laughing was that the joke was on you. He knew that David Squire is the best in the business, and Frank knew that his backup plan to get the original tapes into David's hands was foolproof. You lose, Flaigo. You either die here and now, or you die in a lonely darkened death chamber with only a minister and the man who flips the switch. After they strap you down, then they will open the curtains, and you'll see Frank's family, and, of course, you'll see me. I'll be there at your execution, or I can handle it for you right here and right now. Which will it be, Flaigo?"

Flaigo did not say a single word. He knew he was in a bad fix. He was sure of one thing, however—he was not ever going to end up in a prison death chamber the way she just described it. He knew it was time to make his move. He also knew the chances of winning were slim. Nevertheless, he decided to let the chips fall where they may, so, with all the speed he could muster, he went for his gun inside his coat. He lost. Elizabeth Gardener placed two quick rounds to Benny Flaigo's head before he even got his hand on his gun. Every muscle relaxed immediately, and he dropped like a rock.

Knowing that he was next, Giovetti, thinking that this young woman would not shoot a man in the back, began to slowly walk toward the door. He was wrong. Elizabeth shot him on the outside edge of the back of his right thigh. The impact of the 45-caliber bullet partially spun him around counterclockwise, and as he was turning, he reached for his gun. He was not fast enough. Elizabeth Gardener pumped two rounds into his chest. He was dead before he hit the floor. When she approached his lifeless body, she could see that his right hand was still wrapped around the handle of his gun inside its holster.

Quietly and very calmly, Elizabeth collected her things and loaded them into her car. After one last look at the dead bodies of the two men who had killed the man she loved, she closed the door slowly, stepped across the sidewalk, got into her car and headed south on U S Highway 1. If she drove two hundred miles and rented a room for the night, she might be able to make it to Columbia South Carolina by tomorrow night.

As she drove along the highway, the relief of knowing

that she had avenged the death of her friend began to sink in with Elizabeth. When she had driven seventy-five miles, she began to allow herself to reflect on the gunfight at the hotel. She thought about how calm she had been during the ordeal.

She thought about the hours and hours she had practiced target shooting with her father when she was growing up and how he had always emphatically made the point that she was never to draw a gun on someone unless she was willing to pull the trigger. Her father's devotion to her safety had paid off. She was surprised at the calmness that came over her at a time when she should have been frozen with fear. Then it came to her. She was not afraid because the spirit of Frank was standing behind her whispering in her ear, *"You can do it. Just relax. You can do it."*

From that revelation, Elizabeth was finally able to start letting go of Frank. She had done the ultimate. She had personally killed at least two of the men who were present when Frank was murdered. She could now face the future with the satisfaction of knowing that his life had been one of honor, duty, and country no matter what Whelan's publicity machine was saying. The thought burned into her mind and heart that he, who she believed ordered Frank's murder, was soon to get his due.

CHAPTER 19

Millie Carter was taking the cornbread out of the oven when the telephone rang. By the time she got to the phone, it had rung four times.

"Well, hello gorgeous. I was just about to hang up. Thought you might be out back doing chores," David Squire said.

"No, I was taking the cornbread out of the oven. Come on over and join us. Joe will be home in about twenty minutes," Millie said with a smile.

"Oh, I wish I could. You make the best cornbread west of the Mississippi River," David said.

After a few more small exchanges, David got to the point of his call. "Millie, I'd like to know how Joe is doing. I know he won't tell me the truth because he has never been one to talk about himself."

"Joe isn't doing well," Millie said. He's getting weaker and beginning to lose weight. I've noticed a drop in his energy level in the last couple of weeks. The doctor said he would have a fairly good quality of life for about two months, and then things would begin to go downhill from there. He told us that about six weeks ago."

The reality that he was about to lose his oldest and closest friend began to settle in on David. He debated in his mind as to whether he should tell Millie what he had uncovered about

Clyde's dirty dealings in Washington. As they talked about Joe's condition further, he decided to tell her everything. That is everything except that Sarah Jennings was involved and was instrumental in getting him on the right track to bring Clyde Bayless down.

"Millie, I have a few things to discuss with you. I've been snooping around into some of Clyde Bayless's business affairs and have uncovered some very interesting things involving a money scam. It appears that our old schoolmate has involved himself in some pretty bad stuff involving a powerful US Senator, who is also dirty," David said.

"Oh my goodness, David. Isn't that risky for you?" she asked.

"Yes, it's a bit risky, but it's worth it, Millie," David said.

Overwhelmed at that comment, tears flowed from her eyes. "Please, David, just stop this investigation right now. Joe couldn't bear it, and neither could I if you got hurt by stepping on the toes of the wrong people," she said.

"I'll be okay, Millie. I'm going to take down the high and mighty Jasper Clyde Bayless if I have to crawl through hell on my hands and knees to do so," David said.

Realizing that she was going to lose this argument, Millie just decided to thank David for his help and let him know that she and Joe loved him like a brother.

"I will not tell Joe what you have revealed to me. He's getting weaker and does not need to be worrying about you. Please, for me, just be careful, David," she said as she choked back the tears.

"Not to worry, little sister. I'll be fine. Besides, I have Walt Austin in on this thing with me," David said. "He's been a tremendous help. He has lent me his entire investigative team."

"Oh my goodness, David. That must be costing you a fortune," she exclaimed.

"No," David said. "Walt wouldn't accept payment for his help. He told me he owed it to Joe and wouldn't take a single penny for his services. Walt is a special kind of man, Millie. He has gone out on a limb more than once during this investigation. I simply could not be where I am without his help.

"I think I'm very close to getting what I need to enter into negotiations to clear up your debt and return the deed to your farm. All I need is a few hours to examine some hard evidence, and I'll be ready to drop the hammer on our little nemesis."

With as much control as she could muster, Millie said, "Please promise me you won't do anything that will get you hurt, David. We would never get past it."

"Now is not the time to sugarcoat anything I'm doing up here, Millie. It's been a struggle, and I'm dealing with powerful forces of evil, the kind that don't take any prisoners. But I promise I'll watch my back," David said.

After he had hung up the phone, David thought about the things that Millie had said to him. He knew the points she made were valid. He knew her fears were too, but he simply could not stop now after being so close to victory.

Millie had only been off the phone with David for a few minutes when she saw Joe's pickup turning into the driveway. She barely had time to regain her composure.

After parking his truck, Joe did a quick panoramic look around the farm he had lived on all of his life. After stepping onto the front porch, he sat down in the swing and reflected on his life and the decisions he had made. The thought of his sweetheart being left to make it on her own was very hard to swallow. It was constantly on his mind, and he was sure his stress was working against him in his battle against the cancer.

"A penny for your thoughts?" Millie asked playfully as she stepped onto the porch.

With a smile, Joe said, "You're not trying to cheat me, now, are you? My thoughts are worth far more than a penny."

"Oh really?" She asked. "Tell me what you're thinking about."

After a long beat, Joe looked into the eyes of the woman he loved so much and quietly said, "You."

After what David had revealed to her a few minutes earlier, and now Joe saying this sweet thing to her, Millie could take it no more. The tears freely ran down her face as she took a seat beside him on the swing and laid her head on his shoulder. The two of them sat there for two minutes without a word between them.

Joe spoke first. "It's going to be okay, Millie. David will come through for us. I know he will. He's very good at what he does, and he will not let us down."

Remembering what David had just told her, Millie asked Joe, "What if he gets in a dangerous situation? I mean, what if he encounters some really bad people? Then what?" she asked.

"Then he'll grab em by the ear and kick em in the teeth.

Any confrontation with him will not end well for them. Millie, you simply do not know the other side of David. All you know is the country boy we both grew up with from down the ridge. You don't know the warrior he became after we joined the Army.

"I watched him from about sixty yards away one night under a full moon as he demonstrated just how lethal he could be. He killed seven elite Nazi SS troops, including a colonel as they were attempting to stop us from being picked up by a small aircraft in a pasture in France. He broke the necks of four of them and stabbed the other three without firing a shot. He crept up behind them one at a time until he had killed them all. The rest of the Nazi battalion was only a few hundred yards away, and the sound of gunfire would have put more firepower on us than we, and the five French Partisan fighters with us, could have handled.

"The short of it is this. When the heat gets turned up, the David Squire that you have always known becomes a completely different person. He was the most relaxed man I ever saw in the middle of the fog of war. To him, everything was clear, and there *was* no fog. He saw the enemy, and in a very casual manner, he took them down one by one. If he was ever afraid of a fight, I never saw it. Others who were on missions with him came back telling stories about how they marveled that he never fought the enemy from a defensive position. Without exception, he always took the fight to them. Never ran. Just hammered them into the ground. He always completed his mission and got his agents out of France and safely back to England."

Joe turned and looked at Millie as the tears began to dry

on her cheeks. "That's why I am not worried about my old friend. He's been there before, sweetheart. When the bullets start flying, he will stop the sources one at a time until there's no one left to shoot at him. When he's done, he'll walk quietly away and never think of it again. He's an extraordinary killing machine that lives an ordinary life.

"I sort of doubt he's going to be in that kind of danger on this thing, however. I think he's doing more of a Sneaky Pete operation in an attempt to gain crucial information against the goings-on of crooked little Clyde Bayless."

After hearing the soothing words from her husband, Millie decided to let go of her fear. Besides, she had too much other stuff to worry about. Joe's health was slipping every day, and she had things to do to prepare for the time when he would no longer be mobile. She decided to let David handle his business his own way, and she would take care of her sweetheart until he was no longer here.

****

Sarah Jennings had just finished the payroll when the phone rang at her desk.

"Bayless Farms," she said.

"Good afternoon. Do you have a moment?" Millie asked.

Recognizing her friend's voice, Sarah said, "Of course."

"Joe and I would like for you to come out tonight for dinner. You gonna be busy?" Millie asked.

"No, I'm not. I'll be there under one condition. Give orders to Joe that I said I want some of that scrumptious homemade ice cream he makes," she said with a chuckle.

"Coming right up," Millie said. "Just come after work, and we'll sit long and talk much."

"Great. I'll see you then," Sarah said.

As Sarah turned off the gravel road and into Joe and Millie's driveway, Jeff Miller, a local farmer, was standing next to his truck near the tractor shed talking to Joe. The two of them appeared to be having a rather intense conversation about something. When she got out of her car, Sarah waved, and both men waved back as she disappeared past the front of the house. After a bit of small talk, they sat down at the kitchen table while Millie kept a close eye on the boiling potatoes on the stove.

"Joe seemed to be having an intense conversation with Jeff Miller out by the tractor shed. I thought they were good friends. You don't think they're arguing, do you?" Sarah asked.

"They are good friends, and no, they're not arguing. Jeff called Joe about thirty minutes ago and said he had something he wanted to talk about. He said it was about Clyde Bayless. When Jeff said Clyde's name, Joe perked right up," Millie said. "In fact, looking at them through the window right now makes me think that Joe is probably unloading a lot of stored up frustration to his friend about what Clyde has done to us.

"By the way, do you remember Joe and me talking about our old friend that we grew up with from down the ridge? His name is David Squire, and he now lives in Chicago?"

Hesitating to answer the question, Sarah thought for a moment. Then she decided to acknowledge that she remembered him. "Yes, I do remember you and Joe talking about him. Why?" she asked?

"Because he's working on something big concerning Clyde and some crooked dealings with a Senator in Washington, DC. I don't know the details, but I've been worried that he may be in a lot of danger. He called this morning, and we talked for a while. Joe was not here, so David and I discussed a few things about Joe's health, and then he told me that he had uncovered criminal evidence that's very damaging to Clyde's freedom. I became very alarmed when he told me that things were getting sticky right now. I begged him not to continue his investigation, but being the kind of man he is, he would not quit under any circumstances.

"As for what's going on out near the tractor shed right now, I don't know the exact specifics, but I would bet anything Jeff is talking to Joe about Clyde's behavior lately. I think that David has turned up the heat on some people in Washington, and maybe he has informed the right person there that Clyde is a childhood schoolmate of his. It would be just like David to put Clyde on the hot seat in order to flush him out and make him do crazy things. David and Joe loved getting an angle on Clyde when we were kids. They would take a simple thing and blow it all out of proportion just to watch Clyde squirm."

Jeff Miller left about the time Millie finished cooking. Back in the house, Joe gave Sarah a hug and asked her how everything was going at the palace.

She laughed and said, "Oh it's fine, I guess. Clyde is acting a bit strange, but other than that, things are fine."

Sarah could not tell her friends that she was part of David's investigation, not only because he had asked her to keep it quiet, but also because she did not want them to think she was nosing around in their business. And she certainly did not want *anybody* to know the level of loathing she had for Clyde for what he had done to her. She knew it was unhealthy to hate him this badly, but she didn't care, and she didn't want anyone trying to convince her to forgive him.

During the course of the evening, Joe revealed his conversation with Jeff Miller. Jeff said a good friend of his had come to him and repeated a few unsettling words that Clyde used to describe Joe. Joe was amused by what the little clown had said about him, but he knew that Clyde had the upper hand right now, and there was nothing he could do to shut him up.

Sarah had developed a knot deep down inside her stomach since Millie had told her of the danger David was in. She wanted so badly to tell Joe and Millie everything, but she just couldn't. She didn't know how they would react, and she just did not want to cause any more problems than they already had.

Around midnight that night, Sarah lay in her bed staring at the ceiling. Her mind was racing at the speed of light. She did not know what she had got David into, but she knew it wasn't good.

As she lay there, she made a solemn promise to herself. *If David Squire's life is taken from him during this thing, I will kill Clyde Bayless myself. I really have nothing to live for anyway.*

****

Clyde Bayless was very worried about David Squire showing up all over Washington with the wrong people. Clyde knew that only meant one thing—David Squire had him in his crosshairs. Clyde also knew that David would not give up until he had exhausted every avenue—or until he was dead. That part also bothered Clyde. Whelan had already alluded to someone inside the money trail that was now dead. He didn't say that the guy had been killed, but Clyde knew that's what he meant by the way he said it.

It was clear to Clyde that the only way to get David off his back was to remove the incentive for David to go after him. The only thing standing in the way of that was the lawyer dragging his feet on getting the judge to sign the documents to evict Joe and Millie Carter. So he decided to call Thad McRae and push him again.

"Good afternoon, Thad. What's the word on the Carter farm?" Clyde asked.

"Well, we have a small delay because the judge has taken off for a few days to spend a little time at his hunting camp over in the Ozarks. His secretary said he will be back next Tuesday," Thad said.

"Thad, I need that document signed by the judge as soon as he gets back in his office. Do you understand?" Clyde asked.

"Yes, I do understand, Clyde. I would have it signed already, but I had no way of knowing that he was going to be half way across the state," Thad said.

"Okay, I expect to have the signed document in my possession Tuesday afternoon. Do you think you can do that, Thad?" Clyde said sarcastically.

"I believe so," Thad said.

"Good. I'll see you then," Clyde said as he hung up the phone.

Clyde was beginning to get a sick, weak feeling in his stomach about this. He was no stranger to tight situations, but he had never played this far outside the law. He was having a hard time trying to comprehend the possibility that he, the wealthiest man in the county, could actually go to prison. Never mind that being imprisoned with common criminals would be the worst thing that could happen to him. The entire Bayless Company would end up in ruins.

Clyde knew that his son, Billy, simply did not have what it takes to manage the family corporation—not even for a week.

Clyde was getting more irrational by the minute. He had lost a lot of sleep the night before because of the phone call he received from Whelan late in the afternoon. He had always known that if the ship had to navigate its way through rough seas near a coral reef, Whelan would be in the safest part of the ship. Never mind the women and children. Whelan always looked out for one person—himself.

As for the debacle in Washington, Clyde was sure that it started with Sarah Jennings. He couldn't prove it, but he knew it as well as he knew his own name. It was hard for him to believe that one of his secretaries could have pulled the lever that began a chain reaction of events that could bring down one of the most powerful senators in Washington. If that happened, Clyde knew he would soon be doing a stretch in Leavenworth.

Fundamentally, Clyde was a coward who always masked his true persona by surrounding himself with locals who wanted to be seen as big shots. Men like them would wait at the country club for Clyde to arrive so they could see what kind of shoes he was wearing. If he got out of his car wearing tennis shoes, then all of them reached for their tennis rackets. If he had his golf shoes in his hand, they reached for their clubs. They even made sure they drank the same kind of wine from the bar as he did. This was his county, and he was the king. Clyde knew that many in the community disliked him, but he didn't care. He was regarded as the largest landowner in the county, and he relished the stature that accompanied the ownership of so much land.

But this thing with Whelan was over his head, and he knew it. There would be no safety net to catch him if David had the hard goods on him and Whelan. He knew what David was after, and he knew that the time to do something about it was right now. So, he pulled open his middle desk drawer and moved a few things around until he found the business card David left when he came by to plead to Clyde about Joe's farm.

"Squire Investigations," Madge Bellows said.

"Hi, I'm Clyde Bayless. May I speak with David Squire?" Clyde asked.

"Mr. Squire is out of town for a few days, but if this is an emergency, I can have him call you. He checks in with me once or twice every day," Madge said.

"That will be fine. Just tell him to call me," Clyde said. "He knows the number."

"I surely will, Mr. Bayless," she said.

The enormity of this whole thing was clouding Clyde's judgment. It made him lightheaded to think about the ramifications of what had become a real possibility.

We have to stop David Squire. It makes no difference how

that's accomplished. It only matters that we stop him, and we have to stop him right now, he thought.

CHAPTER 20

"Didn't we have some dealings with this guy, Haunce Walters, a few years ago?" Deputy Gladys Pearson asked as she handed Sheriff Raymond Thompson the phone number to Walters Investigations.

After thinking for a moment, Sheriff Thompson looked at Deputy Pearson and said, "Yes, I believe we did. It was about seven or eight years ago. As I recall, he was linked to the killing of a suspect who had stolen rare jewelry from a client who hired Walters to retrieve it. By the time we linked him to the killing, he had an ironclad alibi. We couldn't ever make a case against him, but he will always be under a cloud in that murder.

"I wonder what he's got himself into this time? Two investigators who worked for him were found dead in a hotel room," Sheriff Thompson mumbled as he dialed the number.

"Walters Investigations. How may I help you?" the receptionist asked.

"This is Sheriff Raymond Thompson out in Fairfax County. May I speak to Haunce Walters?" he asked.

"Please hold," the young lady said as she passed him through to Haunce.

"This is Haunce."

"Mr. Walters, this is Sheriff Thompson in Fairfax County. I'm afraid I have some bad news. We found two men shot dead in a motel room on Highway 1. Their identification says they worked for you. One Benny Flaigo and one Alfonse Giovetti. Could you confirm if these two men worked for Walters Investigations?" Sheriff Thompson asked.

After a long pause, Haunce finally gained his composure. "Yes, they worked for me. What happened?" he asked.

"Well, it looks like someone put two 45 caliber rounds into the head of Mr. Flaigo and two rounds into Mr. Giovetti's chest. It's too early to determine if it was a murder," he said.

"They were both highly trained professionals. I find it hard to believe that they found themselves on the business end of a 45-caliber pistol. Were their guns in their hands?" Haunce asked.

"No, neither of them had their guns out of their holsters, although Mr. Giovetti had his hand on his weapon inside his jacket," Sheriff Thompson said. "I need for you to make arrangements to claim the bodies, and I would like to have a conversation with you about this. Do you think you could come over and have a sit down with me?"

"Yes, I can be there in about thirty minutes," Haunce said.

"Good. I'll tell the deputy up front that you're here to see me," Sheriff Thompson said as he hung up.

Haunce thought about the two men that had worked for him for a decade. He hated losing two good men like that, but that was as far as he would allow his emotions to go concerning the lives of Benny Flaigo and Alfonse Giovetti. As far as he was concerned, they shouldn't have allowed that woman to get the drop on them. In fact, he had told them to just follow her to see where she was going.

The hardest part of his interview with Sheriff Thompson was going to be explaining why they were in that motel room with Elizabeth Gardener. He couldn't think of a single reason why they would be there unless they wanted to pressure her to see if she had actually placed the tapes inside a safety deposit box at the bank. No matter what angle he examined, the killing of his two men by Whelan's personal secretary was going to be hard to explain to Sheriff Thompson. He had already dealt with that sheriff before, and Thompson was very thorough with the last investigation into the mess Haunce got himself into in Fairfax County. It took three of his own men to perjure themselves in sworn statements of his whereabouts at the time of a murder of which he was the prime suspect.

As he parked his car in front of the Fairfax County Sheriff's Department, Haunce was desperately trying to come up with an explanation of the connection of his two investigators and Elizabeth Gardener. He knew the first thing Thompson was going to ask was how they knew her.

At the front desk, the deputy in charge pointed him to the Sheriff's private office. After he introduced himself to the Sheriff's secretary, she disappeared for a moment. When she came back, the Sheriff's secretary asked Haunce to follow her.

Inside Sheriff Thompson's office, Haunce quickly noticed the two deputies present.

Sheriff Thompson pointed to an empty chair between the two deputies. "Have a seat, Mr. Walters," he said. "Would you like a cup of coffee?"

"No thanks, I'm in a bit of a squeeze for time right now. I have to make arrangements for the bodies of my two men. So, what happened?" Haunce asked.

"Well, the best that we can tell right now is that Mr. Flaigo and Mr. Goivetti were shot at close range with a 45-caliber pistol. Probably a Colt automatic. Other than that, we don't know what happened. We were hoping you could help us fill in some of the holes," Sheriff Thompson said.

"Well, I'll try. Ask the questions. I'll do my best," Haunce said.

"I guess we can start with the name of the young lady who had rented the room," Thompson said.

Haunce knew this was the do or die moment. He knew if he showed any crack in his explanation, then the entire investigation into the missing tapes for Whelan was going to ruin him and everyone involved. So, to project calmness, he took out a cigarette and lit it.

After he calmly took a long draw of the cigarette, he asked, "What's her name?"

"Mary Barton," Sheriff Thompson said.

Haunce was shocked. Either Flaigo or Giovetti were screwing around on the job, or Elizabeth Gardener had checked into the motel under an assumed name. It didn't matter at this point.

"I don't know anyone by that name. There was no subject of any investigation we are involved in by the name of Mary Barton," Haunce said.

"What do you think your men would have been doing in

that room with this young woman?" Thompson asked.

"I have no idea unless they were allowing their libido to get the best of their common sense judgment," Haunce said.

"That's plausible."

"What is she saying?" Haunce asked.

"We haven't been able to locate her. She did not report the killing, and she's probably on the run. The motel clerk described her as an average size young woman with dark brown hair and blue eyes. He said she had a certain way of carrying herself that projected class. He also said she drove a late model, light blue Ford Falcon," Sheriff Thompson said.

Haunce immediately knew he was describing Elizabeth Gardener. He tried to cover this revelation by taking another long draw from his cigarette before snuffing it out in the ashtray in front of him.

"She doesn't sound like anyone I know, Sheriff," Haunce said.

"And you have no idea why your men would be in the same room with a beautiful young woman?" Thompson asked.

"No," Haunce answered. "It's very puzzling to me. The last time I talked to Flaigo, he and Giovetti were going to have a cup of coffee at a diner near my office. We weren't tailing anyone so it couldn't have been that."

"Well, if you come up with anything, please call me. This man here can help you with the arrangements for claiming the bodies of Mr. Flaigo and Mr. Giovetti," Sheriff Thompson said as he handed Haunce a note with the name of the man in charge of the morgue.

"Thank you," Haunce said as he took the note.

As he drove back to his office, Haunce began to put together a list of things that had to be done to protect everyone involved in the investigation. It was clear that Elizabeth Gardener had probably left the tapes in her safety deposit box at her bank, and if that was so, there was no way Whelan was ever going to get his hands on them.

Back in his office, Haunce called Lyle Brown, his go-to guy for all wiretaps. "Lyle, this is Haunce. I need a tap right now. Can you come by?" He asked.

"Sure," Lyle said. "What do you need?"

"I'll tell you all about it when you get here," Haunce said.

"I'll be there in twenty minutes," Lyle said as he hung up.

Lyle Brown was, at best, a shady character. He had done time in the Louisiana State Penitentiary at Angola Louisiana for stealing a car from a man's carport outside Monroe, Louisiana. When the man tried to stop him, Lyle beat him so badly he required hospitalization. Lyle was caught later the same day and charged with attempted murder. He served eight years at what was commonly referred to as the Alcatraz of the South.

Those who knew him often said that Lyle must have left some of his humanity at Angola State Penitentiary because he had no conscience. He justified every crooked activity he engaged in by dismissing it as necessary.

"Lyle, I need you to tap a phone for me. Can you do it?" Haunce asked.

"Where and when?" Lyle asked.

"Walt Austin's office and I need it right now. They have

information that I need badly. Can you do it right now?" He asked.

Lyle Brown knew Walt Austin well. They had tangled up on an occasion or two over the years, and Lyle thoroughly disliked Walt Austin. There was nothing he would like better than to tap his phone and listen to all his phone conversations.

"Yes, I can get right on it, but you know it's in the middle of the morning, and I'll have to get a van to make it look like I'm with the telephone company," Lyle said.

Haunce knew what that meant. Lyle was about to ask for money up front, so he pulled out a couple of one hundred dollar bills and handed them to Lyle.

"Thank you, Haunce," Lyle said.

"Just get it done as soon as possible," Haunce said.

"Will do, boss," Lyle said as he was leaving.

Haunce needed to know for sure if Elizabeth Gardener had left the tapes in the safety deposit box at the bank, and the only chance he had of finding out was to intercept any phone conversations about the tapes between Walt Austin and David Squire.

Haunce knew if Whelan went down for this thing, then he would take everybody in his world with him, including Haunce. What Whelan did not know, however, was that he would never spend a day in prison. Haunce had vowed that if Whelan implicated him in any part of his little scam, or in the death of Frank Rubenstein, he would kill the senator himself.

****

"Good morning; Sarah, this is David. How are you?" He asked.

The sound of David Squire's voice startled Sarah. She wasn't expecting him to call her at work. "I'm fine," she said. "How are you?"

"I'm fine; can you pass me through to Clyde?" David asked.

"Sure," she said as she buzzed Clyde.

"Hello," Clyde Bayless said.

"Good morning, Clyde," David said. "My office manager said you wanted to talk to me."

"Yes, I do," Clyde exclaimed. "I'll get right to the point. I have to admit I'm a little bit puzzled and downright disturbed at your behavior in and around Washington these days. A good friend of mine, a very powerful Washington politician, has told me that you've been hanging around in all the wrong places lately, and with all the wrong people. He said you've been sticking your nose where it doesn't belong. He told me that he is on to every move you make and he knows your whereabouts twenty-four hours a day. I feel like since we've known each other all of our lives, I should warn you that you could be in a lot of danger. You have to understand that powerful people do not live by the same rules as you."

Clyde was feeling energized now because he figured when he mentioned a powerful politician, David might get nervous.

"You said that powerful people do not live by the same rules as me. I couldn't help but notice, Clyde that you didn't include yourself in that set of rules that we regular people live by. You a powerful man, Clyde?" David asked. "Because if you are, now would be a good time for you to start circling the wagons. I have evidence, Clyde—*hard* evidence that you and Senator Benjamin Duff Whelan are up to your eyeballs in a money scam involving defense contractors. I know the game you were playing, and I know all the players involved. You're toast, Clyde."

"Now you listen to me, Squire, I…"

"Shut up, you little squirt, I'm not finished. The way I have it figured, you're going to do a stretch in Leavenworth or some other government vacation spot for the next dozen or so years. Too bad they closed Alcatraz this year. That would be the perfect place for you and Whelan. Yep, you're up for a nice, long vacation. No cotton to plant, nor soybeans or corn. And you won't have to worry about figuring out how to scam the local farmers out of a few dollars here and there on their harvest when they bring it to your grain elevator or cotton gin to sell. Oh, yes, by the way, you just may be looking at a whole lot more vacation time if you were involved in the murder of Whelan's front man in your little money project.

"Yes, Clyde, I think you're about to get a long-deserved vacation to the big house. Do you know what they do to little punks like you inside prison, Clyde? Never mind speculating. I'm in a good mood today, so I'll just give you a quick description. They're going to make a girl out of you. You're short, fat, and a weakling all the way to your bones. The sharks are going to be swimming around you as soon as they see that terrified look on your face when the clank of that prison gate closes behind you. Yes, you are in for a long, long night. Or maybe I should say a long, long *nightmare*. Well deserved, I might add."

"I don't have any idea what you're talking about, Squire. You think the likes of you is going to bring me down? I'll show you," Clyde almost screamed as he abruptly hung up.

David sat on the side of his bed and laughed for the next ten minutes. He knew he had lighted little Clyde Bayless' fuse. He was probably on the phone with Whelan crying to him about it. Clyde had a lot of attributes, mostly bad, but one thing he did not have was courage.

In light of what had just transpired between David and Clyde, he decided it was probably a good time for him to move to another motel, so he began to pack his things. Two things had just transpired in the conversation between him and Clyde. He knew Clyde was telling the truth when he said that Whelan knew his every move, including the motel at which he was staying. He also knew, just because he knew how the little chicken was, that Clyde was literally discussing with Whelan ways to get rid of him.

So, he checked out of the motel he had been staying in since arriving in Washington. After driving around for a half hour, he found another motel located only two miles from Walt's office. He decided to call Walt and let him know where he was and to ask Walt where he might find a reel to reel tape recorder that he could use to listen to the tapes.

Elizabeth Gardener had given him the list of places on the tapes that were damaging to Whelan. Frank Rubenstein had flagged the tapes many times where the evidence was strong, and David was anxious to listen to them.

"Good afternoon, Walt. I thought I should call and give

you a heads up on a couple of things. First, I decided to move. I had a rather testy conversation with Clyde Bayless an hour ago. I'm sure he's already called Whelan, and they're probably making arrangements to have my legs broken by now, or maybe worse." David chuckled.

"Well, I figured all along that something might be wrong if you didn't stir up a hornet nest at some point during this thing. It wouldn't be like you not to, Major. What did you tell him?" Walt asked.

"Oh, I just reminded him of the sex change he's going to be having in a few weeks," David said.

"In other words, you told him you have the goods on him, and he's about to take the train ride," Walt said.

"You guessed it."

"So, you've jumped into their faces. You've chosen to flush them out. This is about to get very nasty, Major," Walt said.

"Yes, it is, and that's just exactly what I want. They know they're in deep water without a life jacket, and I think we're about to see what they're all made out of," David said.

Walt sat there for a long moment. Finally, he spoke. "Okay, in case I don't have another chance to say this, Major, it surely was nice knowing you."

"You make it sound like I'm down for the count. Cheer up." David laughed. "I have a question. Do you think you could bring a tape player over to my new motel? I'm staying at the Cherry Blossom Motor Courts, room seven. I want to listen to the tapes that Elizabeth gave me."

"I'll have one there in about an hour," Walt said. "By the way, I have a bit of news for you. Two of Haunce Walters's men were killed last night in a motel in Fairfax County on Highway 1. Sheriff Raymond Thompson has been quoted as saying that the shooter was a young woman. I'm sure your first thought is the same as mine."

David thought about it for a moment. Finally, he said, "I wouldn't doubt it. She has a lot of spunk."

As soon as the two hung up, Lyle Brown called Haunce Walters and reported what he heard through his wiretap. He also informed Haunce that the one guy was about to listen to the tapes that a woman named Elizabeth had given him. He also reported that the man talking to Walt had just moved to a different motel. He gave Haunce the name of the motel and the room number. Haunce thanked him and asked that he continue to monitor the calls from Walt's office.

After Walt's courier had brought the tape player to his room, David hooked it up and began to listen to the tapes. After an hour, he decided the evidence on the tapes was overwhelmingly damaging to Whelan and Clyde Bayless, so he figured the only thing left now was to pay Clyde a visit. He decided to call Walt and tell him the news.

"Walt Austin here," Walt said as he answered the phone.

"I've listened to the tapes, and the damage to Whelan and Clyde is devastating. I think I'll head on down to Arkansas in the morning and have a long-anticipated conversation with little Clyde Bayless," David said.

"Wish I could be there to see that." Walt laughed. "From

what I've heard about him, that Bayless guy must be a real piece of work."

"He is, but I guarantee you that he's shaking in his boots right now. He knows I have the goods on him, but he just doesn't know what I actually have. That's the fun part. I think I'll transcribe a few of the telephone conversations between him and Whelan just to show him how much trouble he's in. I don't think there's any doubt now that I'll get what I want from him," David said.

The two men talked a few more minutes, and David asked if he could use the borrowed car to drive to Arkansas. Walt readily agreed to lend his old friend the car. At David's request, Walt also gave him the address of the place where he had rented the tape player so David could return the player.

After Walt and David hung up, Lyle Brown, who was sitting in his van down the street at the telephone jacket listening to the conversation, immediately called Haunce.

"What do you have for me?" Haunce asked.

"Walt Austin and some guy whose name I do not know just had an interesting conversation. The unknown guy told Walt that he had listened to some tapes and that they contained very damaging information to a guy named Whelan and another guy named Clyde. That wouldn't be Senator Whelan, would it?" he asked.

"That's none of your business, Lyle. I didn't hire you to nose around into my case, now did I?" He half asked, and half stated.

Haunce was not going to tolerate one of his men,

especially someone he temporarily hired to do a small amount of surveillance, to start asking questions that did not pertain to his mission.

"So, you just continue to monitor Walt's calls until I say stop. Do you understand me, Lyle?"

Knowing he had hit a nerve Lyle Brown said, "Yes I do. My apologies."

As soon as he finished talking to Lyle, Haunce called Senator Whelan to bring him up to speed on where he was on getting the tapes.

"Whelan here," Duff said.

"Duff, this is Haunce. I have a few things to cover with you. It appears that this Squire guy has the tapes and is leaving town with them tomorrow morning. He's moved from his original motel to the Cherry Blossom Courts. I'm going to send a couple of men over to muscle the tapes away from him. After that shootout on Highway one, I'm running a little short on qualified men. It's going to take a couple of hours to contact the men to do the job, but I'll take care of it. We'll do all we can to do this the easy way, but if we have to put him to sleep, I'm going to be looking at you to cover my back with the police like you did last week.

"Otherwise, Squire told Walt Austin that he had the goods on you and a guy named Clyde down in Arkansas. Just thought I would pass that along," Haunce said.

"Just do what you have to do, Haunce. At this point, we're up to our elbows in mud, and I don't want to wake up in a couple of days and realize it's quicksand," Whelan said.

"I'm on it, Whelan," Haunce said as he hung up.

That's what Whelan was afraid of. Haunce Walters was a bad man who would take great joy in killing a second man in less than a week. Whelan knew that Haunce had him over a barrel, and could run amok of the law because of the dirt Haunce had on him. Whelan could not believe he had allowed himself to get behind the eight ball with a man who had no regard for human life. He had always prided himself that murder was off the table—even in his shady dealings.

As he sat at his desk and blew smoke rings aimlessly into the air, he thought about how this whole thing had developed into a bad situation. Overnight, it seemed, his sweet little deal with Clyde Bayless had gone from being a positive flow of cash to a flock of dead albatrosses hanging around their necks. He knew that if Haunce were unsuccessful in securing the tapes, the walls would be coming down around everyone involved. *If that happens, it'll be every man for himself,* Whelan thought.

CHAPTER 21

At the Rental shop, David returned the tape equipment and bought five additional blank tapes. After he was back in his room, he placed the original tapes into the new boxes and placed the new, blank tapes into the boxes that had contained the original tapes Frank Rubenstein stole from Senator Whelan.

Securing the tapes inside two separate bags, David decided to lie down and relax. He stared at the ceiling as he pondered on the events that had transpired after he arrived a few days ago.

It had been one week since Frank Rubenstein was murdered, and everything had been happening at lightning speed. So many people, he had learned, utterly despised Whelan. He thought about how one man could be elected to public office by such a huge margin of his constituents, yet had so many enemies that wanted to see his head on the chopping block. It was both amazing and disgusting.

He also thought about how he needed to coordinate the meeting between him and Clyde. He knew he had to have Sarah on standby alert with the payoff agreement that Sarah had already asked Thad McRae to prepare. She had told him that she was a Notary, so he'd just have to make sure she was present to witness Clyde's signature as he signed the document. David figured he could serve as the witness. He thought about how much he was going to enjoy that little aspect of the transaction.

The longer he stared at the ceiling, the sleepier David got, and the more difficult it became to concentrate on his plan for the next day. Finally, before he realized it, he drifted off.

****

Haunce Walters was at his desk reading the latest in the killing of his two men, Benny Flaigo and Alfonse Giovetti, in the afternoon papers when a knock at the door brought him out of his deep thought. His secretary entered and informed him that George Felten was waiting for him outside, and had two men with him. Haunce told her to show them in.

"Good afternoon, George," Haunce said as the two men shook hands. "I'm sorry to call you on such short notice, but I have something of a very sensitive nature that has to be attended to immediately. I'm sure you've heard in the news that I lost two men last night out in Fairfax County. There's no one else on my staff that can handle this thing. I thought of you because you've handled situations like this for me before. Are you interested?" Haunce asked.

"So far. What exactly do you want me to do?" George asked.

"I need you to take your men and go over to room number seven at the Cherry Blossom Motor Courts and retrieve a box or a sack containing five large reels of audiotape. Can you handle it?" Haunce asked.

"That depends on how many guns are behind that door when we knock on it," George said.

"Only one man, but he is, indeed, a man whose reputation precedes him. He's no fool, so getting him to open the door might prove to be a little tricky," he said.

Haunce opened the middle drawer of his desk and pulled out three sets of fake FBI badges with identification.

"Take these, and tell him you're with the FBI and want to talk to him about a matter concerning a United States Senator," Haunce said. "He'll probably open the door then."

"You said this man's reputation precedes him. What exactly do you mean by that?" George asked.

"I mean he's big, strong, and knows how to handle himself. Do not give him an opening, or you're in trouble," Haunce said.

"I believe the three of us can handle one man no matter how big or mean he is," George said. "You want this right now?"

"Yes, right now."

"Okay, we'll go get your tapes," George said as he turned to leave.

"George, I need to have a word with you privately, if I may," Haunce said.

George motioned for his two men to wait for him in the outer office.

"We don't really need to send anyone to their happy hunting grounds on this thing, but just remember, the tapes are far more important than his life," Haunce said.

"I hear you loud and clear," George said as he was leaving.

****

Buck Huston was in a meeting with a couple of agents who were filing reports when his secretary came in and handed him a note from Carl Honeywell who was urgently requesting a meeting concerning the Whelan investigation.

"Send him in," Buck said.

He dismissed the two agents he was meeting with as Carl came through the door.

"What do you have for me, Carl?" Buck asked.

"We've been listening to some conversations between Whelan and a couple of interesting men. It seems that something big is about to go down within the next couple of hours between Haunce Walters and a guy named David Squire. We think this Squire guy is probably the one who was with Clarence Grafton when they tapped Senator Whelan's office. Over the last couple of days, we've concluded, from conversations between Walters and Whelan, that he's a private investigator from Chicago. We ran a check on him two days ago, and I have a dossier for you," Carl said as he handed a folder to agent Buck.

"We believe Whelan is in big trouble concerning taped conversations from his office between him and Haunce Walters, and in separate conversations, a man named Clyde from down in Arkansas that we think is involved in the same shady activity as Senator Whelan. We believe Squire is in possession of the tapes and is about to squeeze the senator and this Clyde guy for reasons we do not know. Maybe blackmail. Maybe he wants in on the action. We just don't know, but we do know that Clyde knows David Squire. They seem to have grown up together, and according to the phone conversations, they don't like each other," Carl said. "Our background check on David Squire revealed that he's in good standing with the authorities in Illinois. He has an excellent service record also, serving in the OSS during the War. Another interesting player in this little drama is Walt Austin. He and David Squire served together in the same unit, and, like Walt, David Squire came home a decorated OSS agent. It seems that Squire and Walt are involved in an investigation of Whelan and this Clyde guy.

"We know that David Squire is staying at the Cherry Blossom Motor Courts and is leaving for Arkansas tomorrow morning, possibly to confront Clyde. In a conversation we just observed a few minutes ago, we learned that Whelan has dispatched Haunce Walters to David Squire's motel room to rip the tapes from him. Should we send a crew over to the Cherry Blossom Courts to prevent this?" Carl asked.

After thinking it over for a few moments, Buck said, "I think it would be better if we waited until Haunce Walters gets the tapes in his hands before we make our move. That way we can link him to Whelan and take both of them down at the same time. I think we need to only observe David Squire for right now. He's working with a good man, Walt Austin, and I'm inclined to believe that they are not into criminal activity here. I don't know why they want this evidence on Whelan and the guy from Arkansas, but I'm going to give them the benefit of the doubt for right now. This could be the home run that finally gets the all-powerful pile of ego, Senator Benjamin Duff Whelan, behind bars where he belonged a long time ago, so I don't want to be too aggressive at this point. Just go over to the Cherry Blossom Motor Courts with Agent Wilson, and the two of you watch the show. I need to know who leaves that motel with those tapes. If the last man standing is David Squire, then follow him. If Haunce Walters' men emerge from Squire's room carrying a package, then follow them, but do not make any arrests no matter who ends up with the tapes, until I give the order."

Buck was, for the first time in several years, feeling close to victory concerning a longtime personal goal of his. He could still see the look in Whelan's eyes as he laughed in Buck's face after he had unsuccessfully pursued him on charges that should have landed Whelan behind bars. That look of condescension had burned into Buck Huston's very soul, and he had vowed that one day the almighty senator would make a misstep, and he, agent Huston, would be there to take him down. The thought of finally stopping the man that he knew to be a criminal all the way to his bones was actually making Buck a bit giddy.

Buck decided to wait for an hour or so before contacting Carl. He wanted to be in on the takedown of Haunce Walters if possible, but he was willing to wait in the background if that was best for the investigation. The excitement was about to overtake him, but he decided to just be calm.

A little while later, agents Carl Honeywell and Phillip Wilson were positioned in the parking lot of the Cherry Blossom in a place where they had a view of every room. The two men had worked many stakeouts over the years, including some big takedowns of notorious criminals. Carl's skill at electronics had served him well with the FBI, but he was also good at confronting a suspect when the time was right.

Carl had seen the look in Buck's eyes as he was giving them their assignment back at headquarters. It was clear that this was personal to Agent Huston. Carl did not know why, but he instinctively knew that Buck wanted this one badly, and he intended to do his part to accommodate his boss.

Agents Honeywell and Wilson had been listening to the radio for an hour when three men in a late model sedan drove up to room number seven. Parking one space away from the room, the three men got out of their car and knocked on the door.

The faint knock at the door woke David immediately. He had always been a light sleeper, and lately, he was particularly aware of the danger surrounding him.

"Who's there?" he asked.

"FBI," George Felten said. "We would like to have a word with you if you don't mind."

"What about?" David asked cautiously.

"It's about an investigation concerning a U. S. senator," George Felton said.

David got up, slipped his 45-caliber pistol into his back pocket, put his shoes on, and went to the door. Peering through the peephole, he could see three neatly dressed men standing outside holding up their FBI identification. Before he unlocked the door, David unplugged the power cord of a lamp that was sitting just to the right of the doorknob on a small table. After removing the lampshade, he held the body of the lamp firmly in his right hand as he slowly unlocked the door with his left hand.

David thought that the men on the other side of that door could either be FBI, or they could be bad guys hired by a crooked senator to do bad things.

It happened so quickly. Had David not been prepared,

the three men would have overpowered him. The first man, the biggest of the three was three inches taller than David and outweighed him by about forty pounds.

As the first man rapidly pushed the door open and charged inside, David stepped sideways to the right and greeted him with all the force he could muster as he slammed the lamp body to the temple of the man's head. He fell to the floor like a piece of firewood and did not move another muscle.

One down and two to go. The odds are getting better, David thought.

The next man pushing through the door had to step over the first man before he could get to David. As the second man glanced down while attempting to navigate over the lifeless body of the first, David quickly stepped forward, and with a fast right hook to the jaw, followed by a left jab to the nose, he took the second man down. As he fell backward onto the sidewalk with blood spurting from his nose, David followed him through the door. He, too, was out cold.

David only had one adversary left. He and the man stood staring at each other for a short beat. David spoke first.

"Well, well, what have we here?" he asked tauntingly. "Looks like you've lost your squad. That leaves only you and me, so maybe it's time for the canary to start singing. Who sent you?"

"That's none of your business," George said in a lame attempt to control the dialogue.

"Oh, yes, it's my business, buddy, when you come busting into my room and try to do bodily harm to me. The way I see it, you have two choices. You either answer the question, or I slowly take you apart, while your two friends over there enjoy their little nap. Now, I'm only going to ask you one more time. Who sent you?" David demanded.

The Herculean glare in David's eyes convinced George that the smart thing to do would be to simply back off.

"I just got involved in this case about an hour ago, so I don't know what's going on here. I was given no details of the case, and I didn't ask for any. I was hired to come to room number seven at this motel and collect something that you have in your possession. Nothing more, nothing less. I don't even know your name, and I don't care to know it. You, however, were ready for us, so I have an idea you know who we're working for," George said.

George had been in many street fights over the years but never had he witnessed one man take down two street brawlers with the physical stature of Henry Bowman and Earl Stewart so quickly—and emerge without a scratch. He knew if he pushed this thing, he was going to end up in a very bad way, so he decided to do the only logical thing left.

"Why don't I collect my two boys, and leave quietly?" he asked.

"That might be a good idea," David said.

By the time the two men finished their conversation, Henry Bowman and Earl Stewart were both awake and moaning about the pain that enveloped their heads. Bowman, who had incurred the worse injury, was rubbing a giant knot near his temple. Groaning as George helped him up, he asked what had happened. George told him he got side-whacked by a ceramic lamp.

Nursing a broken nose, Earl Stewart slowly stumbled to his feet and made his way to the back seat of the car where he leaned back and held his handkerchief against his nostrils in an attempt to stop the blood flow.

As the three men drove off, agents Carl Honeywell and Phillip Wilson, who watched the entire fight from beginning to end, quickly concluded that David Squire was the one they should follow.

Inside his room, David collected his things and took them to his car. He then walked across the parking lot to the motel office and paid the desk clerk for the broken lamp. Returning to his car, he drove onto the street and headed south on Highway 1.

****

"You were right, Haunce," George Felten said. "That guy was way more than just a simple street fighter. He clocked both Bowman and Stewart, so after a brief conversation with him outside his room, I decided we needed to back up and regroup. I'll have to get some more men if we're going to get your tapes for you. Bowman and Stewart are all done."

Haunce Walters hated screwing up a takedown. "Okay, I'll go with you. How soon can you have them here?" he asked.

"Probably in about a half hour. Just say the word, and I'll make the call, George said.

"Call them, and make sure they're armed. It's clear we're going to have to do this the hard way," Haunce said.

Haunce never cared one way or the other about the life of someone else. The only reason David Squire wasn't already dead is because of the increasingly sticky mess it was causing for Whelan. Haunce had to keep Whelan clean because the senator was the only person who had the connections to keep him out of jail for killing Frank Rubenstein.

****

Buck Huston answered the phone on the first ring. He was anxiously waiting to hear from Carl Honeywell concerning the stakeout.

"It looks like David Squire won the argument, Agent Huston," Carl said. "We've followed him to another motel on Highway 1. He's checked in at the Patriot Motel near Belle Haven."

"Stick to him like glue. I want those tapes, but I want to retrieve them from Haunce Walters if at all possible," Buck said. "I'll be there in about thirty minutes, and we'll watch the action and let it play out before we make our move. I figure Haunce Walters will make a personal appearance this time, and his men will kick the door in with guns in hand. If Squire resists, they'll kill him.

"Meanwhile, I want you to go to the front desk and inform the motel clerk who you are and what you're doing there. Tell the clerk that if a gunfight begins, he is *not* to call the police. Tell him this is an FBI investigation and we'll let him know when it's time to call the locals to clean up the mess."

Walt Austin was about to leave to meet with a client when the phone buzzed.

"Mr. Austin, Mr. David Squire, is on line one," the receptionist said.

"Thank you," he said. Picking up the receiver Walt said, "Well, I thought you would be long gone by now."

"No, I decided to get a few hours of sleep before I leave. Got a long drive ahead of me. I've had to move to yet another motel. Haunce Walters sent three goons to the Cherry Blossom to take the evidence away from me. Things didn't quite work out the way they hoped, but I figured they'd be back, so I moved a little further down the road," David said.

"Was there any shooting?"

"No, but if they find me again, I firmly believe they will be well armed. Two of them were hurting pretty good when they left, so I figure they won't try any more stupid tricks," David said. "Next time they'll come with guns blazing."

"Do I need to send backup for you?" Walt asked.

"No, I don't think they'll find me here. I'm at an out of the way motel on highway one outside Belle Haven called The Patriot Inn, room one twenty-seven. If I need you, I'll give you a call," David said.

After they had hung up, Walt sat at his desk and pondered the thought of sending a couple of men to watch David's room. He decided to not act on it unless David asked for help, but he called three of his men and put them on standby alert just in case.

****

"Haunce Walters here," Haunce said.

"Haunce, I have some information for you," Lyle Brown said.

"Okay, let's have it," Haunce said.

Lyle Brown briefed Haunce Walters on the whereabouts of David Squire. He said that Walt Austin had offered to send a couple of men to help Squire, but he had declined Austin's offer. Haunce thanked him and hung up.

Haunce was convinced that he had men on their way over to his office that could take care of the situation. George had never let him down, and he knew tonight would be no different.

George soon returned with four men. Haunce, George, and the other four sat in Haunce's office for a few minutes and discussed what they were going to do. Haunce informed them of where David Squire was located.

"We need to hit him hard and fast. I've got a door ram in the trunk of my car. We'll break the door open, rush the room with our guns in our hands, get the tapes, and leave as quickly as possible. If he makes a wrong move, kill him," Haunce said.

The five men sat quietly listening to Haunce talk about murdering David Squire as if it were the same as stealing cookies from Grandma's jar. Before the briefing was over George had already decided that he would not be the triggerman. He was not going down for murder over a simple operation like this one.

"Pardon me fellas; I have to make a quick phone call. You may have a cup of coffee in the outer office while you wait. This will only take a minute," Haunce said.

Senator Whelan was about to leave for the day when his private line rang.

"Senator Whelan here," he said.

"Duff, this is Haunce. We've had a busy afternoon attempting to strip the tapes from Squire. Right now, he's holed up in a motel room outside of Belle Haven. We're on our way over there to take care of this thing. I just wanted to let you know that this is about to get pretty nasty. We tried to do it the easy way earlier today, but he overpowered my men, and they ended up leaving the motel a bit bruised up. This time we're going to get the tapes no matter what it takes. After it's over, if he no longer walks among the living, then you're going to have to step up and pull all the strings you can to make things right. Are you with me?" Haunce asked.

"I don't know many people in the Belle Haven area, so I'm not sure what I'll be able to do if you step across the line again, Haunce," Whelan said.

"You better start thinking of something, Senator because if I go down, so do you," Haunce said firmly.

"I know that, Haunce. Just get the tapes. If you have to kill him, then just don't get caught," Whelan said quietly.

"I won't," Haunce said as he hung up.

Whelan leaned back in his chair and lit a cigar. He sat there for thirty minutes staring at the door to the closet where the tapes were stolen. He had not heard a word from Elizabeth Gardener since she took a few days off. He was sure that she was gone from Washington for good—a good sign that she was in on the theft of the tapes.

The longer he sat there, the angrier he got. He was glad that Frank Rubenstein was dead. He could never testify against Whelan in a court of law, and as soon as David Squire was dead, he would be forever silenced as well. The unpleasant thought of eliminating Elizabeth Gardener entered his mind also, but he had not yet arrived at a place whereby he could kill a woman.

Just don't screw this up, Haunce. Everybody's freedom is relying on you, he thought.

CHAPTER 22

When agent Buck Huston arrived at The Patriot Motel in Belle Haven, Carl Honeywell and Phillip Wilson were in the motel restaurant having a cup of coffee. They were sitting in a window booth near the door with a good view of the room David Squire entered after he checked in at the front desk.

After Buck had taken a seat in the booth, Carl said, "Here's where we are, Buck. I've informed the restaurant manager and the front desk not to call the police if a gunfight occurs. We also placed a note that says "out of order" on each of the three payphones in various locations, so that restaurant patrons won't be calling the police either. We've seen no sign of Haunce Walters, so we do not know if he's going to show up."

"Oh, he's going to show up alright. The agent that's monitoring Whelan's telephone conversations informed me just before I left that Haunce Walters called Whelan about thirty minutes ago and told him where Squire is staying. I have no idea how he knows it, but he made it clear that he was coming here with a few men, and they would be locked and loaded. They're going to do whatever it takes to get the tapes from Squire. That's when we make our move. I want the tapes in Haunce Walters's hands when we take them down," Buck said.

"Are you sure the three of us will be able to achieve that? What if Walters brings five or six men with him?" Carl asked.

"If they do, then they just might get Squire, but I guarantee we will not leave here with that many men under arrest. Squire's going to eliminate three or four of them. Evidently, you didn't read his dossier. His military record is nothing short of Superman himself. Squire is a killing machine, boys. He'll at least even the odds for us so we can easily get the rest of them. Haunce Walters may be a criminal, but he's a very smart man. He will not fight the FBI. When we show up, he'll stop fighting, and take his chances in court. He's not your ordinary goon," Buck said.

Inside his room, David was going about the task of making it into a fortress. He had taken the small desk and the matching chair and laid them down on top of the bed with the seat of the chair next to the top of the table, thus doubling the thickness of the table top as it lay on the top facing the entry door to the room. He then took the door off the bathroom and propped it up on its edge in front of the bed where the table and chair were. He then got all the sheets and covers from the bed as well as all the towels from the bathroom and placed them on the backside of the table and chair. He figured he would just sleep between the bed and the bathroom wall.

He had taken the three lamps in the room and placed them in a position whereby the lights would be shining into the eyes of anyone coming through the door, thus creating a dark area near the back of the room where he would be.

By arranging his room this way, David had created an area near the door where there would be no cover for an intruder to hide behind. He knew they were coming and he knew they would be coming well-armed. He figured he had a few hours before they found him because he was sure they had not followed him. After all, when they left the Cherry Blossom Motor Courts, they were in no shape to continue surveillance.

As soon as he got his protection in place and sat down with a gun in hand with two extra ammo magazines laying nearby, he heard a car pull up to the curb in a parking place just to the right of his room. He got to his feet and crept over to the window and moved the curtain just enough to create a tiny opening to see outside. Six men got out of the car, and without saying a word, one of them opened the trunk.

Haunce Walters opened the trunk of his car; the two largest men reached inside, retrieved the door ram, and quietly made their way to the sidewalk directly in front of David Squire's door. They very carefully laid the door ram down on the sidewalk and walked back to the rear of Haunce's car. Haunce reached inside the trunk and retrieved two smoke grenades and a stick of dynamite with a three-inch fuse. He then called a huddle of his men at the rear of his car.

Pointing to the two largest of the six men, he said, "You two break the door open, and George will throw a couple of these smoke grenades inside the room followed immediately by this stick of dynamite. One stick of dynamite won't kill him, but it sure will make him temporarily disoriented. Immediately after the explosion, we'll rush through the door before he regains his composure and overwhelm him. At that point, it shouldn't be too much trouble to snatch the tapes. I don't really care to have a murder on our heads, so refrain from killing him unless you have to."

"What if he doesn't have the tapes in the room?" George Felten asked.

"Then we do it the old fashion way," Haunce said. "We beat it out of him. They have to be in the room or in his car. No need to break any windows on his car just yet. He would hear it and start shooting as soon as the door is opened. If anybody dies here tonight, I want it to be him. Not any of us.

Handing George the two smoke grenades, Haunce asked the five men, "Are there any questions?"

There was none, so he motioned for the two men assigned to the ram to go pick it up and get in position to open the door. The two men picked up the ram and awaited Haunce's orders.

Because Haunce knew that George was right-handed, he motioned for George to position himself just to the left of the door so he could more easily throw the grenades inside the room while maintaining cover to the left of the door opening. Haunce pulled out a cigarette lighter from his pocket and motioned the two men with the ram to break the door open.

The door swung open with only one violent thrust of the ram. Once the door was open, the two men dropped the ram immediately and moved out of the way. In less than a half second, George threw the first smoke grenade through the door opening. As soon as he pulled the pin on the second grenade, Haunce calmly lit the fuse to the stick of dynamite. In one fluid motion, George moved out of the way, and Haunce stepped forward and threw the stick of dynamite halfway into the room.

David, protected behind his barricade, was surprised by the smoke grenades, so he fired in the general direction of the door. He had barely popped off three rounds when the dynamite exploded on the other side of his barricade. The percussion of the blast was mind-numbing. David temporarily lost all sense of reality. By the time he regained his senses, the six men were all over him. He managed to catch the first one across the jaw, but there were just too many men on him.

When he entered, Haunce quickly grabbed the spewing smoke grenades and threw them outside the door. The smoke, however, was stifling, making it hard to breathe. Haunce immediately ordered two of his men to bring David outside for interrogation, as he ordered the others to search David's luggage for the tapes.

Outside the room, the two men holding David pushed him against the wall in front of his room and stood in front of him while each of them held onto one of his arms. Haunce stepped in front of David, and with a menacing look, asked, "Why don't you make it easy on yourself, Squire? You know why we're here. Just hand over the tapes, and we'll be on our way."

David didn't know what was going to happen to him before this ordeal was over, but he knew the location of the tapes would never be known by the likes of these guys.

"You must be Haunce Walters," he said calmly.

"That is correct, and if you know who I am, then you know that I am a no-nonsense investigator. Now, where are the tapes?" Haunce asked.

"You may be a no-nonsense investigator, but you're not very smart when it comes to covering your tracks. You're going down for the murder of Frank Rubenstein. And now you're going to add another murder to your list by killing me? I say these things because although you may kill me, you will never know where those tapes are. No matter what you do to me, you are going down for what you did to Frank Rubenstein, and so is Whelan. The show is over, Haunce. The curtain is falling on you and ole Whelan, and there's nothing the two of you can do to stop it," David said with a piercing stare.

Haunce quickly punched David in the belly. The man holding David's right arm did not realize that Haunce was about to punch David, so his grip was not as tight as it should have been. When David bent over after Haunce hit him, the man holding his right arm lost his grip. David quickly jerked his arm free, and before either of the men saw it coming, David hit the man holding his left arm squarely on the chin. As the man fell back, David reached inside the man's jacket and grabbed his revolver from its holster. Spinning around, he shot the other guy right above his left eye.

As Haunce reached for his pistol, David did something he didn't usually do—instead of putting a bullet between his eyes, he hit Haunce across the side of his head with the pistol. Haunce fell to the ground unconscious. David quickly spun around toward the door as the first of the three men who were inside searching the room came through the door with his gun drawn. When he saw that David was free, he quickly began to lift his gun, but it was too late. David put a bullet straight through his chest. The man was dead before he hit the ground.

David took no joy in killing these men. They had given him no choice, however, and he was prepared to take them all down if he had to. Next, George Felten emerged from the smoke-filled room. When he saw David with a 38-caliber Smith and Wesson revolver pointed at him, he immediately raised his hands above his head and dropped his gun. The last man to come through the door saw David, raised his hands, and dropped his weapon.

"Turn around and face the wall," David shouted.

The two men complied without resistance. David quickly stepped up and hit each man over the head with the pistol knocking both of them out. Then he gathered their weapons, including Haunce's and walked over to the front of Haunce's car. Standing directly in front of the grill, he calmly put two rounds into the radiator before shooting holes into two tires on the driver's side. Then he grabbed his luggage from the room, jumped into his car, and drove off.

Immediately after the stick of dynamite exploded, Agents Buck Huston, Carl Honeywell, and Phillip Wilson jumped from their seats inside the restaurant, yelled for everyone to get down, ran outside, and took cover behind Buck's car. The three men watched in stunned amazement as David overcame impossible odds took down all six men.

"Get into my car," Buck said to his two agents. "We'll follow him. He's going to stop somewhere down the road. When he does, we'll get the tapes.

They had been driving south on Highway 1 for five miles before Carl spoke. "Buck I've known you since I came to the Bureau, and I've never known you to do anything that would knowingly endanger the lives of your agents. But I have to admit, my friend, this is not too smart. This guy is exactly what you say he is—a well-oiled killing machine, so just what is your plan to keep us from ending up like Haunce Walters, or worse, like those two stiffs Mr. Squire left outside that room?"

"Reason," Buck said quietly.

"Reason? You mean we're going to attempt to talk 'reason' to this guy? He's already demonstrated that he's capable of death and destruction. I'd like to hear this little plan, Buck," Carl exclaimed.

"David Squire is not an evil man. If he's cornered, somebody's going to get killed, but if we talk reason to him, I think he'll hand over the tapes. I do not think he will view us as a threat," Buck said.

"Okay, but if it's all the same, boss, I think I'll let you go through the door first," Carl said.

"I will," Buck said. "I will."

It was beginning to rain as David pulled off the road and into the parking lot of a roadside diner about a hundred miles south of the Patriot Motel. The northeast wind coming off the Atlantic Ocean had a bite to it, and the rain inflicted a bit of sting to his face as he got out of his car and made his way across the parking lot. The sign out front said it was an all-night filling station and restaurant, so he figured he would have some dinner and gas up before searching for a motel to spend the night.

He navigated through the tables until he found an unoccupied booth near the back of the dining room. After his waitress had arrived, he ordered coffee and the daily special—hamburger steak, rice, gravy, and rolls. He sat quietly and relaxed while recapping how the day's events may affect his case against Clyde Bayless. He wasn't worried about being charged with murdering the two men outside his room. People throughout the motel were coming out of their rooms and the restaurant immediately after that stick of dynamite exploded. He knew the eyewitnesses would tell it the way it happened, so he was comfortable that would end well for him.

After he had finished eating, his waitress stopped by and topped off David's coffee one last time. He thought about the relishing moment of demanding that little Clyde Bayless give up the deed to Joe and Millie's farm. He knew Clyde was going to squeal like the little pig he was, but David knew that, before he risked going to prison, Clyde would meet his demands.

As he stared into the nothingness outside the window next to him, a man calmly stepped over to his booth and sat down across from him.

"Relax, Major Squire," the man said quietly. "We're not here to hurt you."

David was stunned that this man addressed him by his former military rank. He just looked at the guy for a moment. A quick look around revealed the man was not alone. Two other neatly dressed men had placed themselves in strategic locations around his booth.

"I'm Agent Buck Huston with the FBI," Buck said as he and the other two men revealed their FBI badges.

"Earlier today three other men flashed badges at me that looked just like those. Theirs were fake, and I have to tell you, it didn't work out so well for them. The short of it is this, Mr. Huston—your badges don't mean a single thing to me," David said as he continued to sip his coffee.

"We know. We saw both fights. My two men here watched as you took apart the first batch of Haunce Walters's goons at the Cherry Blossom Motor Courts, and I joined them down at The Patriot Motel three hours ago. We knew they were coming for you and we knew they would be packing artillery. The way we have it figured, you knew they were coming too, and you were ready for them. I have to admit you put on quite a show.

"We actually *are* the FBI, Major Squire, and we're not here to tear this place up—just to get from you what we need. So, why don't you hand over the tapes, and we'll go away, and you can be on your way?" Buck asked.

David thought for a long moment about what they were demanding of him. He thought about how much trouble he would be in if he assaulted FBI agents in the line of duty. Finally, he settled on the best chance he had of accomplishing his mission.

"May I talk to you alone, Mr. Huston?" David asked.

Buck leaned back in his seat and said calmly, "You're not as big as the FBI, David. If I dismiss these two men, and if you use that as an opportunity to run, you will lose. We will find you, and you *will* go to prison. Do you understand that?"

"I do understand, and I have no intention of getting violent. Quite frankly, I've had enough of that for one day," David said.

Buck directed Carl Honeywell and Phillip Wilson to take a seat two tables over so he and David could talk privately.

"You speak with a southern drawl, Agent Huston. Where are you from?" David asked.

"Greenville Mississippi. I'm a southerner through and through," Buck said.

"That's good. At least we share roots from the same region. I have quite a long story to tell you, so you might as well order yourself a cup of coffee," David said.

"I believe I will," Buck said as he motioned for the waitress.

Buck sat silently as David told him a short version of the back-story about Joe Carter and Clyde Bayless.

He also told Buck about how he got involved in the investigation of Whelan and how he had brought in Walt Austin, a friend from his days in the OSS, to help him with the investigation. Buck could see the passion in David's eyes as he spoke of his childhood friend. When he finished and was about to ask permission to temporarily keep the tapes, Buck raised his hand and motioned for David to say nothing else.

"I don't think you need to go any further, David. Doing so would only implicate you in something that I do not believe would serve you well in a court of law," Buck said.

"I only need them for forty-eight hours. I'll take them to the Little Rock FBI office as soon as I'm done with them. I give you my word of honor on that," David said.

Buck leaned back in his seat and took a deep breath before saying anything. Finally, he spoke. "Walt Austin is a friend of mine. We've worked on a few cases over the years together, and I trust him to be an honorable man. We know all about you and him tapping Whelan's phone line. If it had been anybody other than Walt, he would be up on charges right now. If I allow you to take the tapes back to Arkansas and do your deal with your childhood nemesis, I expect the tapes to be in our Little Rock office within forty-eight hours from right now. Do you understand me, Major Squire?"

With a deep sigh of relief, David said, "I do understand you, Agent Huston. And I will always be grateful to you for what you're doing here."

"Sometimes, David, there's more to doing the right thing than there is to following the letter of the law," Buck said. "Now, be on your way. I'll pick up the tab for your dinner. You need to get on the road. The clock is ticking."

With a slight smile, David rose to his feet and grabbed his coat.

"By the way, David, I have one more question. Why didn't you kill Haunce Walters when he reached for his gun back at the Patriot Motel? Why did you decide to hit him with the gun and knock him out?" Buck asked.

David stopped and gazed across the room for a moment before answering. "I don't know about you, but with me, a fight is always in slow motion. I do not get nervous, and I do not lose my head. I seem to think more clearly and quickly. When Haunce reached for his pistol, my intellect screamed that it would be better for the government's case if he were alive. He's the kind of bottom feeder that will squeal on everyone when the chips fall the wrong way for him. He'll rat every last one of them out even if he doesn't get a better deal with the prosecutors. For that reason, I decided not to shoot him," David said as he turned and walked away.

Buck watched as David, with the swagger of a champion,

weaved his way through the tables and out the front door. Buck knew what he had just done was against all the FBI stood for. Allowing a civilian to walk away with hard evidence that would nail a criminal to the wall was unheard of. But deep within himself, he knew that old country boy from down south would deliver on his promise to return the evidence. He knew that David Squire would keep his word.

CHAPTER 23

"Duff, there's a Mister Haunce Walters on the phone who wants to speak to you," Mary Whelan said.

"Okay, I'll take it in my study," Whelan said.

Whelan knew that if Haunce Walters was calling him at home, then the news was bad. He just hoped it wasn't a disaster.

"This is Whelan," he said.

"The target got the best of us again. He's on the road, now, and we suspect he's driving to Arkansas because of the connection that you mentioned to me earlier. I believe that now's the time for you to give me the address," Haunce said.

Whelan was surprised that Haunce had picked up on the short mention he made to him a couple of days ago on the phone about an old antagonist of David Squire being in Arkansas. After a short reckoning of the situation, he decided not to reveal too much to Haunce until he could talk to Clyde. Haunce played by a different set of rules, and Whelan figured he should always be on a need-to-know basis.

"I don't know where he's going, but I'll find out and call you back in a few minutes," Whelan said.

After the two men hung up, Whelan immediately called Clyde.

"Listen up, Clyde. We have a problem. David Squire has possession of about five audiotapes that will bring down our world. We cannot allow him to expose us. You say you've known him all your life. What do you think he's up to?" Whelan asked.

Stunned by the bad news, Clyde stuttered for a few seconds while he tried to collect his thoughts.

"I think he's coming here," he said.

"To Arkansas? Why?" Whelan asked.

"Because I have something he wants, and he's going to hold the evidence over my head until I give it to him. I don't believe he cares a single thing about your end of the deal. He only wants to make me give up something he wants. I don't know what to do to stop him," Clyde said nervously. "I'm in the farming business. We're civilized down here, and there's no one here that I can call on to prevent a catastrophe for you and me in case he decides to expose us to the FBI."

"I don't even care what he wants from you. At this point, I need this man eliminated, and I need those tapes. Don't worry about him. I've got it covered," Whelan said. "I'm sending a crew to Arkansas tomorrow morning. If Squire is driving, it will be at least late tomorrow or early the next day before he gets there. My crew will fly and will arrive sometime tomorrow and will be waiting for him. You just stay out of the way and let them do what they do, Clyde. This is going to get nasty, so you better be thinking of something to tell the county sheriff if this ends as badly as I think it will. Do you understand me, Clyde?" Whelan asked with the tone of a Drill Sergeant.

With a weak, barely audible voice Clyde said, "Yes I do."

"Good, I'll be in touch," the Senator said as he hung up.

Clyde suddenly felt sick at his stomach. He stepped onto the back porch of his house and paced around for an hour trying to get a grip on the inevitable reality of the situation.

****

David drove most of the night before stopping and crashing at a motel outside Nashville, Tennessee. By nine A. M., he was back on the road.

By 6:30 p.m., he was checked in at a motel in Lake Village Arkansas, a few miles across the Mississippi River from Greenville, Mississippi. After a quick shower, he called Sarah Jennings. She was elated to hear from him. She told David that she and Millie had been so worried about him. He assured her that everything was fine.

"May I come by to see you tonight?" he asked.

"Of course," she exclaimed. "Where are you?"

"I'm a few miles down the road. I'll grab a bite and come on over. How about eight o'clock?" he asked.

"Don't you dare eat on the run like that," she said. "I'll fix your dinner here."

"Well, I find that just too irresistible to turn down, so how about if I get there at around seven thirty?" He asked.

"Perfect. I'll see you then," Sarah said.

David dressed quickly and got on the road to Sarah's house about twenty-five miles away. He was anxious to find out how Joe and Millie were doing, and he figured Sarah would know firsthand how Millie was holding up under all the pressure.

****

Haunce Walters along with George Felton, Henry Bowman,

and Earl Stewart sat across the desk from Clyde Bayless as Haunce introduced his men to Clyde. He was already terrified about the whole thing, but as Clyde observed Earl Stewart's blackened eyes and broken nose along with the tennis ball sized knot on the side of Henry Bowman's head, he knew they had already met David.

"What happened to your nose?" He asked Earl Stewart.

Stewart was in no mood to entertain Clyde, so he just stared into his eyes until Clyde broke eye contact.

"We've had a difficult time getting our hands on the prize, Mr. Bayless," Haunce said with an intense look. "I guarantee it will be different this time. We'll be waiting for him when he arrives. I think it's only fair that I tell you this—do not get in our way, or you could get hurt. This is going to get nasty quickly, but no matter what happens, we're going to get what we came here for. We will not leave without it."

****

David took a deep breath as he stepped out of the car at Sarah Jennings' house. Breathing in the unmistakable smells of the Deep South was a welcome sign to him that he was home. The night was clear and, although the moon had not risen, the Big Dipper and the Little Dipper were both visible in the northern sky. David was reminded of how, as boys, he and Joe Carter navigated at night using the Big Dipper.

"Trying to figure out which constellation you're looking at?" Sarah asked, smiling.

A bit startled because of his deep thought, David said, "Just remembering an age-old navigation trick that Joe and I used when we were boys," he said. "I'm sorry; I didn't see you standing there."

As David made his way to the top of the steps, Sarah moved in close and extended her hand. After David had answered her invitation to shake hands, she did something he wasn't expecting.

"May I give you a big hug, Mr. Squire?" She asked as she put her arms around him. "Thank you so much for what you've done for Joe and Millie. It was a very noble thing to do. I have to say that you are everything they've always said about you."

"Now you're making me blush," David said. "And just so you'll know, Joe would have done the same for me if the tables were turned."

David and Sarah talked at length about how Joe was doing and especially how Millie was coping with everything. They also talked about how David planned to handle Clyde the next morning.

After they had discussed how she would notarize the debt release documents, David started to get up to leave when Sarah stopped him.

"Mr. Squire I want to let you know how ashamed I am for getting you into the mess you had to go through to get to this point. My reasons were of a selfish nature, but I quickly realized you would have done anything for your friends, including dying if need be. That's the part that scared me. When Millie told me how much danger you were in, I was horrified. Of course, she wasn't aware that I even knew you, so I couldn't share my anxiety with her, or quite frankly, anyone else," Sarah said quietly.

"Don't worry about it, Sarah. If it hadn't been for you, I wouldn't be holding the evidence to force Clyde to do what I want him to do," David said.

The two of them discussed a few more things about the impending separation of Clyde and the stranglehold he had on Joe and Millie Carter. After they had both decided that they were on the same page with each other, Sarah turned to a more personal subject.

"May I tell you my motive for bringing down Clyde Bayless, Mr. Squire?" She asked.

Sensing that she needed to get something off her chest, David said, "You may."

Relaxing against the back of the sofa, he listened as Sarah Jennings spoke with an unguarded lust for vengeance against Clyde Bayless.

"When I lost my husband a few years ago, I literally thought I was going to die. It was my twelve-year-old daughter, who kept me going. She was there through my darkest days encouraging me to never give up. She had the strength that I simply could not find in the weeks and months after my husband's death. Eventually, I found an inner peace and realized that I was stronger than I thought.

"Four years later my daughter…"

"You don't have to tell me this if it's too difficult for you," David said quietly.

"It's important to let you know the reasons I carelessly put you in harm's way," Mr. Squire. I have to get this off my conscience, so please allow me to finish.

"My daughter began to date Clyde Bayless' son, Billy when she was sixteen. I didn't really approve of it because I saw him for what he was—a spoiled little boy who was never going to do anything constructive on his own. Nevertheless, Joanie was no different than most other headstrong teenagers, so I let her date him.

"About three months into the relationship, I noticed a change in Joanie. She was no longer the perky little teenage cheerleader that she had been. One evening, I asked her what was going on, and although she was reluctant to talk about it, she finally told me that her relationship with Billy Bayless was over. I did what most mothers would probably do. I assured her that there were thousands of fish in the sea, and there was one out there for her that would be so much better than him.

"What I did not know was the trouble she had gotten herself into with Billy Bayless. I didn't find it out until years later. By then, it was too late. Exactly one week after she and I had that little talk about all the fish in the sea, my beautiful little Joanie was gone.

"She was on the other side of the levee with a couple of classmates on a Saturday afternoon watching the riverboats go by from the river bank when, according to her best friend, Jean, she got into our car and drove as fast as she could right down the hill and into the Mississippi River. When the sheriff's deputies found the car a mile down river and pulled it onto the bank, her hands were still gripping the steering wheel. She had made no attempt to get out of the car as it sank," Sarah said almost inaudibly.

She was having a hard time speaking now, but David decided to do nothing to stop her. It was obvious to him that she was harboring an incredible amount of hurt inside her heart that she needed to vent. So David moved a bit closer to her on the sofa and gently took her hand in his as she continued.

"I came home from work one afternoon about four years later, and Jean and the other girl who witnessed the suicide were sitting on the doorsteps waiting for me. By then they were both sophomores in college and were home for the Christmas Holidays. When Jean hugged me as she usually did, she began crying. I knew then I was about to learn something new about Joanie's death even though it had been years since the tragedy.

"To make a long story short, Billy Bayless got my daughter pregnant, and Clyde Bayless personally took her to an abortion doctor and had the baby discarded. Four years of inner turmoil about why my Joanie would take her own life was suddenly revealed to me. The mystery was over, and after Jean explained the details, I couldn't speak for an hour. That was in December, six years ago.

"Clyde Bayless and his family were on vacation and out of town for the holidays, and it's a good thing they were. I probably would be in prison right now. As it were, I had two full weeks to cool down.

"When Clyde arrived on his first morning back to work, I was in his office sitting at his desk in *his* chair. I know Clyde Bayless well, and I can say with full confidence that when our eyes met, he instinctively knew I had finally found out the truth about my daughter's death.

"Of course he denied everything, and to this day, he has never admitted the truth to me. He said over and over that he would never do something like that. Those two young girls had lived with that awful secret for four years until they could bear it no longer, so they told me. I know they were telling me the truth. They saw her get into the car with Clyde on the day he took her for that awful procedure.

"Since I could never get him to admit to me even in private that he had done that to my precious little Joanie, I decided to figure out a way to get him back. I realize, Mr. Squire, that it goes against all that is good and decent, but I *will* get my revenge on Clyde Bayless if it's the last thing I ever do on this earth," Sarah said.

"Sarah, your life is not my business, but I do have one small piece of advice for you if you're interested," David said.

"Please do, Mr. Squire," she said.

"I know from personal experience that hate will consume you if you allow it. When this is over, release your anger. Just let it go," David said quietly.

"I'll do my best. Thank you for the advice," Sarah said.

"I have to get some rest, now. Give me the debt relief documents, and I'll have them with me tomorrow morning. That way Clyde won't know that you're in on this thing. Make sure you have your Notary stamp with you," David said as he turned to leave.

"I will," she said as she handed him the documents in a large, brown envelope.

Sarah did tell David that Clyde had guessed that she was

in on David's investigation. She figured it wouldn't matter and that she would deal with Clyde face to face when the time came.

****

"Good morning Sarah. I'm sorry to bother you so early, but I just wanted to tell you that I'm going to be at my hunting camp today. I have some things to do before the opening day of hunting season next weekend," Clyde said. "If anyone needs to see me, just tell them where I am."

"Sure thing, Mr. Bayless. Have a nice day," Sarah said as she hung up.

After talking to Sarah, Clyde joined Haunce Walters and his men who had been waiting in the parking lot when Clyde arrived at his office. It was a full hour before he would be open for business. He had decided to call Sarah at home to let her know he would not be in the office until later. He figured having the meeting at his hunting camp in a remote area 10 miles out of town would be the best location to do the deed. Clyde knew he would not have control over the actions of Haunce Walters and his men, and he certainly did not want to see any employees getting hurt.

"We won't meet him here," he explained to Haunce. "We'll go to my hunting camp and wait for him there. It's in the perfect location for what you have to do."

Haunce and his men followed Clyde to the camp, nestled in a clearing behind thick woods, down a gravel road in a sparsely populated area of the county. The nearest house from his camp was over a mile away, and the camp house was a few hundred yards off the road.

When they got there, Clyde asked Haunce to drive his car around back of the house so it would be out of sight when David arrived. After parking the car in a secure place, Haunce joined the rest of the men in the front room of the cabin.

"We'll have two men on each side of the door when he comes in. If he tries anything, he will be so full of lead, you could use him as a boat anchor," Haunce said with an evil smile.

"I don't want any shooting inside my cabin," Clyde said.

"You're not in charge here. I am," Haunce said with a cold stare. "As I said, we came here for one reason, and that is to get the tapes. We're going to leave here with them even if it means killing your old friend."

Clyde leaned his head back on the headrest of his sofa and stared at the wall. He was petrified and did not know what to do. It was clear to him that these men meant business, and there was nothing he could do but sit quietly and let them have their way.

Just as he figured, a few minutes after 8:00 AM, the sound of an automobile coming down the gravel road got their attention. Haunce's men took their place on each side of the door while Clyde stepped onto the front porch as the car turned off the road and into the driveway.

"Good morning, Clyde," David said as he got out of the car.

"Good morning, David. I've been expecting you," Clyde said.

Clyde's comment told David that Clyde had been in contact with someone in Washington—probably Senator Whelan. *Clyde is either ready to negotiate or ready to go to prison,* David thought.

"Come on in," Clyde said as David followed him toward the cabin door.

David was already inside the cabin before he realized Haunce Walters and his men surrounded him. Before he could mount any defense, David had a 45-caliber pistol pointed at his right temple, and a 38-caliber pointed to his left. Earl got into David's face and told him what he was going to do if David made a wrong move.

Finally, Haunce told Earl to step aside. After a thorough pat down, Haunce determined that David did not have the tapes on him. So after they had retrieved his pistol, Haunce ordered David not to move.

"Okay, you know why we're here," Haunce said.

"Yes, I know exactly why you're here," David said.

"Well, how do you like that, boss? Squire here ain't so dumb after all," Earl said with a wicked smile.

"I thought you already learned that back at the Cherry Blossom Motor Courts," David said. "But, of course, you do actually strike me as being pretty stupid."

"Shut up," Henry growled. "You're walking on thin ice, Squire."

"I do want to say one thing before we go any further," David smirked. "You guys just don't know how close you came to getting the best of me back at the motor courts. That enormously loud thud you made when you hit the floor after I introduced you to that ceramic lamp body was terribly distracting, and I almost didn't see the opening your friend here gave me when he tried to step over your lifeless body. Lucky me. I was able to stun him with a right hook and rearrange his nose with a left jab. I actually enjoyed it, quite frankly."

David was choosing his words carefully. He knew that the two men closest to him were common street goons with a collective IQ of a parakeet. If he was going to have any chance at all of coming out on top, these two idiots were going to give it to him.

"Yes, I have to say, that was one of my finer moments. You two guys wouldn't happen to want a rematch, now would you? You look like you could use a little work on that nose. I can see even through the bandages that it's a bit crooked," he said to Earl.

The two men were coming completely unhinged now, and David knew he was going to have to move fast and hard when they dropped their guard. He could see that they were itching to get a piece of him, so he continued.

"So, tell me, big boy, how's that knot on the side of your head?" he asked.

"That's enough, Squire," Haunce barked. "Produce the tapes, or this is going to get pretty bad for you."

"I'm sorry, I don't have them," David said.

"Check his pockets for his car keys," Haunce ordered.

After retrieving the keys, George went out to search David's car.

Now there were only three men left. David knew that if he didn't move soon, it would all be over and Clyde would have what he wanted.

That's when the interference he was looking for occurred. George accidentally hit the horn of David's car as he was searching under the front seat on the driver's side. Thinking they may have a visitor, Haunce stepped over to the window. As soon as he pulled back the curtains, David made his move. Before Earl, who had been distracted by the sound of the horn, could stop him, David executed an OSS maneuver to disarm a man without firing a shot. He jerked the weapon clear, and with one hard swing, he hit Henry in the same spot he hit him two days earlier. Henry didn't have time to cock his weapon. Henry never cocked his weapon until he was ready to fire because the trigger was too sensitive. He went down like a rock. David then grabbed Earl and placed the gun to his head.

"Drop your weapon, Haunce," David demanded.

It was clear to Haunce that somebody was about to die. He didn't care who it was as long as it wasn't him. With that in mind, he slowly made his way back toward David and Earl while pointing his gun at both of them.

"I don't care if Stewart dies, Squire, I'm going to leave here with those tapes. Nobody's going to stop me. You dig?" Haunce demanded.

"You hear that, Mr. Stewart? Your boss here just said he's going to kill you just to get at me. What do you think about that?" David asked in a taunting voice.

Earl had always heard stories about how Haunce had no friends when the brawl began. Now he knew what that meant. He suddenly realized the chances of him surviving this fight were looking slim.

"I didn't bargain for this, Haunce. We're supposed to be on the same team here," Earl said.

"Don't shoot, Haunce," Clyde pleaded.

"Shut up, little pig. I'm running this show. We came here to get the tapes, and that's exactly what I'm going to do. If that means losing one of my own men, then so be it," Haunce snarled.

"If you shoot him, I will tell the sheriff you intentionally murdered him," Clyde said.

"Not if I shoot you too, shorty," Haunce said slowly and deliberately.

The distraction was all David needed. In the half second that Haunce's eyes were focused on Clyde, David pushed Earl into Haunce with all the force he could muster. As Haunce was caught off balance, David stepped forward and smacked Haunce on the side of the head with the butt of Earl's gun. Haunce dropped to the floor, stunned. David then stepped forward and kicked Haunce in the temple area. He was out cold in less than a second.

David immediately spun Earl around, and with lightning speed, he jabbed his fist into Earl's broken nose. Earl went down to his knees

David quickly made his way to the door as an unsuspecting George Felten opened it. Stepping out from behind the door, David placed Henry's pistol to the back of George's head.

"Well, here we are again, just you and me," he said playfully. "It seems like you're always the only one who walks away unscathed. Maybe you're smarter, or more fortunate than the others. You feeling like mother luck is shining her light on you right now, Mr. Felten? I'd be happy to oblige you if you are. Please give me a reason to send you to hell."

"I wouldn't be interested in making a journey like that just yet, Mr. Squire," George said quietly.

"Okay, then take the roll of fiberglass tape on that coffee table over there, and tape your friend's hands behind their backs, and tape their feet together, too. And, by the way, I'll take that paper bag in your hands, and I'll take your piece too," David said.

Removing his pistol from its holster with two fingers, George handed it to David. After frisking him, David watched as George taped the hands behind the backs of the others.

"Now, lie down on the floor face down," David demanded.

After taping George's hands and feet, David walked over to where Clyde was sitting on the sofa. Clyde was frozen. Looking menacingly down at the pathetic little man, David ordered him to stand up.

"Please don't hit me, David. These men were forced upon me by someone else," Clyde managed to say.

"You mean by the senator?" David asked. "I know all about him and all about what Haunce Walters has done on Senator Whelan's orders. You've got yourself in a bad fix here, Clyde. I'm offering you a way out. Now, you and I are going back to your office to take care of a little business."

As the two men walked into Clyde's business, Sarah Jennings quickly noticed the look on Clyde's face as he approached her desk. *He's going to cooperate with David.*

David had brought the blank tapes with him that he had stored in the original boxes with Whelan's handwritten notes describing them. He also had the large brown envelope with him that Sarah had given him the night before. Once inside Clyde's private office, David laid out everything that he had uncovered on Clyde, and when he finished, he demanded the release of the Carter debt and mortgage on their farm—or he would turn over the tapes to the FBI.

"You have two choices, Clyde. Either sign the documents I have in this envelope, or I turn over these tapes to the FBI," he said.

Reaching into the paper bag and retrieving the tapes, he laid them down on the desk in front of Clyde so that he could see Whelan's handwritten notes on each tape box.

"Here's what I have to offer you—these tapes for the debt relief and released mortgage on Joe Carter's farm.

"This is outright blackmail, David Squire," Clyde shouted.

"I know it is, but what you did to my friend and his wife is a hundred times worse. Your intentions all along were to steal his land. Your greed is the reason you're in this situation. Being the largest landowner in the county wasn't good enough. You had to be the king. You always enjoyed when others were forced to bow down to you.

"All you had to do was to be nice to the rest of us when we were in school, Clyde, and we would have brought you into our clique. You couldn't have that. After all, you were the son and future heir to the largest farming operation in the county. Why would you want to rub shoulders with the boys on the other side of the tracks? That would be beneath you. That and that alone is why you don't have a single friend in this county. You think you're better than everybody else.

"There is, however, one little threat that is going to make you realize that you're, in fact, not better than anyone else. This stack of tapes are going to send you to prison for a long time for bribery, possibly an accessory to murder, and maybe that little kidnapping you attempted on me a little while ago at your camp.

"So, what's it going to be, the tapes for the signed documents, or a prison cell where they'll turn you into a girl?" David asked as he stared right through Clyde.

After sitting in silence for a long beat, finally, Clyde spoke. "I'll sign the documents, but I'll always hate you for this, David. You and Joe Carter are trash and always have been," Clyde said with an effort to have at least some control over the situation. Show me the documents," he said.

"We'll need a Notary to witness the signatures," David said.

Clyde hit the intercom button on his desk and asked Sarah to come into his office and bring her Notary seal.

As she came through the door, Sarah immediately noticed the stack of audiotape boxes on Clyde's desk but said nothing. She knew why she was there and wanted to get it done as soon as possible.

"What do I need to Notarize, Mr. Bayless?" She asked.

"My signature and David Squire's signature. He will be witnessing mine, and you will be notarizing both signatures on these documents," he said.

After signing the documents, and after Sarah performed her Notary duties, David returned them to the brown envelope and handed them to her.

"Please hold onto these for me. I'll pick them up on my way out," he said.

Sarah managed to smother her incredible desire to jump up and down with joy as she went back to her desk outside Clyde's office. David wanted Sarah to hold the documents in her hands for a few minutes because of all the risk she had taken for the last few years to build the evidence against the greedy little crook that had done so much personal harm to her.

"Well, that about does it, Clyde. I'll be on my way now. You can tell the senator that you have the tapes so he can call off his hounds now," David said as he turned to leave.

Clyde just sat staring at the door as David closed it behind him. He could not believe the events that had transpired that morning. After a minute, he reached inside a lower desk drawer, pulled out a bottle of moonshine whiskey that a local farmer had given him, and took a large gulp straight from the bottle.

As he stopped by Sarah's desk on his way out, David could see the giddiness all over her face. He had not seen a look like that in her eyes since this whole ordeal began three weeks ago.

"I have to meet with the FBI and deliver something to them. I'll be back by four o'clock. Arrange to be at Joe and Millie's tonight, but don't tell them I'm here. I want to surprise them," he whispered.

"I will," Sarah said as she handed David the envelope.

****

While at a railroad crossing waiting for a train to pass, David began pondering on what his investigation had accomplished. The last three weeks had been both the most difficult and most rewarding of all his years in the business. He had saved all the assets of his oldest friend, who was dying of cancer, and in the process, he had uncovered hard evidence that would bury one of Washington's most corrupt politicians. Although, in the beginning, he had no interest in Washington corruption, and he probably would not have even pursued that part of the case, but Senator Whelan had proven to be an unrepentant criminal.

David had met at least two decent people that had been traumatically affected by Whelan's actions. Aaron Rubenstein was a well-liked sheriff of a Pennsylvania county, and Elizabeth Gardener was in love with a man that Whelan was responsible for killing. Those two people, whom David had immediately become fond of, deserved to see justice for the murder of their loved one, Frank Rubenstein. For that reason, he had planned to give the tapes to the FBI long before he promised Buck Huston he would do so. Now he was on his way to the Bureau's field office in Little Rock, Arkansas to honor his obligation to Agent Huston, Aaron Rubenstein, and Elizabeth Gardener.

A loud knock on the driver's side window of his car brought David back to reality. It was Haunce Walters. A quick check in his rearview mirror revealed that Henry Bowman was standing directly behind his car. Earl Stewart was standing next to the rear door on the driver's side, while George Felten was next to the front window on the passenger's side. All of the men had their weapons drawn.

David knew there would be no negotiations between him and the men outside his car, so he slipped it into reverse, quickly raced the engine, and jerked his foot off the clutch. Simultaneously, he opened his door. Immediately, Henry was pinned between David's car and the car behind him. At the same time, his opened door caught Earl and crushed several ribs, dragging him to the ground. Pulling his 45-calibre automatic pistol and rolling out of the car onto the pavement, David placed a round through the abdomen of Haunce Walters. He went down and did not move.

George, who had run to the driver's side of David's car, stood as still as a statue as David's eyes met his. George knew there would be no reprieve now. He knew the day of his destiny had come. The fiery look in David's eyes coupled with a steady hand and calm demeanor told George that he better make his move because he was going to be shot anyway.

Raising his pistol slowly, George said, "You're going to kill me anyway, so I have no choice."

Without a single blink in his eyes, David put one round squarely through George Felten's left eye.

"Watch out, Mister," a man in the truck behind David shouted.

Spinning around, David saw Henry Bowman, still pinned between the two vehicles, raising his pistol. With two quick rounds through the chest, he slumped over the trunk of David's car.

As David made a quick visual check of the four men, he

could see that Earl was still alive. As he holstered his weapon, David walked slowly over to Earl and kicked his weapon away from him.

Slowly squatting down three feet away from Earl, with a menacing smile, David said, "Man, I bet you wished you were somewhere else right about now, don't you?"

Earl just looked at David without saying a word. Standing to his feet, David calmly walked back to his car and started the engine. Those who witnessed the gunfight watched in disbelief as he drove away while Henry Bowman's body fell to the ground behind his car.

It was 2:30 PM when David gave the tapes to the agent in charge of the FBI office in Little Rock. He waited until the agent called Buck Huston in Washington to confirm that he had received the tapes.

David then drove back to Sarah Jennings's house. As he got out of his car, she opened the door and stepped onto the porch.

"I was worried about you, Mr. Squire. I thought you may be detained," she said.

"Detained?" he asked.

"Everybody knows about the gunfight at the railroad crossing this morning. Nobody who witnessed it knows who the man was that left the scene. The only thing they can say is that he killed two men and left two men badly wounded. From what I've heard, he killed the others in self-defense, so no charges will be brought against him if he comes forward," she said.

David looked into Sarah's eyes and said nothing. The look on his face told her all she needed to know.

"Have you made arrangements for dinner tonight at Joe and Millie's?" he asked.

"I surely have. They're expecting me at 6:30," she said.

"So, I'll arrive at exactly 6:45. I certainly do not want to miss out on a single bite of Millie's cooking." He smiled. "May

I stay here until it's time to go?"

"You certainly may," she said.

Then she surprised David again with another big hug. The both of them stood there on her front porch and just held each other. David needed the comfort as much as she did.

****

David turned off the road and into Joe and Millie's driveway stopping next to Sarah's car. By the time he parked his car and got to the top of the steps, the door opened, and Joe stepped onto the porch with a huge smile.

"Hey Millie, come look who blew in on the wind," Joe said as he gave David a hardy handshake.

Appearing in the doorway, Millie, with a huge smile on her face, stepped onto the porch and embraced David. After inviting him inside, Millie introduced him to her friend, Sarah Jennings. David gave Sarah a nod.

"What on earth are you doing just appearing out of nowhere at this time of the evening?" Joe asked.

"I smelled Millie's cooking and decided to come on over," David said.

With a blushing smile, Millie turned and stepped into the kitchen to check on her apple pie in the oven. She was so excited that she was literally shaking inside. She knew David was not here just for a social visit. In their last phone conversation a few days ago, he told her that he almost had what he needed. She knew David would not just appear unannounced at her front door if he didn't have something huge to share.

"Are you just now driving in from the airport?" Joe asked.

"No, actually I didn't fly this time. I drove. I stayed in Lake Village last night. I had a meeting with Clyde this morning, and he gave me something for you," David said.

Reaching inside his jacket, David pulled out the envelope with the documents he had forced Clyde to sign and handed them to Joe. Taking his time, Joe read over the debt relief document. After he was finished, he leaned back against the sofa and stared into space for a moment without saying a word.

Finally, he said to Millie, "He did it."

That was all he could force out of his mouth. David sat quietly as Joe, and the two women openly and unashamedly cried with tears of joy for five minutes.

After gaining his composure, Joe, looking at the documents again, turned to Sarah and said, "You notarized these documents. You knew about this didn't you?"

With a shy smile, Sarah quietly said, "Yes, I knew about it."

"That's not all she knew about, old friend," David said. "Sarah is the reason we're all sitting her celebrating this wonderful occasion. If it hadn't been for her, I would never have been able to get Clyde to relieve the debt."

Looking at Sarah, Joe asked, "What did you do?"

"Why don't I tell you about it after we have some of Millie's great cooking?" David asked.

After dinner, they all sat around the living room as David explained how Sarah had placed the note into his hand as he met her that first day at Clyde's office. From there, he explained how the trail had led to Washington D C and had involved one of the most powerful men in the U. S. government: Senator Benjamin Duff Whelan.

He also explained Walt Austin's involvement and the fact that if it hadn't been for him, David could never have gotten the evidence he needed. When he explained why Walt refused to take any payment whatsoever for his efforts, Joe just stared at the floor. David could see that the memory of Joe saving Walt's life in France during the War was racing back into his mind. Joe did not say a word, but he did not need to. The expression on his face said it all.

When David was finished with his story as to how the investigation had unfolded, he asked Joe and Millie if they had any questions.

Joe knew David as well as he knew himself. He knew there was no need in asking that which had been rolling around in his mind for the last ten minutes as David explained the story.

Looking into David's eyes, Joe calmly said, "It was you, wasn't it, Major?"

Instinctively knowing what Joe was asking, David slowly replied, "Yes, it was me. They gave me no choice. I had beaten them down in two separate locations outside of D C, and after I got here this morning, Clyde wanted to meet at his hunting camp. They were waiting for me when I got there, so I had to beat them down again. They were sent here by Whelan to get the evidence I had against him and Clyde. They were determined to get it at all costs.

"When I grabbed Clyde, threw him into my car, and left the camp, they were on the floor tied up. I knew they would eventually get free, but I was able to force your fat little friend into giving you back your land deed and forgiving all that you owed him before they caught up with me. I was on my way to the FBI headquarters in Little Rock with the evidence when they pulled up behind me at the railroad crossing at the edge of town."

Slowly leaning forward on the sofa and staring at the floor, David quietly said, "There was nowhere to go, so I did what I had to do. I knew it would not be a simple attack by four men against one. These guys were bad characters, and they had blood in their eyes. I had humiliated them on three earlier occasions, and they simply were not going to let it happen again. I suppose there's no other way to say it. I won. They lost."

Gazing into space with the intensity of a raging bull, Joe said calmly, "Good riddance. They got what they deserved."

"I think I'll be going home now," Sarah said. "For the first time since my Joanie died, I feel that justice is about to be served to Clyde Bayless."

As she was leaving, Joe and Millie gave her a long hug, and then she turned to David. Moving close, she wrapped her arms around him and said, "You will always be my hero, Mr. Squire. You have set me free."

After Sarah had left, Joe and Millie invited David to stay the night, and he gladly accepted the invitation. It had been a long week, and he was looking forward to sleeping with his window open so he could listen to the nighttime sounds of his youth.

The next morning, David woke to the sound of a far-off

dog barking in the woods across the bayou. He figured it was chasing a deer, a common occurrence this time of year in rural Arkansas.

As bad as he hated to do so, sometime after lunch, David said his goodbyes to Joe and Millie. He explained to them that the car he was driving belonged to Walt Austin and he needed to get it back to him before flying back to Chicago.

Millie looked on as Joe gave his lifelong friend a long goodbye hug.

"I want you to know I'll go to my grave owing you everything for what you did for my Millie," Joe said quietly. "I had no one else to turn to. If you hadn't done this, my sweetheart would be homeless after I'm gone."

David turned and hugged Millie, as she wept in his arms, unable to speak. After shaking Joe's hand one last time, he got into his car and drove away.

Standing at the edge of their driveway and watching the dust trail behind David's car as he drove along the gravel road toward town, Joe turned to Millie and said, "He was my last hope for your future. He was my last friend."

EPILOGUE

April 12, 1964

David Squire, Walt Austin, and four other men who served in the OSS with Joe Carter carried the casket of their old friend to his final resting place. As a gentle North breeze trickled over those present, a military detail performed the twenty-one-gun salute. Joseph Alan Carter had served his country with distinction, having been awarded the Purple Heart, the Bronze Star, and The Silver Star medals.

Millie Carter sat stoically under the funeral tent and said nothing to anyone. Sarah Jennings sat next to her along with other members of Millie's family.

David Squire, for the first time since his wife died tragically years earlier, sobbed openly. The memories of fun times with his best friend during their youth suddenly rushed back to him as if to say, "Goodbye old pal. When you're all done with this life, stop by to see me on the other side. We'll talk about old times and have a few laughs."

As the pallbearers placed their corsages on the flag-draped casket, they each stepped back, stood at attention, and gave a quick, sharp salute. When it came David's turn, he did the same as the others. Then he slowly placed his hand on the casket and said, "Thank you for being my friend."

With tears gently slipping down his face, David slowly leaned over and kissed the casket. The realization hit him that his oldest and best friend had just taken his last ride.

Monday, May 4, 1964

Haunce Walters stood before the judge and pleaded guilty to accessory to murder in the death of Frank Rubenstein. There were no witnesses to place him at the scene of the murder. Elizabeth Gardener's statement to the police that Benny Flaigo and Alfonse Giovetti had told her that Haunce Walters was present at Frank Rubenstein's murder was only hearsay since she had killed both of them in her motel room outside of Washington D C.

In return for the federal prosecutor's decision to drop the charges against Walters for chasing David Squire to Arkansas and attempting to kill him at a railroad crossing, Haunce Walters agreed to testify against Senator Benjamin Duff Whelan for conspiracy to commit murder against Frank Rubenstein.

Haunce Walters was sentenced to three years to begin serving immediately.

Later that same day, Metropolitan Police Department Police Captain, Danny Evans pleaded guilty to taking a bribe in return for interfering with a police investigation. The federal prosecutor agreed to ask for a light sentence for Captain Evans in return for his testimony against Senator Whelan for paying the bribe.

Immediately following Captain Evans' sentencing, James Benton, the money courier between Clyde Bayless and Whelan, pleaded guilty to one charge of taking a bribe in return for testifying against Senator Whelan and Clyde Bayless.

Monday, May 25, 1964

Knowing that all the underlings in his money scheme were lining up against him, Senator Benjamin Duff Whelan pleaded guilty to one charge of paying a bribe and six charges of accepting bribes for legislative favors. He was sentenced to eight years in Federal prison. He pleaded not guilty to the charges brought against him concerning the murder of Frank Rubenstein. That trial was scheduled to commence on June 15.

Monday, June 1, 1964

As Jasper Clyde Bayless stood before the judge to receive his sentence for his part in the bribery scheme, the realization of just how small he really was against the federal government wrapped around him like a wet, cold blanket. He stood, shaking all over thinking about how he could have allowed himself to get into such a mess. He had resigned himself to his fate. He would plead guilty to six charges of accepting a bribe in exchange for an eight-year sentence in a Federal penitentiary.

After the judge had sentenced him, two U. S. Marshalls led him out of the courtroom and into a small room where he would give up his tailored suit for prison clothes.

After he had changed, the U. S. Marshalls shackled his hands and feet and led him out the back door where a waiting prison van was parked. David Squire and Sarah Jennings, accompanied by FBI agent Buck Huston, were standing on the sidewalk a few feet from the door, waiting for Clyde to appear. When the two Marshalls escorted Clyde through the door, they stopped in front of Sarah and David.

David stepped forward and spoke directly to Clyde. "The good book says 'For the love of money is the root of all sorts of evil.' You're a pathetic little pig, Clyde, and you're getting what you deserve. I wish I could say I'm sorry, but after what you tried to do to my oldest friend and his wife, I have to say I'm happy. Enjoy being a girl for the next eight years."

Then it was Sarah's turn. She stepped up, and as Clyde looked at her, she said, "If you hadn't done what you did to my Joanie, I would have ignored that little black book under your desk. Her suicide is on your shoulders, Clyde Bayless. May you rot in prison."

Clyde could take no more. He began to cry like a baby. The two U. S. Marshalls had to drag him to the van. He cried uncontrollably as they forced him inside and chained him to his seat.

As the van drove away, David turned to Sarah and looked into her eyes. With a quiet, measured voice, he said, "It's over, Sarah. You got your vengeance, and Clyde got what he deserved. Now you have to figure out a way to leave your hate right here on this sidewalk."

Sarah smiled back at David and said, "I will. I promise I will."

ABOUT THE AUTHOR

Born and reared on a small family farm about three miles from the Mississippi River in Northeast Louisiana, Darral Williams considers himself just a simple country boy with a head full of stories. Since he was in the eighth grade, he knew that one day he would place at least one of his stories on the written page. Life seems to have a way of delaying one's dreams, but Darral never gave up the idea that he would eventually write.

After his retirement from a thirty-year career in the construction business, he finally sat down and wrote his first story. He often says he has no regrets for his first career and insists that if it hadn't been for meeting so many wonderful people through the years from diverse backgrounds, his story ideas wouldn't be nearly as rich in his mind as they are. His number one hope is that you, as the reader, will see his story as vividly in your head as it was in his when he wrote it.

To contact Darral please visit www.darralwilliams.com

www.ingramcontent.com/pod-product-compliance
Lightning Source LLC
Chambersburg PA
CBHW062006190726
48283CB00002BA/412